BLOCKADE:

THE QUARANTINE OF CUBA

Rick,

Blood[y] shipmate

[signature]

Pensacola Fl

12 Nov 16

The Mike Stafford Novel Series

By William E. Dempsey

Betrayal at Bahia de los Cochinos

Blockade: The Quarantine of Cuba

Deception at San Cristóbal

Revenge at Dealey Plaza

(Release in November 2016)

BLOCKADE:
THE QUARANTINE OF CUBA

A Mike Stafford Novel

William E. Dempsey

ISBN-13: 9781519662989
IBSN-10: 151966298x

Cover Art by Chris Holmes

White Rabbit Graphix

Whiterabbitgraphix.com

Dedication

To my wife Kathleen, and sons John and Mike

In memory of Edward G. Kelley, Captain, USN

and

To the sailors who enforced the quarantine, for their

dedication and tenacity

"Unless another war is prevented it is likely to bring destruction on a scale never before held possible and even now hardly conceived."

Albert Einstein

This work is a fictional account of the adventures of a single ship and its crew out of the hundreds of ships and crews that implemented the naval quarantine of Cuba during the 1962 missile crisis.

The italicized captions at the beginning of the chapters, however, are not fiction. They are words taken from the pages of history to provide the reader a sense of the real-world drama unfolding as the crisis reached its peak. Superscript numbers refer to the sources listed in the back.

Crew of the U.S.S. Boyington (DD 953)

Ellingham, William M., Commander, USN, Commanding

Kaestner, John R., Lieutenant Commander, USN, Executive Officer

Officers:

Anderson, Doug, LTJG, First Lieutenant

Caruthers, David, LT, Chief Engineer

Engle, Philip, LT, Operations Officer

Frankel, Henry, ENS, Electronics Materiel Officer

Padgett, Thomas, ENS, Second Division Officer

Quinn, Patrick, LT, Gunnery Officer

Riley, Ian, LT, SC, Supply Officer

Rudolph, James, LTJG, CIC Officer

Sherwood, Fred, LTJG Sonar Officer

Thomas, Duncan, LTJG, Propulsion Officer

White, Hal, LTJG, Communications Officer

Enlisted Men

Bailey, Bill, Machinist's Mate Second Class

Dalton, John, Boatswain's Mate Second Class

Ford, Kenneth, Boilerman Chief

Foss, Harold, Boatswain's Mate First Class

Gandolfi, Anthony, Quartermaster First Class

Gibbs, Jeffery, Seaman Apprentice

Hughes, Sean, Seaman

Jones, Paul, Boatswain's Mate Chief

Kessler, Jerry, Signalman First Class

Kildare, Robert, Seaman

Leach, John, Fire Control Technician Third Class

Maxwell, Joseph, Seaman Apprentice

McGee, Howard, Engineman Second Class

Stafford, Michael, Gunner's Mate Chief

Tibbits, Gene, Gunner's Mate Second Class

Unger, David, Seaman Apprentice

Waller, Mosses, Electrician's Mate First Class

Zarna, Nick, Gunner's Mate First Class

These are the players in this story. The actual crew on a destroyer of this type was around 325 men.

PROLOGUE

The Cuban Missile Crisis

In the spring of 1962, one year after the Republic of Cuba defeated an attempted invasion by a group of Cuban exiles at the Bay of Pigs, the Soviet Union set into motion a plan to arm the island nation with offensive nuclear weapons. The plan, code named Operation *Anadyr*, included basing strategic nuclear bombers in Cuba, establishing a submarine base at the port of Mariel, near Havana, and the construction of missile launch facilities for medium and intermittent range ballistic missiles along the island's northern coast.

On 1 October 1962, the Soviets initiated the first step in the naval portion of their plan, designated as Operation *Kama*. On that date, four conventional Foxtrot class Soviet submarines covertly sailed from a port on the Barents Sea, north of the Arctic Circle. Their mission: Provide reconnaissance prior to the deployment of seven ballistic missile submarines to Mariel and for a large fleet of cargo ships slated to deliver intermittent range ballistic missiles and other offensive weapons to Cuba. To accomplish their mission, the four submarines had to reach Cuba and patrol the waters around the island undetected.

The United Stated discovered the presence of the medium range Soviet missiles in Cuba on 14 October 1962. Ten days later, President John F. Kennedy ordered a quarantine of Cuba to stop the buildup that threatened America. Kennedy chose the word *quarantine* other than *blockade* as the Soviets might have interpreted the latter as an act of war. The U.S. Atlantic Fleet implemented the orders, designating the outer boundary of the quarantine the *Walnut Line*.

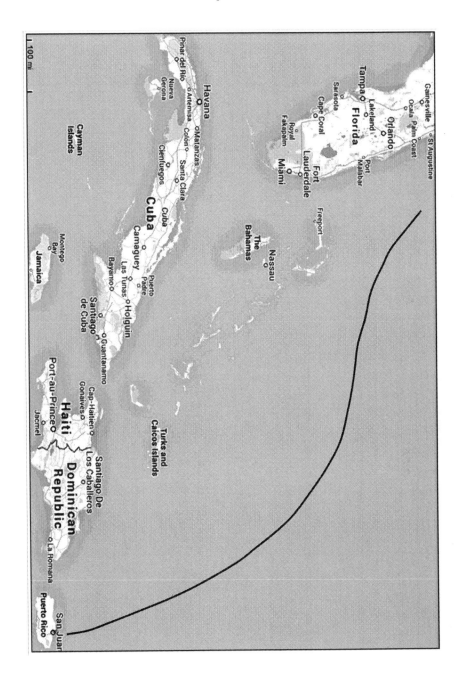

The Walnut Line

PART I

VOYAGE TO ARMAGEDDON

CHAPTER 1

Manchester-by-the-Sea, Massachusetts

Saturday, 20 October 1962

Sandy sat in silence, staring at the letter centered on the table, conditioned by the past, afraid of the future, numbed by the printed words.

"How is this happening? What does it mean, Mike? Tell me I misread it. Tell me I'm wrong. They're calling you back, aren't they?" She looked up at her husband, her eyes filled with dread. "Tell me . . . tell me I'm wrong, Mike. You're not leaving are you? They can't do this to us."

The baby cried.

Mike stood behind her chair. Her long blonde hair cascaded over his hands resting on her shoulders. "Sandy, it's real, you didn't misread it. You're not wrong, but if I don't go, they'll come after me, and I'll end up in the brig, disgraced."

"If you go, you may end up dead."

The baby cried louder, demanding attention.

"Think of us, Mike. . . . Think about Maria and me. You did your duty for the country, for the navy. You spent over twenty years fighting this country's wars and recovered from some horrible wounds. You're retired now and haven't been in uniform for over fifteen months. That part of your life is finished. It's over . . . you did your part . . . your duty is here with us now. They can't ask for more."

"Don't do this, Sandy. You read the message. Come on . . . you were a naval officer, an agent in the Office of Naval Intelligence no less. You know the rules and how the system works . . . you know the law."

"No, no . . . there's been a mistake. That's it, Mike, someone sent this to you by mistake. It's supposed to go to someone else. Just call them and straighten it out."

"No, Sandy, it's not a mistake. It's for real, and it's for me."

"Mike, we have a baby. We can go to Canada or somewhere. I can't lose you . . . we can't lose you. You're human, Mike . . . you only have one life, and you have already put it on the line too many times. We can't risk your going." Her lips trembled as she spoke. Tears streamed down her cheeks and spotted her blouse. She rose slowly and left the room, feeling faint, her head throbbing.

The baby's crying stopped.

Mike paced back and forth, covering the length of the kitchen in even strides, his thoughts a thousand miles away. Images of Cuba formed in his mind. The Bay of Pigs invasion flashed before his eyes. He saw muzzle flashes, heard the dull thuds of recoilless rifles, the staccato chatter of automatic rifles, and the agonizing screams of their victims. He smelled death. Stopping at the table, He picked up the letter and read it again. The words remained unchanged.

DEPARTMENT OF THE NAVY
BUREAU OF NAVAL PERSONNEL
WASHINGTON 2, D.C.

14 Oct 62

To: Michael J. Stafford, 337 62 07, GMC, USN (Ret)
RR 3, Box 5
Manchester-by-the-Sea 3, Massachusetts

Subj: Recall to Active Duty

1. Under Article C-531317(3) (b), BUPERS Manual you are hereby recalled to active duty at your former rate and rating for a period of up to 360 days, or as needs of the service dictate.
2. Proceed to: U.S.S. Yosemite (AD 19), Naval Station Newport, Newport, Rhode Island, for reassignment.
3. Report no later than: 2400 local, 23 Oct 62.
4. Delay Authorized: None.
5. Travel Time Authorized: 01 Day.
6. Transportation Authorized: Individual or commercial.
7. Appropriation/Accounting Data for Travel and Per Diem: 107942.281.16
8. In case of illness or accident, wire: COMCRUDESLANT, Newport.

Stephen G. Miller

Stephen G. Miller, LTJG, USNR

By direction of the Commander, BUPERS

He placed the letter back down on the table, walked to the sideboard, and filled a tumbler with two ice cubes and a generous portion of Bushmills Irish whiskey. Returning to the living room, he sat in his favorite chair and faced the glowing logs in the Inglenook fireplace.

Goober, the family's chocolate Labrador, sensing trouble, sauntered up next to Mike's chair and reclined with a sigh, ready to comfort his master.

Sandy returned carrying the baby and sat on the sofa. Red blotches over her otherwise flawless complexion betrayed the lingering emotional stress, but the crying had stopped.

The baby slept.

Mike finished his drink.

They sat in silence.

"Are you going to go?"

"Sandy, I have no choice in the matter. You know that. I didn't volunteer. They called me up. It's all legal, part of the contract, part of why they send me a check every month."

"When will you leave?" she asked.

"Couple of days. I have to be there Tuesday."

"Is this about Cuba again?"

"I'm sure it is. Cuba has dominated the news for the past couple of weeks. I knew the president screwed up when he backed out of the

Bay of Pigs fight. If they had let us finish the job last year this crisis wouldn't be happening."

"You're no doubt right, sweetheart, but if the invasion had gone as planned you and I wouldn't have met. I guess that's one good thing that came out of the fiasco." Her eyes moistened again.

"Yeah, that may have been the only good thing. Do you want to stay here or go live with your mother until it's over?" Mike said.

"This is our home, Mike—yours, Maria's, and mine. We'll wait right here and pray every night, until you walk back through that door, safe and sound. Promise me you'll be careful."

"I promise."

"And promise you won't volunteer for any crazy missions like you did last time you were in Cuba."

"I promise."

A log in the fireplace popped, a flame erupted, then died, the embers shifted, and the house became quiet.

As Mike and Sandy slumbered, lights in the Pentagon would burn brightly that night and for several weeks to come. The Joint Staff fired out a series of orders to various army, navy, and air force commands causing the eventual relocation of hundreds of warplanes and ships. Within hours, the orders would affect tens of thousands of military men and women. Thousands of military families would suffer the anguish of upcoming separation.

The navy ordered creation of a task force designated TF 135, consisting of the *Enterprise* and *Independence* aircraft carrier task groups, along with dozens of additional cruisers, destroyers, support vessels, and hundreds of aircraft—fighters, bombers, antisubmarine planes, and helicopters. Marine Corps units on both coasts received mobilization alerts. Vice Admiral Alfred Ward, commander of the United States Second Fleet (Atlantic Fleet) put to sea in his flagship, the U.S.S. *Newport News* (CA 148).

The Anti-Submarine Warfare Task Group, an Atlantic Fleet component organized, trained, and equipped specifically to thwart the Soviet submarine threat also received activation orders. It normally patrolled the east coast searching for Soviet submarines as they constantly probed American littoral defenses. The Soviets knew from experience that the ASWTG presented a formidable obstacle to their submarine mission.

In 1959, the Navy converted the seventeen-year-old aircraft carrier U.S.S. *Sibuyan Sea* specifically for the ASW mission. She carried aircraft and helicopters equipped with underwater detection equipment and the ability to attack and destroy enemy subs, and served at the flagship of task group.

Destroyer Squadron Forty-Two protected the carrier and adding another dimension of offensive ASW capability. Rounding out the fearsome package, a hunter-killer submarine, designed to find and destroy other submarines. The American H-K subs are nuclear powered and the best in the world. A diesel powered Soviet submarine has little chance against this foe. The ships and over seven-thousand sailors assigned were mission ready.

Sibuyan Sea received orders while at Naval Station Guantanamo, Cuba, for sea trials after a recently completed overhaul. The carrier put to sea at 0430, 22 October 1962, but her escort squadron of destroyers sat over twelve hundred miles away at Naval Station Newport, Rhode Island, their homeport.

DESRON Forty-Two received deployment alert orders as *Sibuyan Sea* sailed from Gitmo. The following day the squadron received revised orders requiring that all destroyers be prepared to sail with a two-hour notification. Part of the squadron sailed shortly thereafter.

Many sailors were on shore leave, requiring recall notification and a scramble to fill critical personnel vacancies. Most ships sailed shorthanded, creating a human logistics nightmare. Somehow, hundreds of sailors would have to find their way to their ships, over a thousand miles away, in what might be the middle of a shooting war.

⌐ CHAPTER 2

Naval Station Newport, Rhode Island

Tuesday, 23 October 1962

On 22 October 1962, the President called Mr. Robert S. McNamara, the Secretary of Defense, regarding the time when we would be ready to invade Cuba. Mr. McNamara told him seven days. The President said that he wanted to be sure that we were ready in every respect at the end of the seven days.[4]

The following day, 23 October 1962, at a White House ceremony, President John F. Kennedy signed proclamation 3504 that he had announced to the world on the previous evening. In it, he declared a quarantine of the Republic of Cuba, effective at 2:00 P.M. Greenwich Mean Time, October 24, 1962.[5]

The proclamation stated the United States would not allow delivery of offensive military materiel of any kind to Cuba. He ordered the Secretary of Defense to employ the land, sea, and air forces of the United States, in cooperation with any forces made available by other American states, to interdict any vessel or craft destined for Cuba with offensive weapons aboard. Interdicted vessels would be allowed to proceed to any destination other than Cuba. Failure to comply would result in the vessel being taken into custody and sent to a United States port for appropriate disposition, by force if necessary.[5]

Chief Gunner's Mate Mike Stafford stood on pier two, at Naval Station Newport, Rhode Island. Three days had passed since receiving the letter recalling him to active duty. That piece of paper had started events in his life whirling like the blustery wind and sleet now raging across Narragansett Bay.

Pondering the recent past and the immediate future, he looked up at the destroyer tender U.S.S. *Yosemite* (AD 19), moored with her port side to the pier. Fondly known to destroyermen as the "yo-yo," she is the flagship of the Atlantic Fleet cruiser-destroyer force.

Pulling up the collar of his heavy bridge coat, Mike walked down the pier toward the tender's after brow. With noticeable hesitation, he stepped up on it. Climbing haltingly, he reached the gangway where he faced aft, saluted the flag, and then turned toward the quarterdeck and saluted the officer of the deck (OOD).

"Request permission to board, Sir."

The officer returned his salute. "Permission granted."

Mike loosened the top two buttons of his coat, reached into his breast pocket, withdrew his orders, and handed them to the officer.

The officer read the orders and then passed them to the petty officer of the watch, who entered the pertinent information into the logbook and handed the papers back to Mike.

"Do you know where the personnel office is, Chief?" the officer inquired.

"Yes, Sir, I do."

"Welcome aboard, then," the officer said.

"Thank you, Sir, but I don't think I'll be aboard for long."

He passed through the big double cargo doors, walked toward the starboard side until he reached the interior passageway. Turning, he proceeded forward to the personnel office.

"How can I help you, Chief?" a personnel man second class inquired.

Mike handed his orders across the counter without comment. The petty officer read them, walked over to a file bin, and began flipping through a series of folders. He reached the last one and then started over from the front.

Mike took a deep breath.

Finally, the personnel man selected one and looked up. "Misfiled . . . sometimes I think these damn strikers don't even know the alphabet." He read from the folder as he walked back to the counter.

"Don't unpack, Chief. You're to report to the U.S.S. *Boyington*, DD 953, and she sails tomorrow. You can find her tied up over on pier one." He stamped and initialed Stafford's original orders and returned them along with a new set reassigning him to the destroyer.

Mike glanced at the man's name stenciled on his blue chambray work shirt. "Thanks, McGowan." He turned and departed.

After a trip up the hill to the sprawling parking lot to retrieve his suitcase and sea bag, he walked back down to pier one and found the *Boyington* at the far end, moored port side-to. He went through the boarding formalities with the Officer of the Deck.

"Welcome aboard, Chief. I'll have Seaman Hughes, the quarterdeck messenger, help you to the chiefs' quarters. It's kinda tough getting through our narrow passageways with a load like you've got," the OOD said.

"Thank you, Sir, I appreciate the help." Mike saluted again, stepped over the watertight door's coaming, and entered the after passageway. He led the way to the chiefs' quarters as Hughes tagged along behind with the heavy sea bag.

When he entered the chiefs' messing compartment, Mike instantly felt at home. The green, asbestos tile deck; unadorned, gray, metal bulkheads; tables welded to the deck; and the smell of burnt coffee and cigarette smoke brought back memories of the U.S.S. *Jaffey*, his last ship. Both vessels belonged to the Forrest Sherwood class and were nearly identical.

It startled him to see an old shipmate, Chief Boatswain's Mate Paul Jones, sitting at a table with a cup of coffee and a newspaper. "Paul, you old reprobate, I can't believe my eyes."

"Mike, you ol' son of a sea cook. I heard a rumor last week you might join us. Welcome aboard."

"Really, you heard that last week? You always did have the best grapevine going. They pulled me out of retirement—I just got the letter Saturday. What's going on? They told me on the yo-yo that *Boyington* sails tomorrow."

"Well, as you might have guessed, we gotta go down and trim Castro's beard. You must have heard the president a couple of nights ago say on TV that we're gonna blockade Cuba. Belay that, he said, we're gonna 'quarantine' Cuba, but we all know what that means. Of course, when he says 'we,' he means destroyers, and we're the next to go. Most of CRUDESLANT is already down there or on the way."

"What's this CRUDESLANT business? What happed to the DESLANT I knew and loved?" Mike asked.

"Oh, couple of months ago someone had the bright idea of combining the two type commands. I guess they're going to homeport a couple of cruisers here now. One shows up occasionally. It's a terrible idea. You can only imagine how gung-ho the place is going to get."

"Yeah, I noticed everyone on-base wearing blues."

"It gets more chicken-shit every day. Sailors can't go off ship in dungarees anymore."

"Too bad, I always liked this base. By the way, Paul, why does the *Boyington* need another chief gunner's mate?"

"You're not another chief gunner, you're *the* chief gunner. They hauled Chief Banner off last week with what turned out to be an appendicitis attack. They got him up to the hospital, and he damn near died. I recommend staying away from that place, Mike. Lot a the people that go up there die or we never see them again. I don't know what happens to them."

"Yeah, I've heard that happens sometimes in hospitals."

"Hey, let's get you squared away, and then we'll go meet the boss."

"Okay, who is he?"

"Lieutenant Patrick Quinn. He's an academy man, squared away officer, sticks up for his people. I think you'll get along with him just fine."

"Don't think I ever met him. As long as he isn't like that jerk we worked for on the ol' *McCallanan* back in fifty-three, I'll be happy."

"Oh, yeah, thanks. It took me years to get that SOB outta my head. I appreciate you bringing back the memories. Somebody's no doubt shoved the bastard overboard by now."

"Yeah, I wouldn't doubt that a bit."

"But, hey, we gotta great skipper too, Commander William M. Ellingham. He's a good ASW man, but nothing like ol' Captain Schmidt. Man, we gotta lot of catching up to do. Let's take care of business, and then we can hit the beach tonight. There's a bunch of people down at the Blue Moon that'll love to see you."

"Paul, I'm a married man now with a baby girl at home. There are a lot of females around here it's best for me not to meet up with again."

"Oh, man, we sure have a lot to discuss. This is gonna be a great cruise—like the good old days. Come on back to the berthing compartment, and I'll get you a rack and a locker. You can unpack while I find the boss, set up some meetings, and check on my motley crew."

Bosun Jones returned an hour later. Mike waited in the compartment after having stowed his gear.

"Let's go, the lieutenant will meet us in his cabin now," Jones said.

The two walked the short distance to officer's country where Jones knocked on the gunnery officer's open door.

"Come in, Boats."

"Thank you, Sir. This here's Mike Stafford, the best gunner's mate in the whole damn navy."

Lieutenant Quinn and Mike shook hands.

"I've heard some good scuttlebutt about you, Chief. We're up to our ass in alligators right now, but after we get to sea, let's get together and swap sea stories," Quinn said.

"Yes, Sir. Are there any problems I need to know about before we shove off?" Mike asked.

"I think the mounts and loaders are all squared away, but there are a couple of problem seamen that need a little attitude adjustment. Chief Banner tried, but I'm not satisfied that he got these two under control. Listen, I have a department-heads meeting starting in three minutes. We'll talk later. Welcome aboard, Chief."

The two chiefs exited the cabin. Lieutenant Quinn shut the door and headed for the wardroom.

"Okay, next we meet the XO," Jones said. "He's Lieutenant Commander John Kaestner, another good guy, but all business unless you bring up something about hockey or golf."

Mike followed Jones up a series of narrow ladders to the chartroom on the 0-2 level where they found Kaestner and a quartermaster hovering over the table absorbed in some navigational issue.

"Sir, this is Mike Stafford, our new gunner. Chief, meet Commander Kaestner, the XO, and QM1 Gandolfi, the leading quartermaster," Jones said.

Mike shook hands with both men and then turned back to the XO.

"Glad to meet you, Chief Stafford, and welcome aboard. I heard BUPERS pulled you out of retirement with short notice."

"Yes, Sir, they did, but I understand the situation. During my short time as a civilian, I stayed up with the news and world affairs better than I ever could while on active duty."

"Good, I'm glad there aren't any hard feelings. You know it wasn't a decision taken lightly—we may be at war in a few days. There isn't time to train new men in critical ratings, so the cruiser-destroyer commander, COMCRUDESLANT, had to call on the fleet reserve in a number of cases."

"Yes, Sir, I understand."

"Great. Do you have an appointment to meet the captain?"

Mike glanced at Jones.

"Yes, Sir, he's reporting to the skipper at 1500," Jones said.

"Okay, carry on. Good to meet you, Chief, and welcome aboard," Kaestner said. He turned back to the chart he had been working on.

Mike and Bosun Jones left the chartroom and went below to the chiefs' mess for a late dinner. Jones introduced him to the few men still present and they enjoyed a hearty meal.

At 1455, they left for the captain's cabin.

Jones knocked on the door, which elicited a gruff response. "Enter."

Mike led the way into the small office, part of the captain's cabin. He stopped one pace from the desk and came to the position of attention. "Chief Gunner's Mate Michael A. Stafford, service number 337 62 07, reporting for duty as ordered, Sir."

The captain stood and offered his hand, "Welcome aboard, Chief. Have a seat, gentlemen."

"I'm sorry we had to pull you back into the fray the way we did, Chief Stafford, but we were in a tight spot. We lost GMC Banner last week, and we're sailing tomorrow. The way things are looking, we could be back in a shooting war in a matter of days and, well, enough said.

"Your former CO, Fred Schmidt, is an old friend of mine, and he always spoke highly of you, so when BUPERS gave me a list of names to pick from, you were my first choice. Did you find a bunk for him, Bosun?" Ellingham asked.

"Yes, Sir, he's all squared away."

"Good. If you ever need to talk, Guns, the door is always open, no appointment needed. Now, we all have plenty to do and little time, so let's turn-to. We can chat after we're under way."

"Aye, aye, Sir," Mike said. He came to attention again, executed a sharp about-face, and followed Jones out the door.

"That went well. Always good to be handpicked by the commander," Jones said.

"Yeah, but that's a double-edged sword. If the crew thinks I'm some kind of fair-haired boy, I lose all credibility. So please, let's just keep that conversation between us, Paul. Okay?"

"Sure, Mike, I didn't mean nothing, and I understand what you mean about the crew. It'll stay just between us ol' salts. So about tonight, you wanna get off the ship for a last supper and a few beers? If things go down like everyone's saying, it might be our last chance for a while."

"Good idea. I need to go over on the pier and call home to tell my wife what's going on. When I get back, I'll grab a shower and be ready at liberty call."

CHAPTER 3

Chief Petty Officer's Club
Naval Station Newport, Rhode Island

Tuesday, 23 October 1962

Orders flashed from the Pentagon, placing the armed forces of the United States on Defense Condition Three, the third of five readiness postures with five being the least severe.[4]

October 23, 1962—5:40 P.M. Fidel Castro announces a combat alarm, placing the Cuban armed forces on their highest alert. Cuban armed forces subsequently reach a size of 270,000 men following a massive mobilization effort. (Statement by Castro Rejecting the Possibility of Inspection and Noting That Cuba Has Taken Measures To Repeal a United States Attack, 10/23/62; Garthoff [1], p.66.) [1]

The Commander in Chief Atlantic (CINCLANT) identified the Soviet vessels Kimovsk and Gagarin as the first Soviet freighters to be intercepted. Using direction finders, the Navy tracked both ships and designated the Essex carrier group to conduct the interception. They chose the anti-submarine warfare group because of possible submarine escorts with the freighters.[4]

M ike Stafford followed Paul Jones across the brow ten minutes after liberty call sounded. They headed toward the head of the pier and then began climbing the hill to the parking lot.

There were thousands of cars in the massive parking lot, testimony to the number of sailors already deployed. A sign indicated parking for officers and chiefs only, in the first two rows, closest to the piers.

"My car is down at the south end of the second row," Mike said.

They turned down the lane and continued walking. "How about we eat at the Chiefs' Club?" Jones suggested. "The food is good and there'll be some serious partying going on tonight. It's the last night in port for several ships, not just ours."

"Sounds good, and it'll help out the budget. I just took one hell of a pay cut."

"Yeah, I bet you did. Welcome back to Uncle Sam's Yacht Club. We still don't make a decent wage, but think of the glory that'll be showered on us when we come home."

"That might prove to be a big assumption," Mike said.

"You think we might not make it back. Is that what you're saying?"

"After what I saw during WW II and Korea, yeah, it could happen to us. Lots of guys didn't return from those conflicts."

"Not come back? Come on, man, what can the Cubans do to us?"

"It's not the Cubans I'm worried about."

"Oh—you're thinking about the Ruskies?"

"Bingo. I think they're running the island now, and Castro's just a puppet."

They slid into Mike's car and headed to the club.

After a short drive, Mike pulled into the parking lot at the CPO Club. The car in front of them paused at the front door to discharge passengers. Two well-dressed women got out and made their way toward the main entrance.

"Looks like the party's about to start," Jones said, "and I like what I see."

"Hey we're in luck," Mike said. There's an open parking spot there on the end."

"Go for it."

The bosun held the club door open, and they entered. Mike followed Jones into the bar. There weren't any vacant barstools, so they took a table near the back.

A waitress appeared and Jones, with an approving nod from Mike, ordered two bottles of Millers.

That's a real fancy car you got, Buddy. Looks new."

"It's a 1962 Ford Galaxie. I got it as a sort of Christmas present last year, with my bonus check. It's the first new car I ever had and the first car I ever owned outright."

"They're the best kind," Jones said.

"Oh, you like Fords?"

"They're okay, but I meant the paid for kind."

"You're right. My father never had a new car in his life. He always said, 'If you can't pay cash, you can't afford it.' I've never told him, but I bought several on credit. This one, however, I paid cash for."

"What'd it set you back, if you don't mind my asking?"

"Twenty-two hundred dollars, including automatic transmission, turn signals, heater, and radio."

"Man, you damn near stole it right off the lot."

"My brother knows a guy who got the deal for us."

"Fantastic. Hey, Mike, this place is filling up fast. We better finish this beer and grab some chow before a line starts forming in the dining room."

They left the bar and entered the dining room. No one appeared to greet them, so they waited at the desk. Jones looked about, impatiently.

The hostess, a nicely dressed, middle-aged woman, arrived a few minutes later. "Good evening gentlemen, table for two?

"Yes ma'am," Jones said.

She led them to a table near the front window.

A smiling, pert young waitress appeared with pen and pad in hand. "We have a special tonight, gentlemen, fourteen ounce T-bone steak, French fries, and salad, all for a dollar-fifty. We also have two-for-one beer until six o'clock," she said.

"You won my heart, darling. Make the steak rare, the fries hot, and the beer cold. Millers High-Life, please," Jones said.

The waitress turned to Mike.

"Sounds good, make mine the same. Medium-rare for me please."

She jotted the order on her pad. "I'll be right back with your drinks and a selection of salad dressings."

"Cute girl, or are you too married to notice?" Jones said.

Mike opened his wallet and pulled out a photo. "This is my little family, Paul. My wife's name is Sandy. Our baby is Maria and she's four-months old now. I feel like I should be at home with them, not sailing into WW III." Mike paused a moment, looking out the window. "We tied the knot a year ago last July in Norfolk, and Maria came along this past June."

"She's a doll, and the baby's a sweetie too. Where'd you meet such a classy dame?"

"Cuba."

"Yeah . . . she doesn't look Cuban."

"She's not. I met her at Gitmo. She had been an officer, but resigned her commission so we could marry."

"It looks like you landed a great one, and you say she was an officer?"

"Yeah, a jay-gee."

The waitress arrived with their beer, distracting Jones for several minutes. He lit a cigarette then resumed the conversation. "Oh, you always had a way with the ladies. But, you done real good, son. That must be some line of BS you got landing an officer willing to resign her commission for an old, worn out gunner."

"Old and worn out? Give me a break. I'm just entering my prime."

"Yeah, you keep on believing that. Hey, I heard some scuttlebutt last year about you getting stuck ashore down there in 'Cuber,' as our president calls it—any truth to that?"

"Maybe some. Were you down there during the Bay of Pigs invasion?" Mike asked.

"No, I left recruiting duty in January of '61 and went aboard the *Negley.* We were stuck in the yards at Philly until June. Sorry I missed it, but I did have a good time in the city of brotherly, and especially sisterly, love. Did I tell you about the cute little red head I met there?"

Mike took a sip of his beer. "No, and don't say anything about me having a good line. As far as the Bay of Pigs, you didn't miss a thing. Captain Schmidt and I were together on the *Jaffey,* as you know. We were part of the task force designated to support the exile invasion, but Kennedy pulled the entire U.S. military out before we fired a shot. Unfortunately, I happened to be ashore with my striker, and a Cuban exile soldier. We were supposed to be a spotting party for *Jaffey's* five inchers. She had orders to cover the landing, but then the order came down to pull out, so they left without us. We had to hoof it across the island to Gitmo."

"You saying you walked from the Bay of Pigs to Gitmo?"

"Well, that's an exaggeration. We walked a long way, but hopped trains for most of the distance. We made it only because this beautiful, young Cuban girl took pity on us and helped us dodge the police that were chasing us," Mike said.

"I knew it. I knew there would be a beautiful woman in this story."

The food arrived, and conversation stopped, other than Paul's flirting with the waitress.

When she departed, Paul took a long pull on his beer then began slicing his steak. "Go on, why were the police after you, and how'd you manage to make it onto the base. I thought Castro had the place surrounded and locked down tight."

"He did. The police took exception with the idea of three invaders walking free around their country. The details of our escape are still classified, but I can say I made it onto the base and met Sandy there in the Gitmo hospital."

"Hospital—how'd you get hurt?"

"I didn't, but had lost a lot of weight and picked up a few Cuban bugs that had my gut doing flip-flops."

"Oh, so then you weren't aboard *Jaffey* when Schmidt rammed a Russian submarine?"

"No, I had plenty of my own problems to deal with at the time."

"It's a sad situation. Every salt in DESLANT knows at least one story about ol' Captain Schmidt. Guess he pushed his luck one fathom too deep, cuz they beached him."

"Yeah, I know all about the sub and his retiring. They called me back on active duty for a week to testify at the board of inquiry. He's a professor at the Massachusetts Maritime Academy now. We get together every once in awhile for a beer and some fishing."

"That's great. I'm glad to know he's doing okay after the way they treated him."

"Hell of a skipper, and we damn sure need the likes of him now," Mike said.

They finished eating and moved from the dining room back to the now crowded bar. It looked like half the chiefs from the base were there, and the drinks were moving off the bar as fast as the bartenders could pour them. Many of the chiefs' wives were also there, along with a few women who may have been looking for a husband or just companionship.

Mike sat with some old friends in the former group, while Paul circulated in the latter. At 2130, Mike sought him out. "I'm afraid my drinking ability has deteriorated since I retired, ol' buddy. I'm heading back to the ship. You want to come along or stay with the party?"

"Mike, I can't believe you. The night is still young."

A gorgeous blonde in a tight red dress tugged on Paul's arm. "Come on Jonesy, I wanta dance."

"Maybe the night's young, but I'm not. Can you catch a ride, if I leave?" Mike asked.

"Sure, see you in the morning."

"Okay, we shove off at 0800, don't be late. This is one movement you don't want to miss."

"Yeah, yeah, don't worry about me. I'm in good hands, right, Roxie?"

"Oh, yeah, baby. I'm gonna take real good care of you tonight," she said.

Mike threw a casual salute and departed the club. He returned to a very quiet ship. Most of her liberty party would stay ashore until the last possible minute, 0700.

CHAPTER 4

Thames Street, Newport, Rhode Island

Tuesday, 23 October 1962

On the day following the President's announcement, Russia canceled all military leaves and stopped discharges, particularly for personnel in rocket, anti-aircraft, and submarine duties. There were several reports of Soviet long-range submarines along Russian shipping routes.[4]

A Japanese press report said that the Director General of the Soviet News Agency, Tass, visiting Japan, stated, "If the United States sinks a Soviet ship, there will be total war."[4]

All the Communist satellite countries unleashed a propaganda campaign against the United States. However, there were no intelligence reports of the Soviet Bloc planning any aggressive moves or preparing for a major conflict with the United States or other countries of the free world.[4]

The Organization of American States approved the U.S.
quarantine resolution with a 19 to 0 vote highlighting
the reaction of the allied nations to the U.S. action.[4]

Thames Street's sidewalks teemed with pedestrians, civilian and military. Groups of sailors trolled the area looking for a place to spend their last night ashore. Rumors of a long deployment and the possibility of war, electrified the night.

A bar that didn't enforce the legal drinking age stood first on the search list for underage service members. Locations varied from time to time, so trial and error attempts became necessary. Once one underage sailor managed to purchase a beverage, the establishment soon filled with his young and thirsty mates, cash registers rang, and the merriment began.

Young women occupied second place on the search list. Many gravitated to the most crowded bars. On this particular night, Tony's Black Cat Bar answered all criteria. In short order, the word made its way up and down Thames Street and Tony's became the place to be.

The music thundered, the beer flowed freely, and females from all over southern Rhode Island and southwestern Massachusetts flocked in to party with the free spending sailors. Couples packed the dance floor, as Chubby Checker demanded they do the twist.

By eleven o'clock, many of the early arrivals lay crumpled in the dark corners of the bar passed out. Friends carried off the lucky ones. The party, however, continued to grow. A group of local working men gathered in the back around the pool tables, while the sailors tended to remain toward the front of the establishment.

Near midnight, movement at the main entrance caught the bartender's eye. Two big sailors stood framed in the open door. As they entered, many on the dance floor, located at the front of the room, moved toward the wall on the far side. The bartender recognized the two and watched their movements, expecting trouble. He fingered the Louisville Slugger he kept under the bar near the cash register.

One of the barmaids, a well endowed, college girl in a short, tight black dress, danced on the bar. Sensing trouble, she stopped and climbed down, much to the disappointment of the woozy clients occupying stools in front of her station.

A path along the bar parted ahead of the two sailors as they made their way toward the back of the room, most customers judging it prudent to step aside and avoid trouble.

The bartender noticed other sailors in the room scrutinizing the new arrivals from a distance, searching for clues, and sizing up the taller man. Some may have seen and recognized the insignia and chevrons on his left sleeve as belonging to a first class boatswain's mate. Others might have noticed four hash marks on his lower left sleeve signified over sixteen years of naval service. If he behaved well during those years, the chevrons and hash marks would have been gold. He hadn't, and they were red rather than gold. An embroidered patch on his right sleeve near the shoulder indicated his ship, the U.S.S. *Boyington.*

Near the end of the bar, there was a single vacant stool. The taller of the two sailors spotted it, threw his leg over it, and eased himself down.

A civilian sitting on an adjacent stool turned toward the bosun. "You're sitting on my buddy's stool. He's in the can."

"Can't be his cuz I'm sitting on it."

"Yeah? Well, we'll find out when he comes back."

The bosun turned, wrapped a huge hand around a full bottle of beer on the bar behind him. He hoisted it to his lips and drained it in one long, sustained swallow.

"You just drank his beer—I bought it for him."

"Couldn't have been his, cuz it was sitting at my stool. You gonna get this round?"

The other sailor, a husky boatswain's mate second class with three hash marks, listened to the exchange. "I'd like one too, please."

The civilian glared at them incredulously.

The glare went unnoticed by both sailors as they focused on a woman in an extremely short skirt and a form-fitting blouse, bending over the pool table to line up a shot. She flipped her brunette mane over her right shoulder and sank the eight ball. A cheer went up, and she curtsied to the crowd.

A tall, muscular civilian walked up, stopped, and stood in front of the bosun, blocking his view and interrupting his concentration. The big man wore dark green work clothes with his sleeves rolled up to flaunt his bulging biceps and tattoos. Inked on the side of his right

36

bicep, the image of a Mack truck belched smoke from its twin exhaust pipes. His left arm proudly displayed a bulldog, similar to a Mack hood ornament. Above his shirt pocket, the logo of a long haul trucking firm glowed in bright orange and white. The man's name, "Jim," stood out above the opposite pocket, embroidered in luminous orange.

"Yer on my stool, partner," Jim said.

"Ain't your stool, and I ain't your partner, ass wipe."

Jim's friend slid off his stool and stood aside smiling, waiting for the devastating punch about to flatten the obnoxious sailor.

In a movement most people wouldn't have noticed, trucker Jim shifted his weight to his right foot and flexed the fingers of his right hand. The sailor, with the reflexes of an alley cat saw it and reacted. His massive right fist flew through the air like a lightning bolt, striking Jim's nose squarely. It popped like an acorn cracking underfoot. Jim staggered back and fell with blood gushing from both nostrils.

The bosun looked at the civilian standing beside the fallen Jim. "You order a round yet?"

The man scowled and stooped to aid his friend.

The bartender arrived. "What's the trouble here?"

"Can't get a beer, and some guy tripped and fell. I'll have a couple of Narragansett long necks. What're you having, Dalton?"

"The same, Harry, and some peanuts, please."

The barman sneered. "Look, Foss, Tony warned you last time you was here, any trouble and you're barred. He told me to call the cops if you started any fights, so I don't want no more guys tripping and falling near you, understand?"

"Sure, boss. How much longer till we get a beer?"

"Four 'Gansetts coming up."

The lady pool shark walked over, rested her hands on the bosun's rock-hard thighs, leaned forward, and kissed him, long and hard. "What are you doing, Foss, stirring up business for the local hospital again?"

Foss gripped her buttocks with both of his huge hands. "Hi ya, Babs. You're looking mighty good tonight."

She stood up straight, threw her shoulders back, pulled her hair into a ponytail, and then let it loose. Foss admired her chest with a practiced eye as she put on the display.

"What ya drinking tonight, beautiful?"

"Jack-rocks, big boy. Make it a double—care for a game?"

"Not if you mean pool."

"What about you, Dalton, want me to rack your balls?"

"Maybe later . . . right now I'm looking for some stick action."

"Foss, I think this boy made a naughty suggestion. You gonna let him cut your time like that?"

"He's joking, Babs. Go take his money."

Babs won the break and bent low to line up her shot, giving the crowd a full view of her comely legs, enhanced by spike heels. Six balls fell in rapid succession. She returned to the bar and slammed down the first of many double Jacks.

Dalton finished his second beer and ordered four more for himself and Foss, plus two double jacks for Babs.

After buying a dozen beers, six double Jacks, and playing four games, a glassy-eyed Dalton shuffled to the bar, slumped over it, and held his head. He tried to figure out what happened to all his money. Fifty dollars, over a weeks' pay for a second-class petty officer with tens year's service, had somehow disappeared during the games with Babs.

The music reached a deafening level. Two burly men lifted Babs up on the pool table. She hiked up her skirt and began dancing barefooted, drawing a crowd. A circle of lusty fans formed around the table and began encouraging her by throwing dollar bills at her feet.

Her unencumbered breasts undulated to the beat of the music. She unbuttoned her blouse. One button, two buttons, three . . . The thundering music, and Babs's display sent the men into a heated frenzy. They began shouting in unison, "Take it off. Take it off."

Foss slid off his stool and grabbed the first two men he came to by the neck and cast them aside as a small boy might discard toys that no longer held his interest. Closer to the pool table, he snatched two more men and tossed them out of the way. He reached the table and scooped up Babs in his left arm. As he turned to leave, a fist grazed his jaw.

Without flinching or dropping Babs, he grabbed his attacker's hair and using the neatly combed ducktail to gain a firm grip, smashed the man's face down on the hard edge of the pool table. The crunch of disintegrating teeth reflected up Foss's right arm. When the man attempted to stand, red blood splattered across the green-felt table covering. He quivered, and then spiraled to the floor.

The crowd parted as the bartender appeared clutching his baseball bat so tightly that his knuckles were pearl white.

"He started it, Bubba," Foss said.

"Get your ass outta here and don't you never come back, Foss. The cops is on their way, and Tony's gonna be pissed when he sees that table."

"Yeah, yeah. Dalton, grab her shoes and scoop up all the folding money. We're leaving." Foss headed toward the front door with Babs perched on his arm. He carried her with no more effort than a toy poodle required of an average man. She kept her arms locked around his thick neck. Her legs entwined around his narrow waist, causing her skirt to rise up over her thighs. Babs appeared to be either asleep or passed out.

The college girl-barmaid, again danced on the bar, performing a scintillating routine as the jute box boomed Dee Dee Sharp's *Mashed Potato Time*. The dancer emphasized her movements with a bar-towel stretched tightly across her derrière, which she snapped back and forth in time with the music. Her provocative movements completely mesmerized her fans so none noticed Foss, Dalton, and Babs pass by on their way to the front door.

As the trio neared the door, it opened, and trucker Jim filled the entrance. The skin around his eyes, visible above the tape across his nose, had taken on a yellowish hue. Nasal packing forced him to breathe through his mouth. The big man hissed like an angry bull that had spied an antagonizing matador and wanted a kill. His eyes glowed with intense loathing.

"Foss, no trouble—you hear me?" the barman shouted.

"I'm gonna twist your head off and piss down your neck, you sumabitch," Jim snorted.

"Jim, get outta here, now," the barman yelled. As he rounded the end of the bar, he smashed a chair with his baseball bat to underscore the order. The chair splintered, and pieces of wood flew across the dance floor like shrapnel. Women screamed and scattered. Their dance partners hurried after them to avoid the flying shards.

Dalton stepped in front of Foss, who still carried Babs, oblivious of any danger.

"Outta my way punk," the trucker growled. Jim towered over the squat, broad-shouldered sailor. With his eyes locked on Foss, he pounded Dalton's shoulder with a left jab, intended to knock him aside. The sailor didn't move. Surprised, Jim turned his attention from Foss to Dalton.

At that moment, Dalton planted a powerful haymaker square on the poor man's already broken nose.

Jim's eyes crossed, his mouth opened without making a sound, and he toppled backward in slow motion, as a huge oak tree might after a lumberjack planted the final swing of a sharp axe.

Dalton stepped over the comatose body and held the door as Foss and Babs exited. He continued holding it open as two Newport police officers arrived.

The officers nodded their appreciation as they passed him and entered the bar.

Dalton let the door close and started down Thames Street, following Foss.

The police sergeant waived to the bartender as he stepped over Jim's body, ignoring his seriously damaged face. Cupping his hands over his mouth to form a megaphone, the officer shouted over the music and clamor in the bar. "What's the trouble?"

"Some guy fell and hit his nose, Sarge," the bartender yelled back.

"You call an ambulance?"

"Yeah, one's on the way."

"Okay, tell Tony we stopped in. By the way, we'd appreciate it if you'd keep the youngsters back, out of the front window. We don't need any concerned citizens complaining."

"Will do, thanks for coming by, Sarge," the bartender said.

Foss, Babs and Dalton continued down the street toward her apartment.

Dalton stared at his watch, trying to bring the dial into focus. "Hey, Foss, we're supposed to cast off at 0800. You think we oughta head back to the ship?"

"Nah, we got five more hours before liberty's up," Foss replied.

Babs, still clinging to Foss, stirred. "Can't you guys hurry up? I'm cold and I need some serious loving."

CHAPTER 5

Narragansett Bay, Rhode Island

Wednesday, 24 October 1962

The State Department, at the request of the Defense Department, promulgated the following notice to other governments on 24 Oct 62:

Submarine Surfacing and Identification Procedures When Contacted by Quarantine Forces in the General Vicinity of Cuba

U.S. forces in contact with unidentified submerged submarines will make the following signals to inform the submarine that he may surface in order to identify himself: Signals follow: Quarantine forces will drop four or five harmless explosive sound signals, which may be accompanied by the international code signal "IDKCA" meaning, "Rise to the surface." This sonar signal is normally made on underwater communications equipment in the 8kc frequency range. Procedure on receipt of the signal: Submerged submarine, on hearing the signal, should surface on an easterly course. Signal and procedures employed are harmless and are to guarantee the safety of submerged submarines at sea in emergencies.

On 25 Oct 62, DOS requested DOD issue a "Notice to Mariners," for all submarine-possessing nations.[1]

Three trumpeting blasts from a steam horn shattered the tranquility of the harbor as the destroyer U.S.S. *Negley*, previously moored outboard from the *Boyington*, cast-off her lines, and backed into the bay. She maneuvered into the channel then turned south to begin the trip down to the rolling Atlantic Ocean. *Negley* and *Boyington* were under orders to rendezvous in the open sea and proceed together to a destination still under close-hold.

The autumn sun had yet to penetrate the overcast morning, but neither a cold west wind nor lack of sunlight failed to dampen the organized bustle of activity on destroyer pier one or onboard the *Boyington.*

Captain Ellingham stepped out on the open bridge, port side, to observe activities pier side. The engineers had secured all shore services. The disconnected water, electrical, and telephone lines lay coiled on the pier. The deck hands had removed the rat guards and were standing by awaiting their next task.

At 0715, the precise time scheduled in the Plan of the Day, Boatswain's Mate Second Class John Dalton stood near the pilothouse after bulkhead, in front of the 1-MC public address system microphone. His lined face and bloodshot eyes reflected a lack of sleep and the rough night that he had endured ashore in the company of Bosun Foss and their friend Babs.

He wished he'd returned to the ship earlier and had time for a few hours sleep. Getting aboard ten minutes before liberty expired and having a handful of aspirin for breakfast wasn't working out very well.

He drew a deep breath, causing his face to turn scarlet. His hand shook as he pressed the pipe to his lips and blew a series of warbling low and high pitch tones alerting the crew to an announcement. "Now hear this: Now station the special sea and anchor detail. Set material condition Yankee. The officer of the deck is shifting his watch to the bridge. Make all preparations for getting under way." His hoarse voice crackled from loud speakers throughout the ship.

Ellingham turned to see the bridge officers enter the pilothouse. "Get moving on the checklist, Mister Sherwood, we're running late."

"Aye, aye, Sir," Lieutenant (JG) Sherwood replied. As the most skillful ship driver of the junior officers, he held the prestigious position as Officer of the Deck (OOD) when the captain called for the special sea and anchor detail. That group of officers and senior petty officers, manned all critical posts through the ship whenever entering or leaving port or navigating dangerous channels.

The captain moved to the starboard side of the bridge and made a quick assessment.

"I have the deck and conn," Sherwood announced.

The helmsman acknowledged, "Mister Sherwood has the deck and the conn."

Ensign Padgett, the Junior Officer of the Deck (JOOD), watched every move and listened to every command as part of his training. He hoped to qualify for OOD watches in the near future.

Sherwood handed Padgett the checklist clipboard. "Get this finished, the ol' man's upset."

Line handlers on the pier and on deck stood in place, awaiting orders. Mister Anderson, the First Lieutenant, and Chief Boatswain's Mate Jones directed activities on the forecastle, while Mister Quinn, the Gunnery Officer, and Boatswain's Mate First Class Foss managed preparations on the fantail.

Bosun Jones, ignored the wind and cold of the forecastle, and started to wonder if it might not have been wise to leave the club with Mike Stafford earlier the previous evening. His head ached and his eyes burned as his stomach performed acrobatic flip-flops.

The image of a beautiful, fun loving woman formed in his mind. He pictured her hourglass figure, her flowing blonde hair, and that voice, as seductive as Lorelei's song. The idea of missing movement and staying with her crossed his mind in the wee hours of the morning while in her company.

He suggested the option to her, but she reminded him of the consequences and promised a warm welcome upon his return. Now he feared her promise might not have been serious. Perhaps a deployed husband would be returning soon. He couldn't sort his conflicted feelings: love or lust . . . pride or passion. Therefore, he sat aside his physical pains and amorous thoughts, and forced himself to concentrate on the job at hand.

Mister Padgett queried each department involved to ensure all vital positions were manned and ready. He ticked off the items on his clipboard as he received verification. Finally, he turned to the OOD. Checklist complete, Sir. All stations are manned and ready.

Sherwood signed the completed checklist and gave it to the quartermaster. He then addressed the lee helmsman, "Main control, standby to answer bells."

"Main control standing by, Sir."

"Take in the brow and single up all lines," the OOD ordered.

The bridge telephone talker passed the order to the deck crew over the sound powered telephone system.

Dockworkers and deck sailors, working as a team to implement the order, rolled the heavy brow back onto the pier with a resounding thud. Other civilian dockworkers hurried to lift the heavy hawsers over the big iron bollards along the pier as the deck crew pulled them aboard.

"Cast off lines four, five, and six," Sherwood ordered.

The telephone talker passed the command to the fantail over the sound powered phone system.

Foss shouted, "Slack off four, five, and six. When those actions were completed, the men on the pier cast off the after lines and the deck sailors hauled them aboard.

Ellingham and Sherwood watched from the port wing of the bridge as deck hands heaved the heavy, wet hawsers aboard.

While the deck seamen battled the biting wind and strenuous demands of their rating in heavy, canvas, foul-weather jackets, engineering personnel worked below decks, comfortable in shirtsleeves. Lieutenant David Caruthers, the engineering officer, supervised activities at main control in the forward engine room. In the after engine room, Propulsion Assistant, Lieutenant Junior Grade Duncan Thomas, stood by awaiting orders.

Caruthers rang Thomas on the sound powered telephone. "Mister Thomas, they'll be calling for power in a few minutes. Is everything squared away?"

"Aye, Sir. I checked with Chief Ford a few minutes ago. All boilers are on line and ready to deliver 1200 pounds of super-heated steam."

"Very well, stand by," Caruthers said.

"Aye, aye, Sir."

Captain Ellingham paced the open bridge, observing every activity of the topside crew as well as the deck gang as they all went about their work. He monitored every order and watched every step for the safety of his ship and crew.

Sherwood gave the orders and the steam turbines came to life. The powerful engines slowly turned *Boyington's* twin screws, displacing tons of quiescent harbor water and sending vibrations through the hull. The stern swung out, away from the pier, straining the forward mooring lines.

The OOD called out, "All Stop." He then ordered, "Cast off lines two and three."

Bosun Jones shouted orders to deck seaman on the bowlines. They slackened up numbers two and three so workers on the pier could lift the hawsers off the bollards and drop them into the harbor. Sailors began heaving the lines aboard.

A single hawser now tethered the ship to land.

Sherwood joined Ellingham on the port bridge wing. "Captain, we're ready to get under way."

Boyington waited, poised like a champion thoroughbred at the starting gate. Heat from her twin stacks warmed the surrounding air, creating optical distortions when the captain gazed up at the array of wires, halyards, and antennae above the stacks. Excitement filled the air.

"Take her out," Ellingham said.

"Away the number one line," Sherwood ordered.

When the hawser splashed into the water, Bosun Dalton took a deep breath, moistened his lips, and blew his whistle. The long, shrill blast, broadcast over the loud speakers of the 1 MC, resonated throughout the ship and along the pier. "Now shift the colors," he announced.

This signaled the beginning of a sequence of coordinated events.

On the bow, a seaman lowered the jack. As the jack came down, at the stern-rail, a sailor hauled in the ensign fluttering from the flagstaff. Signalmen hoisted Old Glory aloft on the after mast. The wind unfurled her, and the floating red, white, and blue flag proclaimed the ship under way. The quartermaster entered into the log the precise time *Boyington* surrendered her last attachment to land and the journey officially began.

"All back one-third," Sherwood ordered.

Ellingham felt he thrill of the moment. The colors snapped their vivid red, white, and blue against the cold, clear, morning sky. The deck rumbled beneath his feet, and the ship, like a well-trained warhorse, obeyed every command.

Three long, warning blasts from the steam-horn on the after stack warned *Boyington* was under way.

Driven by a stiff westerly breeze, the gasses from her twin stacks combined with the odors of brackish water, fish, oil, and a plethora of other harbor smells and swept back over the piers.

The captain and his wife, Catherine, said their good-byes earlier in his cabin. She now stood on the pier with some of the other officer's wives. He waved and she blew him a kiss. A fresh gust of October wind blew across the bay. The women adjusted their scarves and collars against the cold.

Once out of the harbor and into the channel, the ship turned to head south.

"All ahead one-third, turns for five knots," The OOD ordered. The trip to the open Atlantic Ocean began, *Boyington* trailing one-quarter mile behind *Negley*.

Ellingham relaxed in his elevated bridge chair, and enjoyed the passing scenery. They cruised past the palatial mansions and manicured grounds that lined the shores of Narragansett Bay. A thin layer of snow and ice coated the tops of the shrubs and hedges that huddled in the shade. A formation of squawking seagulls escorted the ship with hopes that some morsel of food might appear in the wake.

At the mouth of the bay, the waterway widened and a rolling three-foot sea greeted the pair. As Block Island fell off to starboard, the wave action gradually intensified. The two ships continued south on parallel courses, separated by one-thousand yards. As the senior of the two commanders, Ellingham would lead the duo to their destination.

Many of the crew were on their first cruise and didn't need a navigational chart to recognize the difference between the bay and the ocean. Their stomachs sounded an alarm. As the ship began to roll, pitch, and yaw, several of the newer sailors hurried to the lifelines, bent over, and spewed their partially digested breakfasts over the side. A stiff breeze caught the vile mixture and hurled it back on the side of the ship and into the pale faces of the sick sailors, bringing on further retching.

Back on the bridge, Ellingham turned his chair to face the pilothouse. Mister Sherwood called out, "Secure the special sea and anchor detail, set the steaming watch."

Bosun Dalton raised his pipe and sounded the long trilling call, known in the lexicon of bosun calls as *Secure*. The call alerted the crew of an activity about to end. He announced, "Now secure the special sea and anchor detail." He then piped *All Hands,* "Now set the steaming watch."

Lieutenant Junior Grade White entered the pilothouse, stopping behind the helmsman.

"There you are. Ready to take over, Mister White?" the Sherwood asked.

"All set."

"Very well, it's all yours."

"I have the deck and the conn," White announced. With the steaming watch set, he would have the officer of the deck watch until 1200.

"Mister White has the deck and the conn. Steering, one-six-five, turns for two five knots, Sir," the helmsman called out. This exchange ensured everyone knew who now conned the ship. Henceforth, the helm would only respond to Mister White's orders and continue to do so until someone relieved him and repeated the procedure. The quartermaster noted the change in the ship's log.

Captain Ellingham slid out of his bridge chair, entered the pilothouse, and stopped at the navigation desk.

Quartermaster Gandolfi looked up, surprised. "Yes, Sir."

"Give me a ring when we reach international waters."

"Aye, aye, Sir," Gandolfi said. The request was unusual, but he would carry out the request without question.

The captain left the bridge and retired to his cabin one deck below. He sat down at his desk and thought about the envelope in the lap drawer. He kept the drawer closed to avoid temptation.

At 1130, the bosun piped *Sweepers.* He then announced, "Now hear this; sweepers start your brooms, sweep down all lower decks, ladders, and passageways."

Fifteen minutes later, he piped *Secure,* and announced "Now, knock off ship's work," followed by the call *All Hands,* and the words, "Mess gear, mess gear, clear the mess decks till pipe down."

Finally, at 1200, he piped *Mess Call,* and said, "Now dinner for the crew."

The sea remained choppy, and the mess line noticeably short—good news for those sailors not afflicted by seasickness. Second helpings would be available before the chow line closed. The navy abhors the waste of food.

The two destroyers plowed on through cold Atlantic waters on a southerly course. Of those aboard *Boyington*, only Captain Ellingham knew their exact destination and mission, although many in the crew had strong suspicions.

CHAPTER 6

Boarding Plans

North Atlantic, Ninety Miles South of Block Island

Wednesday, 24 October 1962

October 24, 1962—morning: William Knox, a U.S. businessman, has a 3¼-hour interview with Premier Khrushchev at Khrushchev's request. Khrushchev states that it is now too late for the United States to take over Cuba, and that he will eventually give orders to sink a U.S. vessel enforcing the blockade if Soviet ships are stopped. (The Soviet Bloc Armed Forces and the Cuban Crisis: A Chronology July-November 1962, 6/18/63; Khrushchev's Conversation with Mr. W.E. Knox, President Westinghouse Electric International, Moscow, October 24, 10/26/62)[1]

Three hours earlier, the captain had waited patiently at his desk for the quartermaster's call. It came a few minutes after nine. "Sir, we're across the line and in international waters."

"Thank you, Gandolfi."

Ellingham pulled open the lap drawer of his desk and withdrew an envelope addressed to "Commanding Officer, U.S.S. *Boyington* (DD 953)." He had opened it at 0630, after a messenger hand delivered it to the ship. Inside was another envelope, sealed, with several red ink stamps indicating the contents had a security classified of "Secret." It also had instructions that the addressee was not to open it until the ship had departed U.S. waters.

After receiving Gandolfi's call, he took his silver letter opener, slit the envelope flap, and extracted the single sheet of paper it contained. The subject line read, "Deployment Orders, U.S.S. Boyington (DD 953)."

He read the orders twice, then placed the paper back in the envelope and locked it in the lap drawer.

Picking up his sound powered telephone, he called the bridge. The JOOD answered.

"Mister Frankel, this is the captain. Have the messenger locate the XO and ask him to join me for dinner, in my cabin, at twelve hundred."

"Aye, Aye, Sir. Anything else, Sir?"

"No, that's all. Thank you, Ensign."

Commander Ellingham and Lieutenant Commander Kaestner met in the former's cabin at noon. "Have a seat, John, lunch is on the way."

Both men sat at the table as Seaman Aguilera, the captain's Filipino steward, entered carrying a silver tray. He wore a crisp, white serving jacket with Mandarin collar and dark blue uniform trousers.

"Are you ready for your dinner, Captain?"

"More than ready, Carlo." Ellingham gestured for him to continue.

The steward gracefully served their dinners and poured coffee. "Do you require anything else, Sir?"

"No, thank you. The meal looks delicious as usual."

The steward backed away from the table and silently departed. The aroma of fresh coffee filled the room.

When the cabin door closed, Ellingham began. "John, the ASW Task Group is now activated. We have orders to rendezvous with the carrier *Sibuyan Sea* and the rest of the squadron Friday to resume our normal anti-submarine warfare mission. However, this time we won't be chasing Soviet subs out of American coastal waters, but protecting the fleet as it enforces the president's orders. We, of course, will also play a role in implementing the blockade."

" 'Blockade,' I thought—"

"My mistake, John," Ellingham interrupted. "I meant to say 'quarantine.' "

"Yes, Sir, although I'm not sure what the difference is."

"'Semantics,' politicians love 'em."

Ellingham continued talking as he sliced his roast beef. "Anyway, the outer boundary of the quarantine arcs past Cuba, in the

Atlantic, approximately five hundred miles off shore. The code name for the boundary is 'Walnut Line,' and the ASW Task Group will patrol the northwestern section of the line from Mona pass west to the Bahamas and north toward Bermuda.

"In addition to hunting subs, our task is to challenge any ship we encounter approaching the line to determine its name, flag, port of origin, destination, and cargo. If they fail to respond, or state they are bound for Cuba it gets interesting. We are to stop and search the ship for offensive war materiel," Ellingham said.

"What do we do if they refuse to answer or stop?"

"We fire a shot across their bow. If that doesn't stop them, we'll shoot their rudder to disable them."

"Sir, isn't that an act of war?"

"Yes, it is. Care for more coffee?"

"No, Sir, I'm fine. Captain, I have some friends who were part of Task Force Twenty-Four last year when the Bay of Pigs invasion began. They all complained about having to stand down just when the fighting started. Do you think President Kennedy will stay the course this time?"

"Yes, I do. There is far too much at stake now. If the Russians fire even one missile from Cuba, they could take out any of a dozen major U.S. cities. The country is at risk, and we are here to protect it. If Castro or his commie friends so much as light a match, I think we will bomb the island back to the Stone Age. If the Soviets try to intervene, we'll hit them too."

"I knew things were getting serious, but I had no idea they had deteriorated this far."

"John, I began my career during WW II then went on to Korea. This situation has the potential to be far worse because both sides have nukes and are fully prepared to use them."

The skipper stepped over to his desk and pulled the envelope containing the secret orders from the lap drawer. "Here, read the official tasking." He pulled the orders from the envelope and handed them to Kaestner.

The XO scanned the orders as he finished eating then handed them back. "Someone picked a clever name for the boundary, 'Walnut,' a hard nut to crack."

"Right, I hope that someone wasn't too optimistic."

"I noticed the orders don't stipulate what the term 'offensive weapons' means."

"I caught that too. Until then, we're on our own. Once we join the task group, we'll probably get further clarification."

"What's our next step, Sir?"

"First, we need to form a couple of boarding parties and train the men what to do and how to do it. Searching a freighter isn't a simple task and the orders aren't much help. 'Block the delivery of offensive war materiel,' is too broad for comfort.

"So, after you leave here, I want you to draw up two boarding parties. Select an officer along with six or eight sailors for each party. Also, list what you think they should be looking for, given our broad orders. Come see me when you're done, and we'll talk it over. Then you can meet with the department heads and the boarding party leaders to get their input and refine the list of items we're looking for," Ellingham said.

"Aye, aye Sir, and thanks for lunch."

"You're most welcome, John. Now get to work."

The bulkhead clock indicated 1355 when Kaestner found the captain on the bridge, sitting in his elevated, leather covered, swivel chair, looking out over dark blue ocean before them.

"Done already, XO?"

"Yes, Sir, first draft, at least.

"Let's lay below to my cabin."

The captain sat at his desk as Kaestner, presented his plan, neatly drawn out on yellow tablet paper. "As I said, Sir, this is the first draft. Here is a list of the proposed boarding parties.

Port Boarding Party

ENS Henry Frankel

BMC Paul Jones

GM1 Nick Zarna

BM2 John Dalton

MM2 Darryl Walker

FT3 George Mashburn

ET3 Peter Stewart

Starboard Boarding Party

ENS Thomas Padgett

GMC Mike Stafford

BM1 Harry Foss

GM2 Gene Tibbits

MM2 Bill Bailey

FT3 Ivan Leach

ET3 Fred Fenster

"How did you select this particular mix of personnel and ratings?" Ellingham asked.

"Sir, I thought it best to have a chief with each officer. Ensigns Frankel and Padgett are both good men and capable officers, but they lack any experience in this sort of mission. In fact, most naval officers haven't had any experience at this sort of thing, me included.

"Chiefs Jones and Stafford have vast experience in a wide variety of missions. Both know how to think on their feet and improvise. Neither will be thrown off guard by the unexpected."

"I agree. Good choices so far, now how about the others?"

"I put a bosun on the teams because knowledge of cargo storage technique is important when searching a freighter, and they are the experts in that field. Since the primary mission is to search for offensive weapons, I included the gunner's mates. The fire control technicians are there to assist the gunners in the event they discover guidance systems or missile related electronics.

"I propose sending the electronics technicians who could spot radio, radar, or sonar equipment and will know the difference, in case some fast talking commie tries to pull the wool over an inspector's eyes. Machine parts and fuels are also of concern so there is an engineer on each party."

"Okay, I follow your logic, but we may need a boilerman on each party, too. Machinist mates know their way around an engine room, but the BTs are the experts on fuels. Once we gain a little experience we can adjust as needed, but this is a good starting point. Have you thought about what the teams should look for?"

"Yes, Sir, here's the list I came up with." He handed another paper to Ellingham.

> Combat gear (belts, canteens, uniforms, etc)
> Conventional arms and ammunition
> Explosives and land mines
> Lubricating oil, diesel, and gasoline
> Rocket or missile warheads
> Rockets or missiles and their launchers
> Ship, aircraft, vehicle, or weapons parts
> Tanks or artillery and their projectiles

Ellingham scrutinized the list. "I would add one more thing, John."

"What's that, Sir?"

"Soldiers—if the fools plan to invade the U.S., they're going to need a lot more men than Fidel has in all his various military organizations."

"Sir, you don't think Castro or Khrushchev is crazy enough to try and invade America, do you?"

"John, two weeks ago I didn't think they were crazy enough to install ballistic missiles in Cuba and aim them at America, so now I don't rule out anything."

"Yes, Sir, good point. What's the next step regarding the boarding parties?" Kaestner asked.

"Meet with the department heads of operations, gunnery, and engineering and the two boarding party officers, to review the plan you just showed me. See if they have any suggestions and get their buy-in. While you do that, I'll brief the crew."

"Aye, aye Sir."

"Another thing, John, in situations like this it's best to ask the junior men to offer their ideas first. They frequently know things or have good, solid suggestions, but are intimidated to speak up after the senior officers have given their input."

"Good idea, Sir, thanks for the tip."

Kaestner departed and the captain turned and picked up the 1-MC public address microphone. "Attention, all hands, this is the captain speaking. As you may have guessed, we are heading for Cuba and will become part of the force quarantining the island. Our primary mission is anti-submarine warfare. Additionally, we will intercept any ship we encounter attempting to cross the quarantine boundary, code named the 'Walnut Line,' to determine the name, flag, origin, destination, and cargo. If their destination is Cuba, or we are not satisfied with the responses we receive, we are to stop and board that vessel to search for offensive military materiel.

"If they fail to stop we are ordered to fire a shot across their bow. If they still refuse to stop, we have authorization to shoot and disable their rudder. This is serious business."

Ellingham paused a few seconds to let his message sink-in.

"We are going to muster two boarding parties tomorrow. Party members will receive their individual roles and missions at that time. That is all."

In the chiefs' mess, Mike, Jones, and Chief Boilerman Ken Ford sat around a table as they listened to the captain's announcement.

"Sounds like the president means business," Jones said.

"I hope so. What do you think, Mike?" Ford asked.

"I just went through a drill like this one eighteen months ago at the Bay of Pigs. The president had better mean what he says this time or the country is down the tubes. End of story."

As *Boyington* and *Negley* continued south toward the rendezvous point, naval intelligence personnel in the Pentagon updated a chart of the North Atlantic with surface contact locations. Information poured in from long-range patrol aircraft and sightings made by ships. American flag vessels and those of our allies reported any Soviet activity they saw. The latest postings indicated an unusually large number of freighters approaching the Walnut Line from the northeast.

Additionally, tiny red flags dotted the chart indicating reported submarine contacts. The analyst knew there were more flags than actual submarines as various detection sources gained and lost the same contact. The ASW Task Group would have to determine which contacts remained active.

U.S. aircraft carriers are primary targets of any foe, so the escorting destroyers concentrated on finding submarines that might be tracking and attempting to target carriers prior to an outbreak of hostilities.

The ASW task groups would also make every effort to disrupt any other missions the submarines might have, such as reconnaissance. The Office of Naval Intelligence (ONI) worried the Soviets might be shipping nuclear missiles to Cuba in their submarines, adding further emphasis to locating them.

In the event a war started, the navy would eliminate the Soviet submarines while American air power destroyed the missile bases in Cuba. As these events transpired, the Soviet Union would remain under microscopic scrutiny. If the Soviets made the slightest offensive move toward America, the Strategic Air Command and the navy ballistic missile fleet would spring into action, targeting the Soviet's ability to wage war.

If the United States and the Soviet Union continued on their present courses, life on planet Earth would undergo incomprehensible changes. The weapons both sides were priming would make the atomic bombs used against Hiroshima and Nagasaki, during World War II, seem like a fireworks display by comparison.

CHAPTER 7

The Misfits

Three-Hundred Miles Northwest of Bermuda

Thursday, 25 October 1962

This morning the United States requested an emergency meeting of the United Nations Security Council. Adlai Stevenson, the U.S. ambassador to the United Nations confronted Soviet Ambassador Valerian Zorin and challenged him to admit the existence of Soviet missiles in Cuba. Zorin, in the presence of the Security Council, refused to answer. Stevenson forcefully demanded an answer, "Don't wait for the translation, answer yes or no!"

Zorin replied, "I am not in an American court of law, and therefore do not answer a question put to me in the manner of a prosecuting counsel...you will have your answer in due course."

Stevenson retorted, "I am prepared to wait for my answer until hell freezes over." He then showed photographs taken by a U-2 spy plane that proved the existence of nuclear missiles in Cuba, just after Zorin had implied they did not exist.[3]

At 0600, the shrill whistle of the bosun's pipe shattered the dreams of over two-hundred sleeping sailors, two thirds of *Boyington's* crew. His droll announcements served to irritate the sleepy men further. "Reveille, reveille, all hands heave-to, and trice up. The smoking lamp is lighted in all authorized spaces. Reveille."

Fifteen minutes later, more annoying bosun calls and announcements. "Now wash down all weather decks. Sweepers, start your brooms. Sweep down all lower decks, ladders, and passageways.

At 0655, "Mess gear, clear the mess deck till pipe down."

Then, at 0700, he announced, "Breakfast for the crew."

Thus began another day at sea. Seldom varying, usually monotonous, occasionally terrifying.

At morning quarters after a series of routine announcements, division chiefs having men in their units assigned to the boarding parties called out those names, and then reminded them of a training session on the torpedo deck to commence immediately after quarters.

Lieutenant Quinn, the gunnery officer, stood on the 0-1 level, next to the starboard torpedo tubes with Ensigns Frankel and Padgett, awaiting arrival of the enlisted men.

After a short wait, all the assigned men stood before the officers. Quinn began, "Okay, men, listen up. I want you to form up by parties: the port boarding party, Mister Frankel's group, over here to my left. Starboard boarding party, you men stand here on my right with Mister Padgett."

After some shuffling around, the men stood in their respective groups silently looking at the gunnery officer, waiting for his instructions.

"Mister Frankel, Mister Padgett, please distribute the contraband lists," Quinn said. He continued talking as the leaders passed the lists around. "You men all heard the captain's announcement yesterday. We selected you based on your expertise and experience for this critical mission. In the event we must search a ship, I doubt we will be welcomed guests. Officers and chiefs will carry side arms and radios.

"The motor whaleboat crew will get you over to the foreign vessel, and you will board as always, in rank order with the officer-in-charge first. Once onboard, the party will remain on deck with the chief, while the OIC and one sailor of his choosing proceeds to meet the vessel's master. The OIC will verify the basic information: Ship's name, registry, port of embarkation, cargo, and destination. He will inform the master that the ship will not continue its voyage until the team completes its search of the vessel. If no contraband items are present, the vessel may proceed. If contraband is present, we will not permit it to cross the Walnut Line. Is everyone with me, so far?" Quinn paused.

No one posed a question.

"The OIC will radio the results of his meeting with the master back to the ship. If the master refuses to cooperate with the search, the party will immediately depart and return to the *Boyington*, whereupon someone higher in the chain of command will decide what action to take. Any questions now?"

"Sir, what if they greet us with weapons? We can't force our way aboard with only two pistols," Bosun Dalton said.

"If they're overtly hostile, the party isn't going aboard. Our job is simply to determine if a ship bound for Cuba is carrying offensive materiel. The bridge will ask the foreign vessel if they will permit a search party to board. If they say 'no,' we'll send the ship back to Russia. They're not going to cross the Walnut Line en route to Cuba without inspection. Anyone else?" Quinn asked. The group stood silent.

"Right. Assuming the party receives permission to search, we hope the master will provide guides. The OIC will remain on the bridge, in radio contact with the *Boyington*. The chiefs will decide who goes where. With or without guides, enter every compartment that could hold contraband. Open boxes, lift covers, do whatever is necessary to see the cargo. Initial the hatch of each cargo hold or compartment door with chalk after your inspection to prevent duplication of effort.

"If any one of you finds something that is on the contraband list, stop searching, go tell the OIC, and prepare to disembark. He will inform the master the search is over, and you are leaving. Once the party is off the vessel, the bridge will advise the master his destination has changed—he won't be sailing to Cuba. Any questions now?" Quinn asked. There weren't any.

"Very well, we're finished here for the time being. If you hear an announcement for your party to form up, meet here, right where you are now standing, and your OIC will provide any last minute information," Quinn said.

The briefing broke up, and the sailors departed for their normal duty stations. Ensign Padgett called to Mike and motioned him toward the port rail.

"What do you make of this situation, Chief?"

"Could get ugly, Sir."

"Do you think we'll have to shoot at another ship?"

"Since the president told the world we are going to quarantine Cuba, we had better do exactly that or hand the keys to the Pentagon over to Castro and his Soviet buddies."

"So you think we will shoot?"

"The president broadcast that speech to the entire world, so every government, especially the Soviet Union, knows our position. The United States must back up its proclamation or lose all credibility. I don't think the president will repeat the mistakes made at the Bay of

Pigs. If we order a vessel to stop and they don't, yes, I believe we'll shoot."

"What if we encounter a foreign vessel, it stops as requested, and we have to search it. How do you see that going down?" Padgett asked.

"If they stop and give us permission to board, they are either running a serious bluff or have nothing to hide. I would bet on the latter."

"So you don't expect trouble?"

"My last skipper often quoted an old saying, 'Hope for the best and prepare for the worst.' I think that would good advice in this situation."

"You're right, Chief. Thanks for your opinion."

"No sweat, Sir. Now I have a question for you. Lieutenant Quinn told me during our first meeting, that a couple of seamen in our division needed an attitude adjustment. Do you know who they are and what they did to get on his bad side?"

"Oh yes, Gibbs and Unger. They're a couple of immature teenagers. I don't think there's any problem there that a couple of year's growth won't cure."

"With all due respect, Sir, we could be in a war tomorrow, and we can't wait a couple of years for two boys to become men. When they took the oath and put on their white hats, they gave up their childhood. I'll have a talk with them."

"Okay, Chief. That'll help, I'm sure."

The two men separated. Mike went aft, looking for either or both of the division troublemakers. He found Unger on the 0-1 level, sitting on the deck next to mount fifty-two, pretending to scrape a rusted area on the side of the gun mount. A cigarette dangled from his lips, he had his chambray shirtsleeves rolled up, and his white hat sat on the back of his head like a beanie.

"Stand up, sailor, and put out that cigarette."

"Hey, Chief, I got work to do here."

"Sailor, those weren't casual suggestions. Now move it or you're going to have to see the corpsman to have that paint scraper surgically removed from your ass. You read me?"

"Yes, Sir." Unger stood and tossed his cigarette overboard.

"As long as you're in my division, you'll wear your uniform properly and act like a sailor of the United States Navy. Now get those sleeves rolled down and square that hat." Unger slowly complied, carefully rolling each sleeve down. When he had both sleeves buttoned, he slowly adjusted his white hat to the proper position.

"Now, you can thank me for saving your sorry life."

"What you talking about, Chief?"

"I'm talking about smoking while you're painting. Many of our paints are flammable, and you could have died in the explosion. That would be a big loss to the navy and this ship because someone would have to spend valuable time cleaning your blood and guts off the deck and everywhere else they splattered, and then repaint the burnt areas. We don't need the extra work now."

"Yeah?"

"Yeah!"

"Okay, Chief, I won't do it again. Our real chief never said nothing about sleeves or setting paint on fire."

"Are you saying I'm not a real chief?"

"I meant our regular chief."

"Listen up, boot, I've been a chief longer than you've been on this earth, and at the rate you're going, your time may be severely limited. I'm as real and as regular as any swinging dick you'll ever meet, and I can become your worst nightmare. You follow me so far?"

"Yes, Sir."

"Don't call me 'sir,' you sorry ass pollywog. I'm a chief, and you'll address me accordingly."

"Yes, Chief."

"Okay, go turn this gear in at the paint locker, and then report to Chief Baker. You're going to spend a month in the scullery. If you survive and return, we'll talk."

"But, Chief, Harris just started mess cooking last week. Our division only has to send one man at a time."

"That's right, but Harris knows how to wear his uniform. He also knows how to prepare steel for painting, as well as when and where it's safe to smoke. He doesn't endanger his shipmates by screwing off and doing stupid things. We may be in a war tomorrow, and I can count on him—you, I'm not so sure of.

"We'll talk when you come back to the division. Now, here's a heads-up, just so you don't make any more stupid mistakes today. Chief Commissaryman Baker is real and regular too. And he's in a foul mood today, so watch what you say and do, or he may want to keep you in the scullery for an extra month or two."

"Yes, Sir—I mean Chief."

"What're you standing there for—haul ass outta here. Move it."

Mike smiled as Unger scurried away. He wondered how cocky the lad would be after a couple of ten-hour days in the heat and humidity of the scullery. If that place failed to render him down, Chief Baker's constant harangue would.

CHAPTER 8

Seaman Apprentice Gibbs
Two-Hundred and Fifty Miles West of Bermuda

Thursday, 25 October 1962

A fleet of sixteen Soviet freighters in the Atlantic en route to Cuba, presumably with a cargo of intermediate range ballistic missiles, reversed course and headed away before reaching the Walnut Line. One ship, the tanker Bucharest carrying petroleum products, however, continued on a southerly course.[4]

The Joint Chiefs of Staff directed CINCLANT to be prepared to strike all Cuban SA-2 sites within two hours if a U-2 aircraft is shot down. They also ordered additional patrol aircraft from U.S. Naval Air Station, Pawtuxet River, Maryland, to augment aerial surveillance of ocean areas, flying from Bermuda and Azores.[4]

In response to the continuing work on the missiles in Cuba, President Kennedy issued Security Action Memorandum 199, authorizing the loading of nuclear weapons onto aircraft under the command of SACEUR (which had the mission of carrying out first air strikes on the Soviet Union).[6]

Mike felt satisfied that he had started one of the division troublemakers down the right path. Having dealt with Seaman Apprentice Unger, he set off in search of Seaman Apprentice Gibbs, but first encountered Chief Boilerman Ford on the fantail.

"Hey, Ken, you just crawl out of your black hole for a reminder of what fresh air and sunshine is like?"

"Yeah, but remind me again when we get back up in the North Atlantic, and you're chipping ice off your mounts while I bask in the comfort of my cozy, eighty-five degree fire room."

"Okay, I'll try to remember to do that. Hey, I've heard some of your firemen bitching about being overworked. What's going on?"

"Oh, I can't seem to get the bilges clean enough to satisfy the XO. He's been on my ass for a couple of weeks now."

"I know you don't fancy deck seamen down in your engineering spaces, but if I had a young gent in need of some career broadening, could you use him, say as a bilge cleaner?" Mike asked.

"You bet. Is he looking to make the navy a career? Maybe I can show him the error in his ways—you know, signing on with gunnery when he could have come to engineering in the first place."

"I haven't done any counseling with him yet, but you're welcome to start. His name is Gibbs. I understand Chief Banner didn't have any luck."

"I see. So he's a problem child?"

"It sounds to me like he thinks he's still in the fifth grade and needs a lesson in the rigors of navy life. I can't see good men doing the nastiest jobs aboard ship while some smart-ass boot skates through the day.

"Mister Padgett told me that when the captain announced we might be boarding ships, Gibbs and his buddy Unger swiped black eye patches from sick bay and strutted around singing 'Fifteen men on the dead man's chest. Yo-ho-ho, and a bottle of rum.' Get the picture?"

Ford laughed. "They may be immature, but that's kind of funny. Sure, I'll take him and introduce him to the bilges straight away. It'll be interesting to see how working down there affects his sense of humor. What's his name again?" Ford asked.

"Gibbs, Seaman Apprentice Jerry Gibbs. Okay, I'll let you know, but I've got to find the little bastard first."

Mike searched all the second division compartments and spaces to no avail. He spent half an hour walking around, asking dozens of sailors if they had seen Gibbs, or knew where he might be. No one had seen him recently or knew of his whereabouts. Finally, on a tip, he located him in the seldom-used after-steering room, stretched out on the deck with his head on a pillow sound asleep.

Mike picked up a metal trashcan and smashed it against a steel stanchion next to the sleeping sailor. It sounded like a grenade going off, and Gibbs leaped to his feet.

"What the hell do you think you're doing back here, sleeping during work hours?"

"I . . . I've been having trouble sleeping lately, Chief."

"Oh, I see. I think I know what your problem is, Gibbs."

"Great. Several guys have told me you know your stuff and are an understanding person. Do you think maybe, I need special permission to sleep during the day? That would help a lot."

"No, in my experience, sailors with a problem like yours simply need more exercise."

"Oh."

"And the best way to get that exercise is to put in a good, solid eight hours of hard work. In addition to your normal steaming watches, that is."

"Eight hours?"

"Eight hours working plus four hours on watch, that's twelve hours, the standard navy work day at sea. You're one lucky sailor, because I just found out that Chief Ford needs some help in the forward fire room. And since second division is obviously getting along without your assistance, I've arranged for you to spend a month with the engineering department."

"But Chief, I'm a seaman apprentice. I don't know a thing about engineering, and it's hot down there in the fire room. I don't think I'd like it there."

"Think about how much better you'll sleep, and the satisfaction from knowing you earned your extravagant pay."

"Extravagant pay? Chief, I make eighty dollars a month, before taxes. My mother gave me a bigger allowance than that in high school."

"Uncle Sam is in charge of your allowance now, not your momma, and apparently he's paying you a lot more than you're worth, because I don't see you doing much to earn it. That however, is going to change. Tomorrow morning, you will muster with engineering, and Chief Ford will give you your assignment."

"Chief, I don't want to do that. If you make me, I'm going to have to write a letter to my father. He and our Congressman are good friends, and if they know I'm not happy, you'll be in a lot of trouble."

"Oh, gee whiz, golly me, you would do that?"

"Yes, I will if you make me work with the snipes."

"Here's the thing, Gibbs. We may be at war in a few days, and the mail gets rather slow during wars. Now that I know how you feel about the fire room, instead of just one month down there, I'm going to make it two. Then, assuming a Soviet torpedo doesn't sink us, and we do make it back to port, you can mail your letter. Now get your lazy ass out of my sight, and if I catch you goofing off again, you'll rue the day you were born."

Gibbs started to leave.

"Oh, one more thing, Gibbs, when you write daddy, be sure to give him my regards, and please spell my name correctly. It's S-T-A-F-F-O-R-D. Got it?"

Gibbs sneered and walked off.

Mike climbed back up to the main deck and stopped in the chiefs' mess looking for Ford, who entered the compartment a few minutes later.

"Did your wayward seaman turn up?"

"Yeah, found him asleep in after-steering. He volunteered for two months special duty with your gang."

"Great, we've got plenty to do, and if we can make the XO happy before Gibbs has to return to second division, I'll see if Chief Chantre can use him in the engine room."

"One other thing, Ken, his daddy knows a congressman, and he threatened to report me if I made him unhappy."

"I wondered why you looked so worried. If he's from such a well connected family, there's only one reason why he's on a destroyer instead of chasing coeds at Yale."

"And what's that, Ken?"

"His daddy wants the apron strings cut and expects us to make a man out of him. Well, his first lesson starts tomorrow morning. BT1 Yost has been pissed off at the world since the XO got the burr in his knickers about the bilges. I'm going to assign this pussy to Yost, and he'll keep the boy's nose in the there until they shine like mirrors.

When Yost finishes, we'll introduce him to one of the engine rooms. Have you heard what the machinist's mates call them on this ship?"

"No."

"They're called 'Chantre's tea parlors.' Every machinist's mate that works for Chief Chantre has his own personal can of Brasso and an endless supply of rags. Those spaces glisten so brightly you have to wear sunglasses when you go down there. That's my problem. The XO keeps comparing Chantre's polished brass engine rooms to my black fire rooms."

"Life ain't always fair, Ken, but glad I could help." Mike patted him on the shoulder and left the compartment. He wanted to find Ensign Padgett and brief him of the corrective steps he had taken with the two misfits. The possibility of a congressional investigation had already slipped his mind.

CHAPTER 9

Rendezvous

Near the Walnut Line

Friday, 26 October 1962

As a result of the increased frequency of low-level reconnaissance missions, additional military targets in Cuba are identified. Military planners consequently revise air attack targeting and plans. The airstrike plan now includes three massive strikes per day until Cuban air capability is destroyed. Some 1,190 bombing sorties are planned for the first day of operations. (The Air Force Response to the Cuban Crisis 14 October-24 November 1962, ca.1/63, p.9.)[1]

The Panamanian-owned, Lebanese flagged merchant ship Marucla, bound for Cuba from the Soviet port of Riga was stopped and searched by a boarding party from the destroyer U.S.S. Joseph P. Kenned, Jr. (DD 850). They did not discover any prohibited materiel and permitted the freighter to continue on to Havana.[4]

The destroyer Joseph P. Kennedy, named for the president's older brother, a Navy bomber pilot killed in action during World War II, was commissioned in December 1945.[10]

Lieutenant Junior Grade Sherwood, the OOD stood in front of the quartermaster's chart. "Everyone stay alert now. We're getting close to the Walnut Line and the rendezvous point. Talkers, pass the word to CIC and the lookouts."

The first hour of duty had crept slowly past the mid-watch. They began the night fortified by strong navy coffee, but another period of uneventful cruising invited boredom into all quarters. Mister Sherwood's announcement brought the bridge back to life.

Twenty-five minutes later in CIC, the radarman assigned to monitor the surface search radar repeater thought he saw the dull glow of a contact. He quickly rubbed his tired eyes while the sweep rotated around and repainted the display on his scope. Positioning the cursor over the contact, he determined its location. "Contact: bearing, zero-zero-five relative; range, one eight miles," He announced.

One of two senior radarmen standing at the dead reckoning tracer (DRT) marked the location with a tiny arrow on the grid paper covering the instrument. Eventually, as the surface search operator provided additional location reports, a line connecting the arrows would indicate the contact's course.

A pinpoint of light below the grid paper, controlled by the ship's gyrocompass moved to denote *Boyington's* ever changing position. The second radarman also periodically marked the destroyer's position with a small "x" of a on the paper to create a picture of the tactical situation for the CIC watch officer or the captain to evaluate.

The officer grabbed his telephone. "Bridge, CIC. Contact: bearing, zero-zero-five relative; range, one eight miles. That's close to the rendezvous point, so it's most likely one of ours."

"Roger, CIC," the bridge telephone talker responded. He then reported the contact to the officer of the deck.

The OOD rang the captain's sea cabin.

"Ellingham," a sleepy voice mumbled.

"Sir, its Mister Sherwood, the OOD. CIC has a surface contact, eighteen miles ahead. They think it may be one of our ships on the Walnut Line."

"Call me when you have it identified, and make sure *Negley* sees it."

"Aye, aye, Sir."

Twenty miles to the east, on a sea that twinkled with reflections from a full moon, a lone submarine cruised slowly, peacefully recharging its batteries. Two lookouts and the captain stood in the cockpit atop the sail, eighteen feet above the water line. The lookouts, using high power binoculars, continuously scanned the horizon in 180-degree sweeps.

One sailor observed forward, the other aft. The safety of the vessel rested in their ability to spot an enemy ship or patrol plane. The captain dared not activate the radar, as its electromagnetic beam might give away their presence. Their reconnaissance mission required the utmost stealth.

Two sailors enjoyed a saltwater shower, on the open deck aft of the conning tower. The captain permitted the crew that luxury whenever he could. Washing away the stink of eight hours inside the hot, steel cylinder proved a great morale booster. When submerged at these southern latitudes, the atmosphere inside becomes an oppressive brew of fumes from human sweat, hot oil, and battery acid. It causes skin to break out in painful rashes and tempers to flare. Now, after eight hours on the surface, under diesel power, fans had flushed the rancid air and life on the boat improved.

"Comrade Captain Petrov, I'm sorry to report the batteries are fully charged, and we may dive anytime you wish," the chief engineer reported.

"Why do you feel sorry, Ivan, continuing our mission for the glory of mother Russia should make you joyous."

"Yes, Sir. It should, but a clean body, on a beautiful night with a cool breeze blowing through what remains of my hair, makes me feel even better."

"All right, thank you, Comrade Chief Engineer. Let's clear the decks and prepare to dive. The captain looked aft at the phosphorescent wake, and then slid through the hatch and down the ladder into the command center two decks below. "Dive. Flood the forward tanks. Set bow planes at eight degrees. All ahead one-third."

Twenty minutes later, they cruised one-hundred and fifty feet below the surface of the Atlantic, on a westerly course, at seven knots.

On *Boyington,* the radarman manning the surface search radar repeater reported another contact.

The CIC officer picked up a radiotelephone handset and keyed the transmitter calling the command section of the ASW Task Group, aboard the aircraft carrier U.S.S. Sibuyan Sea. "Checkbook, this is Siena, over."

"Siena, Checkbook, go ahead."

"Checkbook, Siena, we are approaching two-six north by six-eight west and have two contacts at zero-zero-five relative, one five miles out."

"Roger, Siena, you have Excalibur and Silver Spur. Proceed on your present course to rendezvous. Checkbook out."

The call signs were those of the U.S.S. Bartow and the U.S.S. Browning, respectively. *Boyington* and *Negley,* now reunited with their squadron, had traveled over eleven hundred miles since leaving Newport.

CIC notified the bridge.

The OOD called the captain again. "Sir, we have radar contact with *Bartow* and *Browning.* CIC has confirmed the contacts with Checkbook. Our orders are to proceed to the rendezvous point."

"Very well, I'll be up in a few minutes."

Ten minutes later, the bosun of the watch called out, "Captain's on the bridge."

"Where are they now, Mister Sherwood?" Ellingham asked.

"Eleven miles out, Sir, still bearing zero-zero-five."

"Very well." The captain picked up the radiotelephone handset on the destroyer squadron tactical network and called the commodore's staff, "Adeline Alpha, this is Siena actual, over."

"Siena, Adeline Alpha, over."

"Adeline Alpha, Siena. We are eleven miles out and closing, over."

"Roger, Siena, welcome to the party. We're looking for uninvited guests. Take ASW station three between Brewmeister and Fullback."

The call signs were for the U.S.S. *Keffer* and the U.S.S *Spenser*.

"Roger, Siena out."

"Mister Sherwood, do we have a fix on *Keffer* yet?" Ellingham asked.

"Yes, Sir, she's in position two of the ASW screen. The formation is steaming east at twelve knots."

"Very well, set a course to intercept. Let's get on station, and look smart about it."

"Aye, aye, Sir," Sherwood said. He turned to the talker, "Have CIC plot us a course to intercept Keffer."

The 1JS talker passed the word.

The CIC officer had anticipated the request and had the answer ready. He sent it to the bridge seconds later.

"Helm, steer one-seven-five, all ahead full, make turns of two five knots," Sherwood called out.

The helmsman repeated the course and speed orders as he turned the wheel.

"Comrade Captain, I have two fast moving contacts four-thousand meters dead ahead on a southerly course," the sonar operator reported.

"Very well, halt transmissions and follow them passively. All ahead full,"

The sonarman and helmsman both responded and set about implementing the orders.

Thirty-five minutes after receiving orders from the DESRON Forty-Two, *Boyington* took her station one mile southwest of *Sibuyan Sea* and two miles behind *Keffer*. *Negley* had also found her position in the formation.

One hour later, on the Soviet submarine, the captain fretted. "Down periscope," He turned to his number two, his face ashen. "We have arrived in the middle of an American fleet. Within the radius of less than two kilometers, I saw an aircraft carrier and three destroyers. Emergency dive to one-hundred meters and rig for silent running. I do not think they detected us yet, but we will be lucky to survive this situation."

The seven ships of the ASW Task Group all had their sonar equipment on-line and pinging. S2F Tracker aircraft patrolled the skies in a radius ten miles out from the carrier searching for submarines with their Magnetic Anomaly Detection (MAD) gear. However, Soviet submarine B-115 miraculously went undetected. Unusual sea conditions and the noise generated by the fleet masked sonar reception within the circle of American ships.

CHAPTER 10

Gibbs Reassigned

Three-Hundred and Fifty Miles North of Mona Passage

Friday, 26 October 1962

At 10:00 P.M. EDT, the United States raised the readiness level of SAC forces to DEFCON 2 for the first time in U.S. history. While B-52 bombers went on continuous airborne alert, SAC dispersed 183 B-47 medium bombers to various military and civilian airfields, throughout the country. Over 150 intercontinental ballistic missiles stood on ready alert and seventy-five nuclear-armed B-52 sorties flew per day to orbit points within striking distance of the Soviet Union.[7]

Additionally, the Continental Air Defense Command placed 520 aircraft on alert and the Tactical Air Command moved 511 fighter aircraft to Florida. During a two-day period, the USAF airlifted 2,000 marines and 1,400 tons of equipment to Naval Station Guantanamo.[8]

Three Soviet ships, the Vishnevsky, Okhotsk, and Sergev Botkin, en route to Cuba, changed course and headed back toward to their ports of departure.[4]

The bosun's announcement blared throughout the ship: "Now hear this, all hands to quarters for muster." At 0755, *Boyington's* off-watch crew, dressed, shaved, and fed, sauntered toward their designated stations.

Second division sailors gathered on the fantail and formed up in two rows. Chief Stafford and GM1 Zarna stood in front of the formation, facing the men.

Mike looked over the formation and saw Seaman Apprentice Gibbs in the back row. "Gibbs, I told you to muster with the engineers today. What the hell are you doing here?"

"Chief, I need to talk to you—in private."

"Meet me after quarters. You have ten minutes to get your story together, and it had better be good because now you've pissed off two people, Chief Ford, and me."

"Yes, Sir."

"Gibbs, you knuckle head, what did I tell you yesterday about that? Now try again."

"Yes, Chief."

"Better. See, you can learn to follow simple instructions.

"Mount captains—make sure your routine maintenance is up to date. I'll be around today to inspect and I don't want to see any—"

Petty Officer Zarna interrupted Mike's announcement, calling out, "Attention on deck." The division came to attention. Zarna and Mike each executed an about-face movement, placing their backs toward the formation and facing their division officer.

Mike saluted, "Second division, all present, or accounted for, Sir."

Mister Padgett, the division officer returned the salute. "Division—stand at ease. . . . Men, we're on-station now at the Walnut Line and are providing ASW coverage. We received word that Soviet freighters are heading our way, and there may already be enemy submarines in the area. You can expect to spend some time at general quarters and at your ASW stations. When you hear the word to man your battle stations, do so smartly and stay alert. Additionally, the captain assigned six second-division men including me to the boarding parties, and we can expect to see action there. So again, stay sharp. We are on the cusp of war with Cuba and possibly the Soviet Union. The nation is depending on us."

"Chief, take charge of the division."

"Aye, aye, Sir." Mike saluted. Ensign Padgett returned the salute and departed.

Mike and Zarna executed about-face movements and again faced the formation. "Division, attention . . . dismissed. Gibbs, over here," Mike said.

Gibbs approached Mike tentatively as the other sailors departed for their workstations.

The bosun's pipe boomed from the loud speakers. "Now, all hands turn-to. Commence ship's work."

Mike leaned against the side of the big gun mount. "Okay, sailor, what's your story?"

"Chief, I'm sorry about that stuff I said yesterday. I'm not going to write a letter to my dad or anyone else, okay."

"Fine, but you're still going to engineering for sixty days. I told you that, and I told Chief Ford you'd be there this morning. Now you made me look bad, so I'm thinking about making it ninety days."

"I'm sorry, Chief. Here's the thing . . . I'm terrified of tight places. Whenever I'm in a closed in space, like in a telephone booth or an elevator, I freak out. I looked down the hatch into the fire room yesterday and panicked. I can't do it, Chief. I don't think I can even go down that long, steep ladder. If I try to squeeze in between all that machinery, I'm afraid I'll go crazy."

"Gibbs, all ships are full of tight places. You wanted to be a gunner's mate. All our spaces, the mounts, the magazines, the equipment rooms are all small and tight. What the hell were you thinking?"

"Maybe I shouldn't be here at all."

"Well, you are here, and we're in the middle of the fricking ocean. This isn't like a bus where you can get off at the next stop." Mike turned and opened the small door on the side of the five-inch gun mount. "Get in there."

"I . . . I can't."

"Yes, you can, and yes, you will. I'll leave the door open and be right here. Now get in."

Gibbs trembled as he placed his foot on the two-rung ladder. His knuckles turned white as he squeezed the handgrip alongside the opening and pulled himself up into the mount.

Inside, equipment filled nearly all the space. Gibbs immediately hit his head on a steel arm protruding from the apparatus. His eyes moistened, and his face turned red. He tried to rub his head where he had bumped it and hit his elbow on another piece of equipment. All color drained from his face, leaving a moist alabaster sheen.

Mike feared that if he passed out, he might seriously hurt himself.

"Come back out, Gibbs."

The shaking sailor backed out of the mount.

"You are either claustrophobic or one hell of a good actor, Gibbs."

"What's 'claustrophobic' mean, Chief?"

"It's a fear of tight places."

"Yeah, well, I already told you that."

"So you did. Here's what I'm going to do, Gibbs. Forget about the fire room. You're going to first division. You can chip paint and swab decks in the nice fresh, open air all day long with the deck hands until we get to port where the medics can check you over. If you are claustrophobic, your navy career is over."

"First division, that sounds like hard work, Chief."

"It is, and the bosuns aren't fond of slackers, so you better turn-to when they say to and keep chipping or swabbing until they say 'secure,' or you'll wish you were back in that gun-mount. Let's go."

"Where are we going?"

"First we're going to apologize to Chief Ford for breaking our promises to him, and then we're going to meet Chief Jones, your new boss."

Mike asked a fireman, they passed on the mess deck, where he could find Chief Ford. He learned Ford had a problem in the fire room, so the two headed forward.

They saw Chief Jones on the forecastle, instructing a new seaman on how to coil a Flemish to his exacting standards. As they approached, Jones bellowed at a two-striper. "No, clockwise, I said. Don't you know what that means?"

"Yes, Chief," the terrified seaman apprentice responded.

"Then start over. Coil the line flat on the deck in a clockwise direction and keep the fakes snuggled up tight."

"Keep what tight?"

"Fakes . . . fakes, didn't you learn a damn thing in boot camp, or were you sleeping all day there too?"

"I . . . I'm sorry, Chief. I don't know what a 'fake' is. Some of this stuff is too hard to remember. Maybe I had fallen asleep when they explained this stuff at Great Lakes."

"Okay, Abernathy, I'm going to tell you one more time. I'll speak real slow, so listen up good, cuz if you forget again, I'm putting you on mess cooking for the rest of your life. A 'fake' is a single turn of a line when you coil it down. You got it now?"

"I think so, but Chief . . .

"But what?" Jones roared.

"How can you put me on mess cooking for the rest of my life? I only enlisted for four years."

"Because, if you can't remember how to do this simple job, you're too stupid to deserve a discharge. The navy don't just hand out discharges cuz you put in four years—you have to earn it. The civilians don't want no ex-sailors coming back home and drawing unemployment cuz they're too stupid to do simple jobs like faking down a line or coiling a Flemish." Jones turned away from the puzzled seaman.

Mike smiled while Gibbs, standing beside him, shuddered in fear as he stared up at the six-foot-two, two-hundred and forty pound, red-faced bosun.

"What's up, Chief Stafford?" Jones asked.

"I've got a volunteer for you, Chief Jones. This is Seaman Apprentice Gibbs, who has discovered he can't work in tight, confined places like a gun mount. He would like to join the deck gang until we get to port and can have the medics check him over."

"Are you serious? In over twenty-five years at sea, I can't ever remember a sailor volunteering for the deck gang."

"Then it's your lucky day, Boats."

"Okay, maybe it is. Bosun Foss is up on the oh-one level doing some deck repairs. Come on, Gibbs. Let's go meet him. You two will hit it off because he likes it out on the weather decks, regardless of the time of day, or what kind of weather we're having. In fact he loves it most out here during storms."

Jones patted Mike on the back, grabbed Gibbs's arm in his meaty paw and dragged him aft, toward the amidships ladder.

CHAPTER 11

Refueling Detail

Four-Hundred Miles Northeast of Mona Passage

Friday, 26 October 1962

October 26, 1962—1:00 P.M.: John Scali, State Department correspondent for ABC News, lunches with Aleksandr Formin at the Occidental Restaurant in Washington at Fomin's request. The two have met together on several previous occasions. Fomin, officially the Soviet embassy public affairs counselor, is known to be the KGB's Washington station chief. Noting that "war seems about to break out," he asks Scali to contact his "high-level friends" in the State Department to ascertain whether the United States would be interested in a possible solution to the crisis. According to Scali's notes, Fomin's proposal runs along the following lines: "[Soviet] bases would be dismantled under UN supervision and Castro would pledge not to accept offensive weapons of any kind, ever, in return for [a U.S.] pledge not to invade Cuba." Following the lunch, Scali goes directly to the State Department to report on the meeting to Roger Hilsman. (Document 43, John Scali's Notes of First Meeting with Soviet Embassy Counselor Aleksandr Fomin, 10/26/62)[1]

The U.S.S. Randolph ASW Group joined the quarantine patrol forces. She was prosecuting one of three active submarine contacts. The Essex group and P2V's from Bermuda were holding the other two under surveillance. Eight destroyers were in company with Randolph.[4]

Mid-Evening: The U.S.S. Cony, part of the Randolph task group, investigates a sonar contact, possibly C-19 (Cony Deck Log Book, 10/26/62)[2]

The huge aircraft carrier loomed close enough that Mike thought he could hit it with "Betsy" his old 30-30 Winchester, if he had it, but he didn't. It was probably still in the barn, back home, he hoped.

He had been standing on the forecastle enjoying the pleasant breeze as Bosun Jones walked off with Gibbs in tow. When he finally decided to go break the change of plans to Chief Ford, he saw the carrier and realized they were on course to come alongside. That meant refueling time. He walked back to the anchor windlass, a good spot to observe the process.

Once the destroyer slipped into position, less than a hundred feet separated the two ships, and the huge carrier cast a shadow over the much smaller destroyer. The colliding bow-waves turned the sea into a fulminating cauldron between the vessels, forcing water over the destroyer's main deck aft of the bulwark.

Proximity of the vessels required flawless ship handling. Mike knew both captains would either have the conn of their ships or be on the bridge closely overseeing procedures. Only senior quartermasters would be trusted at the helms during this maneuver as the slightest misstep could spell disaster.

The bosun's pipe trilled from the loudspeakers. He then announced, "Now station the refueling detail. The smoking lamp is out throughout the ship while taking on fuel." He repeated the announcement to ensure all hands heard. Fire and fuel oil were a dangerous combination onboard ship

On deck, a choreographed ballet of activity began. A mix of twenty seamen, including the two misfits, Gibbs and Unger, arrived and formed a queue along the main deck, port side. A chorus of their laughs and complaints filled the air.

Five men, led by Bosun Dalton, took up positions at the forward fueling station on the 0-1 level, port side, directly below the bridge wing.

Mike turned his attention back to the *Sibuyan Sea*. A sailor on the carrier's refueling detail raised a special shotgun, aimed, and fired at the destroyer. The gun launched a projectile with a lightweight line attached. It arced across the foaming chasm between the two ships and landed on the 0-1 level, atop the forward three-inch gun mount.

Dalton concentrated on the dangerous task about to begin. "Come-on, Matthews. Haul ass and get that line back here. It's layin' across mount thirty-one."

The seaman ran forward, grabbed the line, then dashed back and fed it through a pulley down to Seaman Hughes, the lead man of the queue below on the main deck.

Hughes passed the line back until all twenty men each had a firm grip. They began pulling, and a succession of heavier lines paid out from the carrier. The final section, a steel cable, increased the effort required of the sailors.

When the cable arrived at the 0-1 level refueling station, Seaman Matthews snapped the end fitting to a stanchion and shouted, "Secure."

Bosun Dalton stood adjacent to the fuel trunk. "Okay, look alive there. Get the line off the cable. Come on, move it. We ain't got all frickin'day," he shouted. The roar of the waves nearly drowned out his commands.

Matthews disconnected the line from the steel cable that now tethered the two ships. The heavy, hemp line, having brought the cable over from the carrier, now served another purpose. The other end connected to a heavy, eight-inch diameter fuel hose on the *Sibuyan Sea*.

"Let's get this done. Heave away," Dalton yelled. The detail below pulled the heavy line drawing the hose, suspended from pulleys that rolled across on the steel cable.

The tug-of-war became a grueling challenge. Dalton exhorted the sailors below. "Heave, heave," he bellowed. The thundering of the waves and the cacophony of ship noises combined to smother the big man's shouts.

On the main deck, the twenty-man detail pulled with all their might. Dalton continuously shifted his gaze between the hose inching across from the carrier and the men below. He demanded the detail pull harder.

Occasionally, a wave would cause a sudden shift by one of the ships tightening the slack in the line, and the entire detail would be dragged foreword, fighting for purchase on the wet steel deck.

Hughes struggled to keep his grip. The men aft of him began slipping and falling, only to rise and pull harder. Seawater soaked their shoes and trousers, and their hands ached as they tried to maintain their grip on the line.

When the hose arrived at the refueling station, three seamen wrestled it into the fuel trunk, a large diameter pipe that ran from the refueling station, on the 0-1 level, down to the fuel bunkers below the water line. A seaman secured it in place.

Dalton signaled the carrier to begin pumping, and the thick Navy Standard Fuel Oil (NSFO) gushed through the hose and down into *Boyington's* nearly empty fuel bunkers.

The detail on the main deck relaxed, rubbing their sore hands.

"Four months and three days and I'm through with this bull shit," Seaman Struthers declared.

"Lucky bastard, I got over two more years left," Seaman Yeager responded.

A sickening metallic clank rang out, and the big hose snapped loose from the fuel trunk. Under high pressure from the pump on the carrier, it thrashed about like a berserk serpent, spewing forth a stream of black oil that coated the ship and sailors at the fueling station and on the main deck below.

Dalton yelled at his men trying to get the thrashing hose under control. In spite of their best efforts, they were unable to maintain their footing on the oil-coated deck, let alone hold onto the slippery hose.

Oil sprayed out over the water and alongside the ship. Captain Ellingham, on the open bridge directly above the refueling station, knew immediately what had happened. He stepped back into the pilothouse and grabbed to the 1MC microphone. "On the *Sibuyan Sea*, belay refueling. I repeat, belay refueling operations." The announcement blared from loudspeakers on *Boyington's* weather decks and reverberated loudly in the steel canyon between the two ships.

The captain returned to the open bridge as a sailor on the carrier leaped for the oil pump's bright red cut-off switch, but there were hundreds of gallons of oil still in the hose.

Ellingham glanced down toward the detail manning the hose line two decks below. At that moment, Seaman Hughes lost his footing and slid aft, feet first, flying along the oil-coated deck, propelled rapidly by waves crashing over the gunwale.

Two men leaped to grab him, but their sudden movement caused them to slip and fall.

The ship rolled to port and Hughes's legs passed under the lifelines and over the side. His flailing right hand touched the lower lifeline cable as he passed under it, and his fingers reflexively locked around the line. He hung there by one arm while powerful waves smashed his body against the hull. His mates, skating on the oily deck, struggled to reach him while trying to avoid the same fate.

The captain spun around and dashed into the pilothouse, where he again grabbed the public address microphone. "At the refueling station, cast-off the refueling gear. I repeat, at the fueling station, cast off all refueling gear. Ellingham ran back to the port bridge wing.

Dalton, his voice hoarse and cracking, yelled at the men fighting the thrashing hose. "Let that damn hose go and get out of my way."

Slipping and sliding, grabbing one another for support, the refueling crew abandoned the station and moved forward, their faces black and their work uniforms dripping oil. Dalton stepped into the danger zone, a five-pound hammer in his right hand. With a well-aimed swing, he knocked loose the clamp, releasing the steel cable and hose. Both flew into the sea.

Ellingham turned to the pilothouse door. "Helm, hard right rudder, All Stop."

The carrier pulled away as *Boyington* slowed and turned away. The distance between the ships increased and the wave action alongside diminished.

Two sailors now lying flat on the oily deck to avoid slipping overboard, each wrapped an arm over the lower lifeline for their own support and safety. Reaching over the gunwale, they grasped Hughes's left arm just as his grip failed. Pulling with every ounce of strength in their bodies, they dragged him back under the lifeline onto the safety of the deck. The three lay exhausted, gasping for breath.

The captain stepped back into the pilothouse, picked up the interior communications handset, and called Commander Kaestner in secondary conn. "XO, secure your station. Have supply get a case of soap and all the towels they can find, and lay aft to the fantail. Then find a couple dozen men to form a new refueling detail. Rate doesn't matter. Any enlisted man not on watch is eligible. We have to get back alongside *Sibuyan Sea* and refuel ASAP."

Ellingham then radioed the carrier and arranged another refueling in thirty minutes.

Chief Boatswain's Mate Jones stepped out onto the main deck at the bulwark and took charge. He yelled at the line handlers, "You men get back to the fantail and strip down. Throw all your clothes overboard—shoes and everything. They're all ruined."

Jones surveying the oil soaked bulkhead saw Bosun Foss at the torpedo deck rail, contemplating the chaos below. "Foss, turn-to, and breakout the fire hoses. Start with a saltwater wash-down. Get the fueling station first, then the sides and decks. Every second counts. We gotta get back alongside *Sibuyan Sea* and refuel."

Turning, he yelled up to the refueling station. "Dalton, you, and your men get the hell outta here. Get back to the fantail, strip, and get that crud off your bodies as fast as you can."

With that, he disappeared into the athwartships passageway.

One team of six seamen manned a powerful fire hose and began blasting the deck and bulkheads around the refueling station with saltwater. Another team started on the main deck at the bulwark hosing the oil-covered port side bulkheads and decks with another high-pressure stream of saltwater.

Twenty-five naked sailors stood on the fantail scrubbing their oil-soaked skin and hair under low-pressure saltwater hoses. A trail of oil-soaked clothing floated in *Boyington's* wake.

A corpsman administered first aid to several men who had oil in their eyes.

When Mike saw the hose come loose, he knew what would happen and what the immediate needs of the ship were. He ran aft crossing the forecastle toward the starboard side. He entered the athwartships passageway and at the central passageway, stopped to let the chief hospital corpsman pass. The chief, with the help of another sailor, was walking Hughes into sickbay for treatment of shock.

Mike started rounding up a work party. He met the XO on the mess deck, the three men he had recruited in tow.

"Chief, the bosuns are hosing down the deck now. Round up a new refueling detail. As soon as the decks are safe to walk on, we're going back alongside the carrier and try it again."

"Aye, aye, Sir," Mike said. "Got these three already."

He turned to the little group. "Harrigan, you run forward to the operations and first division compartments, round up anyone you find and bring them back here. Jackson, go aft to second division and engineering and do the same. Fenster, you check supply and the mess cook's compartment. Bring anyone not on watch back here."

Bosun Jones entered the mess deck through the forward door. "What're you doing, Mike?"

"Trying to form up a new refueling detail. Did you see what happened?"

"Yeah, I'm heading aft to help clean up the crew that got soaked in oil." Jones dashed off.

Mike soon had twenty-two sailors corralled on the mess deck, waiting to replace their shipmates on the fantail.

Later, when *Boyington* again pulled alongside *Sibuyan Sea*, Mike took Seaman Hughes's place at the head of the queue, and Foss replaced Dalton at the 0-1 fueling station. Fifteen minutes later, the carrier began pumping barrels of NSFO into the destroyer without further disruption.

By 1030, the deck crew had rescrubbed the port side bulkheads and decks with fresh water. They began preparing to repaint a few areas where the high-pressure wash down had stripped the paint away.

At noon, the mess decks were crowded with exhausted, hungry sailors. Mess cooks, under the watchful eye of a commissaryman, portioned out the chow: meat loaf, powdered mashed potatoes, brown gravy, and canned carrots, with chocolate chip cookies for dessert. The beverage choices were Cherry Kool-Aid, coffee, and water.

The unfortunate event of the morning caused superficial damage to the ship, but more importantly, had nearly cost the life of a seaman. The incident had a dampening effect on the morale of the crew.

The officers and chiefs, sensing the mood, planned a busy afternoon. Lieutenant Commander Kaestner received permission to conduct a general-quarters drill.

By the end of the workday, a more cheerful mood prevailed. However, the senior leaders knew far greater challenges awaited ship and crew. Their immediate task became apparent. They had to condition the young sailors to recover from traumatic events immediately and press on with the mission. War is an ugly business that allows no time for emotions or grieving, and the threat of war became greater with each passing hour on the Walnut Line.

CHAPTER 12

Esmeralda

Four-Hundred and Fifty Miles North of Mona Passage

Saturday, 27 October 1962

During the morning of 27 October 1962: Premier Nikita Khrushchev publically announced that the Soviet Union was willing to remove its offensive missiles from Cuba if the United States would remove its offensive missiles from Turkey.[4]

At a tense meeting of the Executive Committee, President Kennedy resists pressure for immediate military action against the SAM sites. At several points in the discussion, Kennedy insists that removal of the American missiles in Turkey will have to be part of an overall negotiated settlement. The Committee ultimately decides to ignore the Saturday letter from Moscow and respond favorably to the more conciliatory Friday message. Air Force troop carrier squadrons are ordered to active duty in case an invasion is required.[9]

Later that night, Robert Kennedy meets secretly with Ambassador Anatoly Dobrynin. They reach a basic understanding: the Soviet Union will withdraw the missiles from Cuba under United Nations supervision in exchange for an American pledge not to invade Cuba. In an additional secret understanding, the United States agrees to eventually remove the Jupiter missiles from Turkey.[9]

The Fifth Marine Expeditionary Brigade completed loading at West Coast ports and sailed for the Panama Canal. The Air Force activated forty-two Air Reserve Transport Squadrons and recalled 14,215 air reservists. An additional eight wings, three-hundred and eighty-four aircraft were activated in-place, along with two wing headquarters and support units, which included 21 squadrons of C-119's and three squadrons of C-123's.[4]

Captain Ellingham shouted, "Get a course to intercept."

"Aye, aye, Sir," Lieutenant Caruthers, the OOD responded.

The excitement level rose in CIC and on the bridge. A navy P2V Neptune patrol plane, flying out of Bermuda, spotted a freighter heading toward Mona Passage, a gateway to the Caribbean between the islands of Puerto Rico and Hispaniola. The commodore gave *Boyington* the mission to intercept and search it, if necessary.

Lieutenant Junior Grade James Rudolph worked out the course and speed *Boyington* needed to cut off the freighter, based on the datum and speed of the freighter reported by the Neptune. He stepped into the pilothouse and handed the solution to the OOD.

"Helm, steer zero-one-five, make turns for two five knots," Mister Caruthers ordered. He turned to the captain. "We should intercept the contact in about two hours, assuming she stays with the present course and speed."

"When we're about half an hour out, muster the port boarding party. Give Mister Frankel a heads-up. I'm going below," Ellingham said.

"Aye, aye, Sir."

Lieutenant Caruthers called the captain's cabin at 1435. "Sir, its Caruthers. We have the contact on radar nineteen miles north. Thirty-four minutes to intercept."

"Okay, alert the port boarding party. I'll be up in a few minutes."

"Aye, aye, Sir," Caruthers said. "Bosun, call away the port boarding party and whaleboat crew."

As Ellingham set the telephone handset down on his desk, the 1MC speakers vibrated with the bosun's pipe and announcement. "Now hear this. Now hear this. Now muster the Port boarding party, on the oh-one level. This is not a drill. Port boarding party, muster on the oh-one level. Motor whaleboat crew, man your stations, and prepare to launch."

Ensign Frankel and Chief Jones met at the small arms locker. GM1 Zarna, the armorer, arrived seconds later, unlocked the room and issued holsters, web belts, M-1911 .45 caliber pistols, and ammunition to each. The two men signed for the pistols, strapped on the gear, and then double-timed their way to the 0-1 level.

Electronics Technician Third Class Stewart arrived with walkie-talkies and handed them to Frankel and Jones.

"Are the batteries fresh?" Jones asked.

"I put new ones in before I came up," Stewart said.

The XO came down the ladder from the signal bridge. "Is everyone present, Mister Frankel? Are you ready to go?"

"Yes, Sir. All present and ready."

Kaestner addressed the group, "Men, we don't know yet what we're dealing with here. It could be an innocent freighter on its way to the Caribbean or a Soviet preparing to run the quarantine. We'll assume the latter. Make sure you have all the gear you'll need. Check the radios now and again before you board, if it comes to that. Lock and load your pistols. I'll brief you again as soon as we make contact with the freighter. Mister Frankel, carry on."

"Aye, aye, Sir." As the XO departed, Ensign Frankel looked over the checklist he had prepared. "Okay, men, if you need a head call, go now. Nothing's going to happen in the next fifteen minutes, but get back here *pronto*."

Several yards aft of the boarding party, the bosuns lowered the boat to the 0-1 level for boarding. The coxswain jumped in to double-check fuel and supplies prior to launching.

The boarding party suited up in their life jackets and waited to board.

"Sir, visual contact reported: Freighter off the port bow; range, three oh-double-oh." The 1JV telephone talker on the bridge relayed a sighting from the 0-3 level lookout.

The captain stepped out onto the port bridge wing, and focused the contact through his binoculars. Lieutenant Caruthers stood next to the skipper. He called out, "Steady as she goes, all ahead one-third, turns for fifteen knots."

The lee helmsman repeated the order, and the ship slowed.

Boyington made a sweeping turn aft of the freighter and approached on its starboard quarter. She flew the Spanish ensign, and the name *Esmeralda* appeared on the stern plates, along with Cádiz, her homeport.

"Mister Caruthers, call her on the international channel and ask the quarantine questions," Ellingham said.

"Aye, aye, Sir. Caruthers entered pilothouse and picked up the radiotelephone handset, "*Esmeralda,* this is the United States Ship *Boyington,* over."

"U.S. ship, this motor vessel *Esmeralda,* you talk, okay."

"What is your cargo and destination, *Esmeralda*?"

"We carrying textiles, olive oil, and some good Spanish wine to Cartagena and Veracruz."

"Thank you, *Esmeralda.* Have a pleasant voyage, *Boyington* out."

Caruthers turned to the captain who had entered the pilothouse. "She's carrying wine, olive oil, and cloth, Sir. They're on their way to Columbia and Mexico."

"Okay, prepare a report for Checkbook, and tell radio central to get it out ASAP. The Caribbean patrol will follow-up to make sure they told us the truth." He turned to the bosun. "Secure the boarding party and the whaleboat crew. Helm, steer one-nine-five; all ahead full, turns for two oh knots."

Two miles away and thirty feet below the surface, a predator had witnessed the meeting of the two ships.

"Down periscope. The Americans came alongside the Spaniard and did not even stop them. Maybe our freighters won't have such a hard time after all, Comrade Captain Lieutenant. Perhaps the U.S. Navy is a big paper tiger, and we have nothing to fear."

"I am not so sure, Captain Petrov. Would they react the same if the freighter had a Soviet flag?"

"We shall see."

"Comrade Captain, the destroyer has started searching with its sonar again," a petty officer called out.

"Dive, dive. All ahead full," Petrov shouted. "Planesman, take us down to one-hundred meters."

The afternoon sun bore down on *Boyington's* torpedo desk as Ensign Frankel addressed his boarding party. "Sorry, men, I know you were all ready to go—maybe next time. Stow your life jackets. Detail dismissed."

The boatswains winched the whaleboat back up and stowed it in the steaming position.

Frankel and Jones looked at each other, sighed, and headed for the small arms locker to turn in their weapons. "This is crazy, Chief. I feel disappointed and relieved at the same time," Frankel said.

"I know exactly how you feel, Sir, but I don't think it's crazy, just a waste of adrenaline."

As the excitement of the surface contact encounter diminished, an announcement from the 1JS telephone talker reignited tension on the bridge. "Sonar has a contact: bearing, two-zero-two; range, four oh-double-oh; depth one five oh and diving."

Ellingham ran to the attack director, which indicated both the true and relative bearing to the sonar contact, its course, and the attack angle. "Mister Caruthers, come about hard to port, steer zero-eight-zero."

"Helm, come about hard to port, steer zero-eight-zero. All ahead flank," the OOD ordered. "Bosun, sound general quarters, set ASW condition one. CIC, notify DESRON Forty-Two we have a contact."

Boyington rolled hard as she turned sharply behind the departing freighter and increased speed. The GQ alarm bell clanged away as the crew involved repositioned to ASW battle stations.

"Sir, contact is now at two-hundred feet and still diving."

One mile to the west and forty fathoms below the surface, tensions also rose. "Comrade Captain, the destroyer is turning toward us and closing fast, range two-thousand meters," the sonarman announced.

"Add five degrees to the bow planes. As soon as we are under the thermocline, level out and rig for silent running."

Ten minutes passed. "Captain, sonar lost the contact," the telephone talker reported.

Ellingham sighed, "Let's circle around awhile and see if she pops up again."

"Helm, left standard rudder, Bosun, secure from general quarters. CIC, notify DESRON Forty-Two we lost contact and will stay on location to continue searching," the OOD said.

Two decks below, Mike met Chief Boilerman Ken Ford in the Chiefs' mess. Bosun Jones entered as they were sitting down at a table.

"Sorry you didn't get to have any fun on that Spaniard, Paul," Ford said.

"Yeah, Dalton hoped they might have some *señoritas* in the crew. He's always ready to party," Jones said.

"I don't know about the Spaniards, but the Russians have women in their crews. Maybe he'll find a nice *babushka* in the galley of one of those Soviet freighters before this is all over," Mike said.

"Yeah, he needs a good stout woman to slap him around when he gets out of line," Jones said.

"That might just work out. The language barrier would keep him from insulting her and keep her from pissing him off. It could be a match made in heaven. He hasn't had much luck with English speaking women, I understand," Ford said.

Jones filled his mug and headed for the door. "Good idea. I'll try to it sell to him."

Ken walked over to the coffee urn and refilled his cup, a big handsome mug with "U.S.S. Blandy" arching over a coat of arms, glazed on the side. "Hey, Mike, what happened to your man? He didn't show up at quarters this morning like you told me. I got BT1 Yost's hopes up that he'd get a new bilge cleaner today. Now he's damn near heartbroken. I thought he was gonna cry," Ford said.

"I'm sorry about that, Ken. Gibbs convinced me he's claustrophobic and would go nuts in the fire room." Mike filled a cup and sat back down at the table. "Tell Yost I'm sorry. Hey, nice looking mug you got there, Ken."

"Thanks, I got it on the *Blandy,* when you were lollygagging around on the *Jaffey*. But getting back to Gibbs, if he's afraid of things being tight in the fire room, how the heck is he gonna work in a gun mount or any of your other spaces?"

"You're right. I stuck him in mount fifty-three after quarters yesterday morning, and he damn near passed out. I sent him to first division until we can get the medics to check him over. I think he'll end up getting kicked out and going home to mommy."

"It's too bad Gibbs didn't work out in gunnery. There's probably a kid somewhere who wanted destroyer duty and got stuck on shore in some place like Bermuda, or Key West because Gibbs got this billet," Ford said.

"That would be a real shame, wouldn't it? If you find out where that guy is, let him know I need a new striker," Mike said.

"You sound like a man planning on staying. I figured you for a citizen-sailor, in only for the duration."

"Yeah, I slipped back into the lifer-mode there for a minute. I'm outta here as soon as this business is over. Listen, Buddy, I better get moving. The fifty-one crew have some kind of problem with the loader. Catch you later," Mike said.

"Okay, later," Ford replied.

CHAPTER 13

Trouble on the Mess Deck

One-Hundred and Forty Miles Northwest of Turks Island Passage

Saturday, 27 October 1962

October 27, 1962—6:00 A.M.: The CIA intelligence memorandum contains information compiled as of 6:00 A.M., reports that three of the four MRBM sites at San Cristóbal and two sites at Sagua la Grande appear to be fully operational. The mobilization of Cuban military forces is reported to be continuing at a high rate, but the CIA advises that Cuban forces remain under orders not to engage in hostilities unless attacked. (Document 47, CIA Daily Report, The Crisis USSR-Cuba: Information as of 0600 27 October 1962.)[1]

At 1636 EST, an afternoon flight of low-level reconnaissance aircraft reported they were fired on by what appeared to be a 30 mm cannon. Since JCS had issued the order to strike surface-to-air sites if a reconnaissance plane was downed, this flight received cautious evaluation. Two of the eight-plane flight returned with engine trouble at 1604 EST.[4]

Mike heard loud shouts coming from the mess deck as he headed aft. The workday had ended with the forward five-inch loader back in operation. He was tired and hungry as he walked back to the chiefs' quarters to clean-up for supper. When he entered the mess deck, a near riot blocked his path. The two Masters-at-Arms, Chief Jones and GM1 Zarna, fought a losing battle as they tried to restore order.

"Paul, what the hell's going on?" Mike shouted. He could barely make himself heard above the clamor.

"The fricking scullery's busted. There ain't no clean trays, and half the crew ain't eaten yet. Give us a hand."

Mike jumped on top the nearest table. With a red face and his chiseled jaw protruding like a man ready for a fight, he shouted over the din. "If you've eaten, get the hell outta here now. If you haven't eaten, get in line out on the weather deck, and you'll get fed shortly."

No one questioned him. The noise level dropped, and the sailors began leaving.

Mike jumped down from the table, and looking in the galley, saw CS2 Hastings, the duty commissaryman in-charge, standing behind the serving line. He walked over to him. "That's right, isn't it, Hastings?" he whispered. "You'll be feeding them soon, won't you?"

"I got the food, but no trays. We ain't never had a problem like this before. The scullery quit working, and the dirty trays are piling up. The electricians are working on it, but so far it's still broke."

"Okay, just keep the food hot. Do Chief Baker and the supply officer know what's happened?"

"Don't know, ain't seen neither of them."

"Well, since the mess cooks aren't real busy right now, send a couple out to find them. This is a big problem."

"Okay, Chief."

Mike headed for the scullery. Two electricians had the machine opened up and were sweating away in the tiny, hot, humid room. Electrician's Mate First Class Moses Waller stood next to the machine looking at a schematic drawing, while his striker checked voltages.

"Moses, have you figured out what the trouble is yet?" Mike asked.

"No, Chief, but we're getting close."

"How much longer?"

"We'll have it up and running in ten minutes, unless we need some part that's not onboard."

"Okay, that's great."

"Chief, that's ten minutes after we figure out what the problem is."

"Oh, okay, smart-ass, then get back to work."

Mike returned to the galley. "Hastings, there may not be any trays for quite some time. Why don't you make some hot dogs? The men can eat them without trays."

"Good idea, Chief. I'll send the jack-o'-the-dust down to the freezer to get some right away."

Mike turned as the supply officer stormed into the galley with Baker, the chief commissary man on his heels. "What the hell's going on here, Hastings?" Lieutenant Riley barked.

"Sir, the scullery's broke, and we ain't got no trays. I'm gonna make some hot dogs so's the men can eat without trays, Sir."

"Good thinking, Hastings," Riley said. He headed to the scullery to check with the electricians.

Hastings smiled and gave Mike a covert thumbs-up.

As Mike passed the open door to the starboard weather deck, he noticed Seaman Apprentice Unger, leaning against a lifeline stanchion, smoking a cigarette and smiling to himself.

Mike stepped out onto the weather deck. He squinted as the sun, low on the western horizon, flashed across his field of vision. "Come on up here with me for a minute, Unger." Together they walked forward to the bulwark, away from the sailors in the chow line. "Tell me exactly what happened there in the scullery."

"I don't know what happened, Chief. Like usual, the heat and humidity in there had me sweating buckets. As fast as I could, I scraped off the trays and stacked them to go through the steam wash. Then, all of a sudden, the machine just stopped. I kept hitting the button to start it up again, but nothing happened. That's all I know."

"Did Hastings look at it?"

"He tried, but it didn't start for him either."

"Okay, carry on."

When Mike returned to the mess deck, he walked back to the scullery door. The electricians were putting the machine back together. "Is it fixed now, Waller?" he asked.

"Yeah, a wire broke off one of the control boards, down underneath the washer—a real bitch of a place to get to. Good thing my striker's a wiry little guy. I've never seen a trouble like this in the eighteen years I been riding tin cans. I couldn't squeeze underneath that thing in a month of Sundays. On top of that, this damn little room is hotter than Hades. I bet the temperature in here is higher than the fire room during GQ."

"You may be right, not a great place to work. Is that your striker over there drinking Kool-aid?" Mike asked.

"That's him, hero of the day."

"He can't weigh more than 125-130 pounds—about the same as Unger, the mess cook assigned in here."

"You're right, Chief. Can't remember when I weighed 125 pounds, maybe in kindergarten. Good thing I got a skinny striker or we'd never been able to fix it."

"Okay, Waller, glad you solved the problem."

Mike walked over to the electrician striker. "Good job on the scullery, Evans. Waller told me you're the only guy on the ship that could have fixed it."

"Thanks, Chief. Any of the other guys in the electrical shop could've fixed it if they could've squeezed under the machine. I just happen to be the only one who would fit under there."

"Well, you did it, and you get the credit. I'll tell the XO when I see him."

"Thanks, Chief."

Mike turned as Bosun Jones entered the mess deck.

"What say, Mike. Hey, thanks for helping restore order. What a mess, and it couldn't have happened at a worse time."

"Yeah, it was almost like someone planned it."

"What you getting at?"

"I find it quite curious. That kid Unger is another one of my problem children. I put him in the scullery as punishment, so he's pissed off at the world. Lieutenant Quinn told me he's been a screw up since he came aboard. I found him goofing off on the job and decided he might learn to appreciate being a gunner if he learned how some of the others in the crew spent their working days.

"Then Waller, the electrician, tells me that he's never seen an equipment failure like this before, and only a skinny guy could get under the machine where they located the fault," Mike said.

"I get your drift, but do you think Unger is smart enough to have pulled off something like that? I mean, he's been working his ass off in there, and it has to be one of the worst jobs on the ship. During chow time, those dirty trays fly through the window, and he couldn't just stop washing and crawl under the machine to unhook a wire, could he?"

"Yeah, good point. It might be my imagination working overtime. But right after we got things under control, I saw him standing out on the weather deck, smirking like a little kid that just messed his pants and doesn't think anyone knows it."

"Well, we got no proof, so's all I can say is watch him."

"Yeah, guess so," Mike said.

CHAPTER 14

The Trap

One-Hundred Miles North of Caicos Passage

Saturday, 27 October 1962

On the morning of 27 October, a U-2 piloted by USAF Major Rudolf Anderson, departed its forward operating location at McCoy Air Force Base, Orlando, Florida. At approximately 12:00 PM EDT, a SAM missile launched from Cuba struck the aircraft killing Anderson. The stress in negotiations between the USSR and the U.S. intensified, and only later was it learned that the decision to fire the missile was made locally by an undetermined Soviet commander acting on his own authority. Major Anderson was the only combat casualty of the Cuban Missile Crisis, but eleven more airmen would die in accidents before the emergency ended. [13]

The U.S.S. Randolph (CVS 15), with an escort of eight destroyers, joined the quarantine. One of her destroyers, the U.S.S. Cony (DDE 508), began investigating contact

C-19, detected by an air patrol. Later, destroyers Beale (DDE 471) and Murray (DDE 576) joined Cony. Beale attempted to signal the submarine with grenades and sonar, but the sub didn't respond. Later, the Cony again challenged it with grenades. Although aware of the U.S. notification that grenades would be used, initially the Soviets believed they were under attack. That evening with her batteries running low, the sub surfaced and was identified as Soviet vessel B-59.[2]

W hen Mike finally entered the chiefs' mess after the mess deck debacle, those present stood and applauded. His face turned from its usual deep tan to a pale red.

He sat down with Ken Ford, and the mess cook served his supper.

"Way to take charge, Mike."

"Thanks. I thought a full-scale riot might erupt at any moment. Jones and Zarna were trying, but couldn't get control, and the folks in the galley didn't lift a fork to help."

"I heard Hastings had the duty as commissaryman-in-charge, but he's in over his head even when things are going smoothly," Ford said.

"Saw that . . . he seemed clueless," Mike said.

"Yeah, well, they have to work with what they got."

"Ken, I've a nagging suspicion that Unger may have sabotaged that scullery machine. Listen to this, and tell me what you think." Mike related the suspicions he shared with the bosun earlier.

"Wow, if that's true, he's looking at a court martial."

"Right, and that's why I have to get proof, one way or another. A court martial would ruin his life, but if he's guilty, it has to be done."

"Agreed, but how can you prove it?"

"I don't know, but I thought maybe if you, Jones, and I put our heads together, we could figure something out."

"Okay, Jones has to be on the bridge for eight o'clock reports and he's always busy until then. Let's try and meet right after he's done," Ken suggested.

That night the three chiefs met on the 0-1 level to discuss what course of action they should take. A cool breeze from the southwest floated across the open deck and starlight reflected, like tiny electric lights, from the gently rolling sea.

Mike began, "I think the first thing to consider is access. If Unger did commit an act of sabotage, the time he had to do it is limited. I don't know how he could pull it off during messing hours when the machine is in operation. There are too many people milling around, and he couldn't stop working and crawl under the machine, even for a few minutes."

"He could have done it at night." Jones said. "They turn out the lights and close the galley after serving mid-rats. But if someone tried to sneak into the scullery between then and 0400 when the cooks start to work, they would have to turn on the lights or use a flashlight, and odds are someone on the mid-watch would have seen him."

"What about after the evening chow when all the trays have been cleaned and put away? The scullery man has to clean the machine. No one would pay any attention to him crawling around then. It would just look like part of the job," Ford said.

"By golly, I think you've got it, Ken. Sure, it's perfect. If Hastings looked in on him, he would praise the kid for doing a good, thorough job. He could have loosened a wire, then the next day, with the machine in heavy use, the vibration caused it to come off, and bam . . . the scullery is out of business," Mike suggested.

"Just to make sure, I'll start locking the scullery door after he's done cleaning," Jones said. "No one needs to get in there between 1800 and 0630 the next morning when the early risers finish morning chow. I think you nailed it, Ken. If he did something to damage the machine, he would have had to do it between about 1730 and 1800. We can get Zarna to help, and between the four of us walking up and down the passageway during that thirty minute window, we may see some unusual activity."

"Sounds like a plan. You go lock the room up now, Paul, and I'll brief Zarna in the morning after quarters," Mike said.

They all started to leave, but Mike turned back. "Hey, Paul, I forgot to ask. How's Gibbs, my other problem-child working out?"

"Oh, that's another story. I put him to work in Harry Foss's gang, chipping and resurfacing the deck we're standing on. Foss said the kid is doing okay. He hasn't caused any problems and works hard."

"Interesting, maybe we got his attention."

"Yeah, Harry's good at that. Not many men stand up to him for long, that is. If he could quit getting into brawls ashore, he'd be a chief," Jones said.

"Do one thing, if you can. Put Gibbs in some confined space and see what he does. See if he freaks out. He might have fooled me with his claustrophobic act," Stafford said.

"Will do," Jones replied.

Mike and Ken headed aft toward the chiefs' quarters.

Jones went to the master-at-arms shack, on the port side of the mess deck, to get the key and lock the scullery.

No one had locked the room in years, so it took considerable time just to locate the key. Then he had to find a squirt-can of oil and lubricate the lock, before he could get the key to work in the tumbler. Finally, with the door locked, Jones returned to the MAA shack, put away the oilcan, hung the key in its rightful place, and cleared away some lingering paperwork. Shortly after the mid-watch picked up their sandwiches and left the mess deck, Jones turned off the light, stepped out of the tiny office, and locked the door.

The bosun paused in the shadows of the dimly lit mess deck when he saw Unger coming down the passageway from the mess cook's berthing compartment. The young sailor stopped at the scullery and tried to open the door. He appeared surprised to find it wouldn't open. He repeatedly turned the knob while pushing on the door, apparently thinking it might be stuck.

Jones quietly covered the twenty feet that separated the two men. "Got a problem there, sailor?"

Unger tensed in surprise and spun around. "Oh, Chief, you scared me. I didn't hear you coming."

"I stopped by the MAA shack to clear out some paperwork. What're you doing?"

"W-well, I-I just wanted to make sure I had everything squared away for morning chow."

"I see. The XO has decided to secure all non-critical spaces when not in use. I locked this door a few minutes ago. I'll open it in the morning before the chow line forms. You'll have plenty of time to check things out before the first dirty tray arrives."

"Okay, Chief, I just hope everything works. You know the problem we had earlier when the machine broke down—damn near had a riot. There'd be trouble if that happened again."

"Yes, there would be. So you get up here when mess-gear is piped and check it out."

"Okay, Chief. See you in the morning."

"Right, good night."

A pleasant breeze continued through the night air as *Boyington* patrolled on an easterly course at fifteen knots through a calm Atlantic, one part of the cordon of steel that closed the Walnut Line to the enemies of America.

PART II

THE END OF THE BEGINNING

CHAPTER 15

Svetlana

Two-Hundred Miles Northeast of Nassau, Bahamas Islands

0600 Sunday, 28 October 1962

If there was an official end to the Cuban Missile Crisis, it occurred on this date.[4]

At 0430 local, one of the approaching Russian ships, the Groznyy, had reached the quarantine line and stopped. She remained dead in the water all day and did not proceed into the area where she would be subject to challenge.[4]

October 28, 1962, Secretary Khrushchev wrote President Kennedy stating...the Soviet Government, in addition to earlier instructions on the discontinuation of further work on weapons construction sites, has given a new order to dismantle the arms, which you described as offensive, and to crate and return them to the Soviet Union.[11]

In spite of the encouraging turn of events, however, there was no slackening of quarantine operational matters. The Joint Staff approved a proposal that the line of destroyers be withdrawn to a new, closer-in position for more efficient search and utilization of ships. The Soviet freighter Belovodsk was reported en route and approaching the quarantine zone with a deck load of crated helicopters.[4]

Mister Anderson, the OOD, hung up the radiotelephone handset and turned to the captain. "Sir, we just received orders to intercept a freighter heading for the Walnut Line. She failed to respond to one of *Sibuyan Sea's* patrol planes. The pilot thinks she's going to try to run the line."

"How far away is she?" Ellingham asked.

"At last report, twenty-five miles northeast of our present position and heading this way at an estimated eighteen knots, Sir."

"Is the plane still tracking her?"

"Yes, Sir."

"Okay, let's get up there at flank speed and check her out. Alert the starboard boarding party and the whaleboat crew to get ready and standby."

"Aye, aye, Sir," Anderson said.

The captain stepped out on the starboard open deck. A red-amber aura on the eastern horizon heralded the rising sun. The strange colors flooded the bridge with an eerie glow.

Anderson's voice filled the pilothouse as he passed the requisite orders. The bosun's announcements then blared throughout the ship.

Ensign Padgett, leader of the starboard boarding team, arrived at the small arms locker, followed by Gunner's Mate Zarna.

"Guess we gotta live one, Sir," Zarna said. He unlocked the door and grabbed two pistol belts he had pre-equipped with weapons and ammunition. "Here you go, Sir. Verify the weapon's serial number, sign the log, and it's all yours."

Padgett strapped on his belt as Mike arrived and went through the same routine. "Okay Chief, let's get topside and see what mischief we can get into today."

"Have you seen the sky, Sir? Not a good omen."

In CIC, the watch officer called the aircraft tracking the freighter. "Red Rover Three, This is Siena. Have you made radio contact with the freighter?"

"Negative, Siena, no response so far. If you're taking over, I'm heading home, my fuel situation is nearing critical, over."

"We got it Red Rover Three, Siena out." The watch officer reached for a handset, and advised the bridge of this development.

Captain Ellingham shouted from the bridge. "Time-to-intercept, Mister Anderson?"

"Twenty minutes or less, Sir, we're closing fast. CIC has radar contact. Checkbook advised they have designated the freighter as surface contact 'sierra one-seven.' "

Ten minutes passed. "Mister Anderson, the way this contact is behaving may mean trouble—let's go to general quarters.

"XO, are the boarding party and the whaleboat ready to go?" Ellingham asked.

Kaestner, who had returned from the torpedo deck, paused. "Yes, Sir, the starboard boarding party is armed and ready, and the whaleboat crew is standing by to launch."

The 1JV talker continued relaying CIC's radar range and bearing to the target.

"Now general quarters, general quarters. All hands man your battle stations. This is not a drill. Set material condition Zulu." The bosun's announcement filled every compartment on the ship then the incessant alarm bell began ringing.

The announcement set off an organized chaos throughout the ship. Sailors heading forward or to higher decks used starboard passageways and ladders. Those running aft or to lower decks use passageways and ladders on the port side.

The last man through each watertight door or hatch shut it and dogged it tight. Damage control parties broke-out tools, equipment, and materials to deal with catastrophic conditions such as fire or loss of watertight integrity.

Men in exposed stations donned life jackets and steel helmets. Torpedo tubes, depth charge racks, and hedgehog launchers are manned, armed, and ready to fire.

"Sir, the oh-three lookout reports a ship off the starboard bow, range four five double-oh," the 1JV telephone talker reported.

Lieutenant Anderson donned his helmet. "Captain, all battle stations are manned and ready."

The sun, now cresting the horizon, ignited a plateau of gossamer clouds into a fusion of bright pink and orange.

Anderson stood on the open bridge, his binoculars focused on the freighter. "Conn, approach on her port side, then circle around to approach on the starboard side."

"Aye, aye, Sir," Mister White, the conning officer, replied. "Helm, come right to zero-one-zero, turns for two oh knots," he ordered.

When *Boyington* arrived to within five-hundred yards of the freighter's bow, Mister White reduced the speed to ten knots. The two ships passed in opposite directions port side-to-port side.

"Helm, come about hard to port, steer one-nine-zero, turns for one eight knots," Mister White ordered.

As the destroyer swept around the freighter's stern, Anderson noted the vessel's name, *Svetlana,* with a homeport of Leningrad. The red Soviet flag with a gold hammer and sickle flew from her mast.

The two ships cruised along side-by-side in moderate seas.

"Mister Anderson, hail the freighter and ask the quarantine questions," Ellingham ordered.

"Aye, aye, Sir." Anderson picked up the radiotelephone handset and called on the international distress frequency. "Svetlana, this is the United States Ship *Boyington*, over."

No response.

He called again, still no response. "Captain, they're not answering."

Ellingham walked out on the open bridge and called aft to a signalman. "Kessler, use those new codes and query them with the signal lamp. Identify us and ask their destination."

"Aye, aye, Sir," the signalman responded. Then with codebook in hand, he began tapping out the message on a signal lamp, but received no response.

Ellingham waited on the bridge as the signalman sent, then repeated the message. Svetlana did not answer. He picked up the radiotelephone handset on the tactical network. "Checkbook, this is Siena actual, over."

"Go ahead, Siena, this is Checkbook."

"Checkbook, Siena, we are tracking surface contact sierra one-seven, cruising on one-nine-zero at eighteen knots. She is the *Svetlana*, out of Leningrad and flying the Soviet flag. Red Rover Three attempted to make radio contact, but didn't receive any reply. Now, we have tried repeatedly to contact her by radio and signal lamp, and she isn't responding, over."

"Roger, Siena. Stand by."

Several minutes passed. "Siena, this Checkbook. Stay with contact sierra one-seven and advise when you reach the Walnut Line, Checkbook out."

"Roger, Checkbook, Siena out."

Ellingham turned to the OOD, apprising him of Checkbook's orders.

"Bosun, secure from general quarters, stand-down the boarding party and whaleboat crew. Conn, put another five-hundred yards between us and the Soviet," Anderson ordered.

Ensign Padgett and Chief Stafford stood on the torpedo deck with the freighter looming off to port.

"What do you think is going to happen now, Chief?" Padgett asked.

"Most likely nothing, unless they cross the blockade line. But if we get there, and they still refuse to stop or turn around, things could get interesting," Mike said.

The two men departed to return their weapons to the small arms locker.

Boyington steamed on a parallel course, one-half mile to the west of the Soviet freighter *Svetlana* for five hours.

At noon, the OOD interrupted the Captain's lunch. "Sir, we just crossed the Walnut Line. I called Svetlana on the radio and tried the signal lamp again, but still no response."

"Okay. I'll be up in a few minutes," Ellingham said.

When he returned to the bridge, the captain scanned the Russian ship with his binoculars, but didn't notice any activity on her weather decks. He returned to the pilothouse and called the task group commander. "Checkbook, this is Siena actual, over."

"Siena, Checkbook, go ahead."

"Checkbook, Siena. I'm tracking contact sierra one-seven. We've just crossed the Walnut Line, and they still refuse to respond to our radio or signal lamp queries. Advise, over."

"Stand-by Siena."

Ten minutes passed before the task group called back. "Siena, this is Checkbook, over."

"Checkbook, Siena actual, over," Ellingham said.

"Siena, Checkbook. Fire one shot across the bow of sierra one-seven, the vessel you have identified as the Soviet ship *Svetlana.* After firing, advise her reaction, over."

Captain Ellingham repeated the order to ensure a correct understanding. After receiving verification, he hung up the handset and looked across the one-thousand yard gap between the two ships. *I hope you know what you're starting here, you Communist bastard.*

"Mister Thomas, call the Svetlana one more time."

Seconds ticked away. "No response, Sir," Thomas the OOD said.

"Very well. Sound general-quarters and close the gap to five-hundred yards," Ellingham ordered.

CHAPTER 16

First Shot

Two-Hundred and Thirty Miles East of Nassau, Bahamas Islands

1200 Sunday, 28 October 1962

Relations between Cuba and the Soviet Union deteriorated with Fidel Castro accusing the Soviets of backing down from the Americans and deserting the Cuban socialist revolution. Castro called for a campaign of terrorist agitation in Latin America. Venezuela reported an intercepted radio broadcast from Cuba ordering raids on their oil fields. They believed that similar orders had gone out to Communist groups in other Latin American countries as well. A later report stated saboteurs blew up four oil-company power stations in the Lake Maracaibo district, knocking out one-sixth of Venezuela's oil production.[4]

Throughout the night surveillance and position reports arrived at the CNO Flag Plot including the report of a

Soviet submarine on the surface northeast of the quarantine line.[4]

Captain Ellingham selected a number on the sound powered telephone and turned the crank. "Gunnery, this is the CO. We have orders to try to stop this would-be blockade-runner with a shot across the bow. Aim all five-inch mounts toward her then when you're ready, we'll have fifty-one send the rude bastards a greeting."

"Aye, aye, Sir," Lieutenant Quinn said.

Dark, low hanging clouds now filled the sky as *Boyington* continued on a course parallel to Svetlana, five-hundred yards off her starboard side. Both ships were cutting through the increasing seas at eighteen knots. Waves were breaking over the destroyer's bow with increasing frequency.

"All battle stations manned and ready, Captain," Mister Anderson reported.

The destroyer's five-inch gun mounts rotated toward the *Svetlana*. Her fire control directors tracked the vessel, feeding range and bearing data to computers that controlled the lateral positions of the mounts and elevation of the gun barrels. The rough sea caused the system to reposition the big gun barrels with each roll of the deck, moving the barrels up and down, keeping them locked on target.

At 1216, local time, the U.S.S. *Boyington* fired her first warning shot of the Cuban missile crisis. The forward gun mount roared. A donut shaped ring of silver and black smoke formed at the tip of the barrel with a central core of red-orange flames licking at the salt air.

The pungent odor of burnt gunpowder wafted across the bridge. A seventy-pound projectile screamed across the bow of the freighter and splashed harmlessly into the Atlantic Ocean, ten miles away, before the Soviet ship's master could draw a breath.

Ellingham and Anderson stood on the portside wing of the open bridge, their binoculars focused on *Svetlana*. "Watch the stern. If they cut power that rooster-tail of seawater will disappear," Ellingham said.

Minutes ticked away, then the turbulence at *Svetlana's* stern abated, and her propeller wake flattened.

"All stop," Anderson shouted.

The two vessels coasted on, surrendering momentum, rolling slightly in increasing seas.

"See if they are interested in talking now, Mister Anderson," Ellingham said.

Another agonizing wait ensued.

"Sir, they addressed us as 'American pirates' and asked if we intend to sink their vessel."

"Tell them that all depends on how they respond to our questions, and then start running the quarantine checklist."

It took Anderson five minutes to surmount the language barrier and obtain answers to the standard quarantine questions.

"Captain, here's what I learned. They confirmed the ship is the Soviet freighter *Svetlana*. They sailed from Gdansk, Poland, with a cargo of agricultural machinery, and they're bound for Havana, Cuba."

"Very well, tell them we're going to send a party over to look at their 'agricultural machinery,' and once we've inspected it, the ship may continue on to Havana."

Another five-minute delay took place before the Russians responded. "Sir, they said you can send your pirates over, and they can look all they want to, but *Svetlana* is behind schedule and will keep steaming while they look," Anderson said.

"Negative, tell them to heave to. They aren't going anyplace until we've cleared them," Ellingham said.

Anderson radioed the answer and waited.

"Captain, they said to come aboard and get it over with quickly."

Ellingham nodded, and then called the commodore, Adeline Alpha, to advise what had taken place.

"Bosun, call away the starboard boarding party, and prepare to launch the motor whaleboat. Gunnery, center line the mounts," Anderson ordered.

Fifteen minutes later Ensign Padgett, Chief Stafford, and the starboard boarding party sat in the motor whaleboat with pistols locked and loaded, radio checks completed, and adrenaline surging.

Bosun Jones bellowed, "Away the whaleboat." The boat falls squeaked as they slowly lowered their load to the sea.

The sky turned darker still as the little boat plowed through four-foot swells. The coxswain labored against the running sea to turn the boat alongside the rusty freighter at a point where the Russian sailors had dropped a Jacob's ladder.

With trepidation, Ensign Padgett struggled to haul himself out of the bobbing whaleboat, onto the moving ladder, as the freighter slowly rolled and yawed. He began climbing up to the gangway. Mike followed, and then the others in rank order, the junior man last.

On deck, three swarthy merchant seamen, none of whom spoke English, greeted them with stolid faces. One of the three motioned for Mister Padgett to follow him. Padgett selected Gunner's Mate Second Class Gene Tibbits to accompany him, and they departed. Mike and the remaining four American sailors waited at the gangway with their two Russian minders.

Mike keyed his walkie-talkie, "Siena, Starboard Two. Starboard One is on his way to the bridge. All is well, so far, over."

"Roger, Starboard Two, Siena out."

Mike could see Captain Ellingham and Mister Anderson standing on the open bridge assessing activities on the Svetlana through their binoculars.

A light rain began to fall.

Ensign Padgett and Petty Officer Tibbits entered the freighter's massive bridge.

Two Russian Merchant Marine officers greeted them. The younger man spoke in broken English. "I am first mate. The master wishes you say what right you have to shoot his vessel and force us to stop. We are on high sea. What you do illegal by international law."

"We did not shoot your vessel. We shot across your bow to signal you to stop, since you failed to answer our radio call or signal lamp messages."

The mate translated, and the master, obviously not happy, spoke rapidly in Russian.

"The master, he say you are pirates with no right to stop him."

"The United States announced a quarantine of Cuba beginning at 1400 GMT on 24 October 1962. Your government is well aware of that fact. If you are not carrying any of the prohibited materials, you may pass. If we find any offensive military materiel, however, you will turn back and leave the area," Padgett said.

The first mate translated. As he spoke, the master became increasingly agitated. When he completed the translation, the red-faced master spat out a lengthy response.

"The master, he say this act unlawful on the high sea, and you no can stop him. He gives you five minutes to look at cargo, then he sail to Havana."

Ensign Padgett walked out onto the open bridge, keyed his radio, and related the conversation to Mister Anderson on *Boyington*.

When Anderson repeated the master's response, Ellingham took the walkie-talkie. "Mister Padgett, this is the CO. Tell that communist son-of-a-bitch that if he tries to move, I'll blow his rudder off."

Ellingham went into the pilothouse and updated Checkbook. He received permission to fire at the rudder if the freighter attempted to move.

Five-hundred yards to the east, Padgett re-entered *Svetlana's* bridge and relayed Ellingham's message.

After another translation, the Russian master's face turned a brighter shade of red and dripped perspiration. He began shouting, and sailors on the bridge reacted.

Padgett felt *Svetlana* begin to get under way.

The first mate turned to the American officer with alarm flashing in his eyes. "The master he say we leave. He order me say you and American sailors now hostages until we get Havana. He say, you tell captain he pick you and sailors up in Havana if no more shooting. He say you tell captain that if he stop us, you and sailors in big danger. This is what my master he says. You understand, yes?"

Padgett nodded and turned to go out on the bridge. He froze in his steps when he saw three Russian sailors holding pistols, aimed at him and Tibbits.

CHAPTER 17

Hostages Taken

Three-Hundred and Ninety Miles Southeast of Nassau, Bahamas Islands

1330, Sunday, 28 October 1962

President Kennedy responded to Secretary Khrushchev's with a telegram, saying in part: I am replying at once to your broadcast message of October twenty-eight even though the official text has not yet reached me because of the great importance I attach to moving forward promptly to the settlement of the Cuban crisis.... I consider my letter to you of October twenty-seventh and your reply of today as firm undertakings on the part of both our governments, which should be promptly carried out. I hope that the necessary measures can at once be taken through the United Nations as your message says, so that the United States in turn can remove the quarantine measures now in effect. I have already made arrangements to report all these matters to the Organization of American States, whose members share a deep interest in a genuine peace in the Caribbean area.[12]

Ensign Padgett stood on *Svetlana's* bridge, terrified, as he stared into the barrel of a Russian pistol. One of the merchant sailors stepped forward, removed the officer's pistol from its holster. A second sailor frisked him for hidden weapons. They then checked Tibbits over, but found nothing.

The first mate said, "You go now and send message to captain."

Padgett moved to leave, and one of the gunmen walked over and poked him in the ribs with his pistol.

With a shaking hand, Ensign Padgett lifted his walkie-talkie, called his ship, and told Captain Ellingham what had happened.

Five-hundred yards across the water, Ellingham held the walkie-talkie to his ear. "Okay, stay cool and do what they say," he said. "We're staying right here beside you, and we'll get you out of this mess."

Ellingham had put *Boyington* in motion when he saw the freighter begin to move. After hearing Padgett's report, he immediately called Checkbook and informed the admiral directly of the situation.

Back on the *Svetlana* Mike Stafford held the walkie-talkie to his ear, listening to the conversation between Padgett and Ellingham. As he turned to tell the others what had transpired, two armed Russian sailors walked up, joined the minders, and surrounded the Americans.

One of the Russians disarmed Mike and took his radio. Another sailor then frisked the other Americans.

The merchant seaman in charge motioned for Mike and his men to follow him into the ship.

They climbed up three decks where the Russian waved them into a small berthing compartment, furnished with two bunk beds and a chair. When all five were inside the cabin, the sailor closed and locked the door.

"What's going on, Chief?" Bosun Foss asked.

Mike told the group what he had heard on the radio when Ensign Padgett called Captain Ellingham.

"Well, ain't this a fine kettle of fish. When I get a chance, I'm gonna bust that son of a bitch Russian in the snot locker so fricking hard, he'll be sneezing outta his ass."

"Foss, didn't you understand a word of what I just said? The captain said we should do what the Russians say, and he'll get us out of here," Mike said.

"Ain't no frigging, Russian communist, son a bitch, bastard gonna lock me up in one of their stinking ships and get away with it," Foss said.

"Settle down, and let's see what develops," Mike said.

Machinist mate Bill Bailey, sat on a lower bunk bed, next to Fred Fenster. "We're in serious trouble here, ain't we, Chief?" Bailey asked.

"Well, it's not exactly Fleet Week in New York City, but the only thing we can or should do right now is stay calm and count on Captain Ellingham to get the situation under control," Mike said.

The Russians had also locked Padgett and Tibbits in a berthing cabin, down the passageway toward the bridge.

"What do you figure they're going to do with us, Sir?" Tibbits asked.

"I don't know. Unless we end up in a war, they'll probably turn us loose when we get to Havana. But if a war starts before then, it could be bad news for us."

On the aircraft carrier *Sibuyan Sea*, the rear admiral in command of the ASW Task Group talked to his immediate superior, the vice admiral commanding the Atlantic Fleet who bore full responsibility for enforcing the quarantine of Cuba.

"Get some help up there and block it. The Soviets are not going to flaunt the quarantine, and that freighter is not going to Havana. Let me know as soon as you figure out how to get our men back," COMLANTFLT directed.

"Aye, aye, Sir. We're on the way now," the ASW Task Group commander said.

The *Sibuyan Sea* and her escorts raced north at thirty knots on a course to intercept *Boyington* and the *Svetlana*.

Immediately after ordering the ASW Task Group to block *Svetlana* and to get the boarding party back, the Atlantic Fleet commander flashed a SITREP to his boss, the commander-in-chief of the United States Atlantic command, CINCUSLANTCOM. Within the hour, a White House staffer briefed President Kennedy on the situation.

The door to Mike's cabin opened. A Russian entered, grabbed John Leach by the arm, pulled him out into the passageway, and took him away. Another Russian entered with a cart carrying four bowls of steaming borscht, a mound of black bread, and four big mugs of black coffee. He then withdrew and locked the door.

"What do you think them stinking commies are going to do with Leach, Chief?" Foss asked.

"Must've figured out this cabin only sleeps four and we're going to be here for a while. Hey, this soup's good. Try it."

"I ain't eating no damn Russian slop," Foss said.

Bailey and Fenster each took a bowl and began eating.

Foss picked up a piece of hard black bread, spat the first bite of crust on the deck, and then slowly began chewing the remaining piece.

Down the passageway, Padgett's door opened, and the Russian sailor shoved Leach into the cabin. A cart of soup, bread, and coffee followed.

"What's going on? Where are the others?" Padgett asked.

"About twenty feet aft, in a cabin like this one, Sir."

"Is everyone okay?"

"Yes, Sir, everybody's fine. They were getting this same chow when I left. Guess I'm bunking with you guys now."

A high-pitched whistling sound followed quickly by a thundering roar caused the men to look up involuntarily. They all knew the sound; *Sibuyan Sea's* fighter aircraft were buzzing *Svetlana* at a very low altitude.

"The cavalry has arrived," Leach said. "I bet that got the Russian's attention on the bridge."

On the bridge, the master shook his fist at the jets as they roared away. Turning to starboard, he saw *Boyington* increase speed and steer to port as if to cut off his ship and herd her back north.

The master, knowing the Americans wouldn't risk a collision with a ship more than twice the size of theirs stayed on course.

The destroyer cut back at the last moment, and the Russian Master uttered a curse of contempt.

As the autumn sun began its descent, *Svetlana's* master scanned the sea with his binoculars. When he turned to the southwest, a stunning sight came into focus. Arrayed across the horizon and heading directly toward him were an aircraft carrier and five destroyers. He ran to his radarscope to see what else might be awaiting him.

The jet fighters buzzed *Svetlana* again, rattling the bridge windows.

He changed course, ten degrees to starboard. So did *Boyington*.

The master again looked ahead with his binoculars as the approaching task group adjusted course to block him.

A horrendous boom rattled the freighter's bridge as *Boyington* fired another five inch round across Svetlana's bow from less than half a mile away. The roar of the blast and the shell screeching over his ship caused the master to duck.

"These Yankee pirates are not going to intimidate me," he shouted.

The helmsman shuddered in fear. He whispered to another sailor, "The Americans are not going to let us go to Cuba, and our crazy master thinks he can force his way past them."

"Shut-up, Ivan. You could be shot if he hears you talking like that."

CHAPTER 18

Negotiations

Three-Hundred Miles Southeast of Nassau, Bahamas Islands

1800, Sunday, 28 October 1962

One of the most startling disclosures, revealed years later, was that each of the four Soviet submarines deployed as part of Operation Kama carried a nuclear-tipped torpedo, which greatly raised the dangers of an incident as the U.S. Navy carried out its efforts to induce the beleaguered Soviet submariners to bring their ships to the surface.[2]

(In comparison to the ten-kiloton Soviet torpedoes, the atomic bomb dropped by the U.S. on Hiroshima, Japan, on 6 August 1945 was a fifteen-kiloton weapon. Use of a tactical nuclear device during this period would undoubtedly have triggered the launch of intercontinental ballistic missiles from both sides and the beginning of Armageddon. Author's note)

T he American hostages stayed keenly alert trying to imagine the events transpiring outside their cabins. First, the roar of jet fighters and now the unmistakable sound of *Boyington's* five-inch gun signaled an escalation of the confrontation. The portholes of both their cabins were on the freighter's port side, revealing only a vast expanse of empty ocean. *Boyington* remained on the freighter's starboard side.

On *Svetlana's* bridge, the master fretted. His anger had gotten the best of him, and now he faced quite a predicament alone, thousands of miles from home, with a fleet of angry warships closing in on him.

When the freighter's owners offered him a big bonus to run the American blockade, or quarantine as they called it, he hadn't considered anything like this. It looked like easy money. He hadn't mentioned the bonus or possible danger to the crew.

During World War II, he had dodged German submarines in the North Atlantic and been shot at by Nazi warships in the Baltic and North Seas, but he had been much younger then and felt invincible. Now he wasn't so sure, but he had made a stand and couldn't lose face by capitulating.

Then another thundering explosion shook *Svetlana's* deck like an earthquake.

The helmsman shouted, "Comrade Master, we have lost steerage. She will not answer the helm."

The first mate ran back into the bridge from the open wing. "Comrade Master, the Americans are shooting at us, and they are not warning shots. The last one hit us in the stern."

The master grabbed the ship's intercom. "Bridge to engineering, what has happened—we have lost steerage."

"Comrade Master, I think the Yankees are shelling us. Did you not feel the ship shake?" the chief engineer asked.

"Yes, you idiot, but I want to know why I cannot steer my ship. Find out and report immediately."

The two F4-B Skyhawk fighters returned, again shaking the windscreens on *Svetlana's* bridge as they roared over at an altitude of two-hundred feet.

The freighter continued to flounder, pushed about by the rolling sea, unable to steer.

The bridge telephone rang. "Comrade Master, there are two big holes in our stern above the water line. A shell took out the steering gear. We have no control over the rudder," the engineer reported.

"Well, fix it, you fool." The master hung up before the engineer could explain.

He lifted his binoculars and looked across the bow. The aircraft carrier loomed large directly ahead with its escort of destroyers.

The speaker on the radio tuned to the international distress frequency crackled, and then an English language message echoed around the bridge. "*Svetlana,* this is the US warship *Boyington*, do you copy, over."

"Where is the first mate?" the master shouted.

"He went below to see the damage to the stern, Comrade Master," the helmsman said.

"Well, get him back up here, now." he roared.

"*Svetlana, Svetlana,* this is the U.S. warship *Boyington*, do you copy, over."

The master picked up the microphone. "I cannot understand your gibberish, you fools. Stop firing at my ship."

Mister Rudolph, the OOD reported the strange response to the Captain. "Sir, it sounds like they are answering us, but the response is in Russian, I think."

"Oh great . . . find out if any of the other ships in the task group heard them and has a Russian speaker who can tell us what they said."

As Mister Rudolph chased down an answer to that question, a voice rose above the static from the speaker on international distress channel. "This is *Svetlana*. What do you say to us?"

Ellingham reached for the microphone. "Svetlana, this is Captain Ellingham on the U.S.S. *Boyington*. Are the Americans aboard your ship safe?"

"Yes, they safe. You no shoot us again. Yes?"

"If you release my men, there will be no further shooting."

"My master say, you shoot his ship again, he shoot American sailor in head."

"Tell him, he cannot win this confrontation. If he harms my men, I will blow your ship out of the water, and everyone aboard will die. There is no negotiation. Free my men, and everyone on *Svetlana* lives. Harm them, and everyone dies."

After a pause, "My master say, you not sink his ship when American sailors aboard. But you sink *Svetlana* if American sailors gone."

"I will tow *Svetlana* to San Juan, Puerto Rico, if you will free my men when we get there. You can have your ship repaired and return to the Soviet Union from there, but you are not going to Cuba."

Following another long pause, the mate returned to the radio. "My master say, San Juan same as America, and he no trust Americans."

"Pick another port then, but there aren't many that can do the sort of repairs you need."

Ellingham endured another lengthy wait. "He say, we go Caracas."

"I can't tow you that far. You will have to wait for a tugboat, and it will take a day to get one out here."

"He say that is good."

"I will arrange a non-American tug if you release my men before you leave here."

"Master he say, no. You will sink *Svetlana* as soon as men gone."

"I do not want to sink *Svetlana*. I only want my men back. You can call Cuba and have a Soviet plane fly out to monitor the transfer. We get our men, you get a tow to Caracas, and the Soviet air force can watch the whole thing. Do we have a deal?"

"You wait, the master sends message to superiors now. I call you with answer."

The door to Mike's cabin on *Svetlana* opened, and a sailor shoved in a food cart, again laden with borscht and black bread.

"Is this the only thing these poor bastards ever eat?" Foss asked.

"I know one thing," Bailey said. "I need to use the head before I can face another bowl of that stuff." He rose and began banging on the door, but no one answered. "This could become a serious problem, real soon."

Minutes passed, and Bailey displayed signs of being even more uncomfortable. Finally, there were footsteps in the passageway. He began knocking furiously.

A Russian sailor opened the door. Bailey, with various hand signals communicated his urgent needs. The sailor waved for him to follow, locking the others in the cabin.

When Bailey and the Russian returned, the others indicated similar needs. One at a time, the sailor escorted them to the head.

When all four were back in the cabin together, Foss said, "I told you idiots not to eat that Russian slop. See what it done to ya."

"Foss, if all you're going to eat until we get out of here is that black bread, it's going to lock you up tighter than the skin on a snare drum," Bailey said.

"I'll take my chances," Foss said.

———

On *Boyington*, the first mate's voice rang out. "U.S. ship, *Svetlana* call you."

"Go ahead, *Svetlana*," Ellingham said.

"The master, he say okay, you get tug, he let American sailors leave."

"All right, *Svetlana*. It will take a while to set up the tug. I'll call you when it's arranged."

"Okay, good bye."

Ellingham picked up a different handset. "Checkbook, Siena actual, over."

"Siena, Checkbook actual, go ahead."

Ellingham addressed the admiral. "Checkbook, *Svetlana* agrees to release our men if we provide a non-U.S. flag tugboat to tow him to Caracas for repairs. He also wants a Soviet plane from Cuba to monitor the transfer, and then follow him to port. He understands we will not allow him to enter any Cuban port, period. That's the best I could do. Over."

"Bravo-Zulu, *Siena*. Great job. When's the transfer? Over."

"As soon as I can get a tug up here. Over."

"Let me arrange the tug, Siena. Payment will become an issue, and we may need some State Department help. I'll advise ASAP. Checkbook out."

"Roger, Checkbook. Siena out."

CHAPTER 19

The Storm

Three-Hundred Miles Southeast of Nassau,

Bahamas Islands

Monday, 29 October 1962

October 29, 1962—10:00 A.M.: At the morning ExComm meeting, President Kennedy orders that U.S. Navy ships maintain their quarantine stations. Low-level reconnaissance flights are directed to resume, but no U-2 missions are authorized. (NSC Executive Committee Record of Action, October 29, 1962, 6:30 P.M. Meeting No. 12)[1]

During the day, an earlier stand-down of Cuban military preparedness apparently had ended, and Castro announced publicly he had ordered his forces to fire on all planes violating Cuban airspace. There also were indications that Cuba was tracking U.S. aircraft with radar at all times during their over-flights.[4]

A t 0300 Monday morning, Commander, ASW Task Group, messaged *Boyington* to advise an ocean-going tug had departed the Dominican Republic with an ETA at *Svetlana's* location of 2000 local time.

The duty radioman woke the captain to deliver the priority message. Ellingham pulled on his bathrobe, climbed up to the bridge, and called *Svetlana*. It took the Russian bridge officer ten minutes to get a sleepy first mate to the radio.

"Yes, hello U.S. ship."

"*Svetlana*, this is Captain Ellingham. Tell your master that a tugboat will arrive at around 2000 local time to tow his ship to Caracas. Once you have the towline attached, I expect to see my seven men on deck and ready to leave."

"That is agreement."

"We will stand by here to wait and assist as needed. The weather is predicted to deteriorate further tonight, *Boyington* out."

"*Svetlana* say good bye."

Just before sunrise, the U.S.S. *Browning* arrived to relieve *Boyington* so she could sail five miles south to rendezvous with *Sibuyan Sea* and refuel. The wind had picked up, causing the sea to become quite choppy with four to five foot waves. The refueling detail struggled more than usual with their task.

At 0830, *Boyington* returned to station near *Svetlana*.

On board *Svetlana*, a Russian cook proudly served a breakfast of steaming fish pie and black coffee to the *Boyington* sailors.

"In all my life I ain't never seen nobody eat like these fricking Ruskies. No wonder they're as screwed up as they are, eating slop like this all the time and drinking that damn vodka like it's water," Foss said.

As Foss complained, Mike and the two other men ate. "Never had fish pie for breakfast, but it's not bad," Mike said.

"I've never even heard of it before, but it is good," Fenster said.

"I wonder if we'll ever get to search this ship," Bailey said.

"I wonder if we'll ever get off of this stinking tub," Foss added.

"Come on, Foss. If you'd seen the POW's coming out of the Japanese prison camps after WW II, you'd realize they're treating us damn good," Mike said.

"Yeah, I've seen pictures of those poor guys," Fenster said.

"Fricking Ruskies, I get the chance, I'm gonna kick the living shit outta every one I can get my hands on," Foss said.

At the other end of the passageway, Padgett, Tibbits, and Leach also breakfasted on fish pie, and no one complained.

"Mister Padgett, after this adventure, are you going to make the navy a career?" Leach asked.

"I don't know. We have to get out of here first. I've enjoyed the navy so far, but I have three more years on my commitment before I have to decide."

"What was your major in college, Sir, if I may ask?" Leach asked.

"Geology, at the University of Florida."

"No kidding, I have been thinking about going to Florida when I get out."

"Great school, good professors, beautiful coeds. I think you'd like it. Do you have a major in mind?"

"Yes, Sir, electrical engineering . . . beautiful coeds, you say?

"All over campus . . . You can't go wrong with engineering, especially with the training and experience you're getting here."

"You must mean 'there,' Sir. We ain't getting nothing but sore asses here," Tibbits said. "You know, if I ever get sent to jail, I hope I get hard labor, because I'd go frickin' crazy sitting in a cell like this day after day."

"Oh, yeah, right, but best to stay out of jail, Tibbits. I wonder what's going on. We haven't heard anything for quite a while," Padgett said.

As the early morning hours dragged past, the wind velocity continued to increase. Commander Kaestner stood in the pilothouse looking out one of *Boyington's* portholes and reckoned they were in at least sea state four, with six-foot seas occasionally washing over the forecastle. Unlike the freighter, *Boyington* headed into the wind and rolling waves. The XO's real concern remained *Svetlana,* drifting over a half-mile away. If the storm worsened, and she couldn't get her bow into the wind, she could capsize. The old freighter only had a single screw, so along with the absence of rudder control, she lacked even the limited ability to effect steerage that dual screws might afford.

By noon, *Boyington* faced eight-foot waves, howling winds, and a driving rainsquall.

Svetlana floundered at the mercy of the sea. Without steerage, her broad hull acted like a sail, forcing her to stay athwart the wind and hammering waves. She began to take serious rolls. Cargo deep in the holds strained against the tie-downs.

On the bridge, men struggled to remain at their duty stations. To prevent losing their footing and flying across the compartment, they grasped stanchions with one hand and held on for dear life, while attempting to accomplish their assigned duties with the other.

The master retired to his cabin after learning a tugboat would be towing his ship to Caracas. It would arrive in a few hours, and this nightmare would end, at least until he got home. He curled up in his cabin with a bottle of vodka and soon became unfit for duty or even aware of the storm and its dangers.

The first mate knew from experience that he would not see the captain again, perhaps for several days. He took charge as he always did when the master escaped into a bottle. He believed the master had grossly mishandled the situation with the American blockade and their boarding party, so his initial order was to send a sailor to release the hostages from their cabins. "Bring their leaders to me on the bridge," he instructed.

A Russian sailor opened the door and motioned for Mike to accompany him. They stepped into the passageway, and the Russian rushed forward without relocking the cabin door. Instead, he unlocked the door to a second cabin and entered it.

Popping back out, with Mister Padgett close behind, the sailor hastened toward the bridge.

When Padgett cast a glance over his shoulder, Mike noticed a stunned expression had replaced his normal self-confident countenance. The ensign nodded, and then started after the Russian sailor.

The other Americans cautiously stepped out of their cabins into the passageway.

Mike paused, trying to assess the situation. The men clustered behind him, bracing themselves against the bulkheads.

After a few steps forward, Padgett glanced over his shoulder. "Come on, Chief, I think they want both of us on the bridge."

"You guys stay here till we find out what's going on," Mike said. The men retreated to the security of their former cells.

Mike hurried to catch up with Padgett and the Russian sailor, but the severe rolls the ship was taking slammed him into a bulkhead every few steps.

When they reached the bridge, the Russian sailor returned to his duty station while Mike and Padgett grasped the long counter fronting the after bulkhead.

The first mate stood near the helm, his left arm wrapped around a stanchion. "We have big problem, no steering. Cargo come loose."

The roar of the storm forced the men to converse in shouts.

"We have a boatswain and a machinist in our party. We could help," Padgett said. "The storm is getting worse."

"Yes, bad storm. No steering. Tugboat come help us tonight."

"We can't wait for the tug. Tonight will be too late. We must do something now or we're going to capsize—roll over." Padgett released his grip on the cabinet, made the shape of a boat with his hands, and turned it over emphasizing his point. As he did, the ship rolled, tossing the officer to the deck. Mike, holding onto the cabinet with one hand, helped him regain his footing with the other.

"You will help us save ship?" the mate asked.

Svetlana took a horrific roll to starboard, the forecastle completely awash. Windblown seawater pounded the bridge windows in gusts that sounded like cannons firing. The ship fought to right herself.

"We'll help, but we must start now."

"Okay, Russian and American sailors save ship. You call me Sergi."

"Right, I'm Tom." He pointed to the chief, "Mike."

Sergi nodded to each while repeating their names. "No helm, ship make big roll and cargo shift. We fix now," Sergi said.

"Chief, get Foss and Bailey up here," Padgett said.

Mike found the rest of the boarding party back in their cabins, lying in their bunks or holding fast to the stanchions. "There's no way to get back to *Boyington* in this storm, so we've got to help the Russians save the ship or we're all going down with it. Foss, they need help securing some cargo that's coming loose."

"I ain't doing nothing to help these frickin' bastards. Chief, have you already forgot they had us locked up like prisoners, feeding us slop?"

"That was the master's doing. He's out of the picture now—the first mate is in charge. He ordered the cabins unlocked and set us free. Now head up to the bridge, Foss. You too, Bailey. The rest of you stay here so I can find you when I need you," Mike said.

The three fought their way forward. As he stepped over the coaming into the pilothouse, Mike came face-to-face with the huge Russian sailor who had taken him and his men prisoner. He stood next to Sergi, sharing a stanchion between for support. The man was at least six foot-four with broad shoulders and massive arms.

"This Svetlana bosun, Boris," Sergi said. "American bosun and Boris fix cargo."

"Foss, give the man your hand," Stafford said.

"I ain't gonna shake no frickin'—"

"Belay that, Foss," Padgett said. "Shake the man's hand, or I'll see you busted to seaman deuce if we get out alive."

Foss begrudgingly shook hands. Boris motioned for him to follow, and they staggered off.

"Okay, what about the steering?" Padgett asked.

Sergi waved, "Come, I show."

Padgett, Stafford, and Bailey, queued up behind the first mate and departed the pilothouse through a door in the after bulkhead that opened to an interior passageway.

Weaving behind Sergi, they caromed off the bulkheads, as they made their way aft on the bridge deck, and then began descending a steep ladder. At times, their feet flailed in midair when a sudden roll took the next step from under them. They continued down, each with a death grip on the handrails. Finally, six decks below the bridge, Sergi stopped at a landing and opened the door into the steering-gear room.

Stepping out onto a catwalk, a foul odor assaulted them, while dirty water sloshed about below the grated platform.

Seawater splashed in through a jagged hole in the starboard hull made by *Boyington's* inert five-inch training round. The newly created porthole sat four or five feet above a red line painted on the hull indicating the water line. As the shell passed through the room, it had taken out the heavy steel connecting-shaft that determined the rudder's position, and thus the ability to steer the ship.

The shell had then exited through the hull on the opposite side, leaving the former iron supporting braces hanging from the overhead like grotesquely twisted tentacles. Seawater poured in through the port side breach, opposite the starboard hole.

The catwalk was mounted five-feet above the water line, but the malodorous, oil-contaminated water surged up through the grates with the more severe rolls, soaking their shoes and trousers.

A Russian in oil-spotted coveralls entered. Sergi introduced him as Dmitry, the chief engineer. He said something to Sergi in Russian, and the mate shook his head.

The scowl on the engineer's face suggested he wasn't happy with the situation or those present. Mike ignored the Russian and marveled at the accuracy with which his men had put *Svetlana* out of commission, even as he realized how their skill had put his life and those of the boarding party at risk.

CHAPTER 20

The Jury-Rig

Three-Hundred Miles Southeast of Nassau, Bahamas Islands

1400, Monday 29 October 1962

October 29, 1962—10:48 P.M.: CINCLANT informs the JCS that, in view of reports that Cuban forces have nuclear-capable FROG short-range missiles, he intends to modify invasion plans so that U.S. air and ground forces engaged in operations against Cuba would also be armed with tactical nuclear weapons. CINCLANT assures the JSC that the nuclear weapons would be employed only if Cuban or Soviet forces initiated the use of nuclear weapons. The JCS agrees to allow U.S. invasion forces to be armed with nuclear-capable weapons but specifies that the actual nuclear warheads should not be introduced into Cuba without further JCS authorization. (Summary of Items of Significant Interest Period 300701-310700 October1962; CINCLANT

Historical Account of Cuban Crisis, p. 95; The Air Force Response to the Cuban Crisis 14 October-24 November1962, ca 1/63. P.11; Secretary of Defense's Report for Congress, 12/29/62)[1]

T he five men braced themselves against the catwalk's safety rail and held on tightly. Violent tremors passed through the room when the storm raised the fantail out of the water and the ship slid down the leeward side of the wave, smacking the bottom of a trough. More seawater then flooded in through the portside hole.

Machinist Mate Bill Bailey scratched his head with his free hand as he stared at the tangled mass of steel brackets and supports. Mike and Ensign Padgett silently waited for his appraisal. The first mate and chief engineer stood behind them, shaking their heads. The ship rolled, pitched, and yawed in the fury of the storm, filling the air with agonizing steel groans.

"Anything come to mind, Bailey?" Mike asked. His shouted question was barely audible over the ambient noise level.

Bailey pointed below the catwalk. "That shaft coming straight up there out of that bearing chase is from the rudder. Right above it is the shaft from the servomotor. All this twisted-up stuff in between supported the bearings that kept the connecting shaft in place. That bent up thing dangling over there was the connecting shaft, that once joined the rudder to the servomotor. See the couplings on each of the shafts? Somehow, the shaft was ripped right out without damaging either the rudder or motor shaft."

"Can you jury-rig something?" Padgett asked.

Bailey nodded, "If we can get some materials and tools. First, we need a torch to cut this junk out of the way."

"Do you understand, Sergi?" Padgett asked.

"No, what is 'torch'?"

Bailey mimed gestures indicating he wanted to cut the metal.

Dmitry got the idea and turned to Sergi. "Acetylene cutting tool—I have." he said in Russian.

"Ah, Dmitry explain. Yes, we have tool," Sergi said.

"Okay, you guys see what you can do here. Sergi, let's go check the cargo," Padgett said.

Sergi nodded agreement, and they departed.

Bailey and Mike followed Dmitry to his shop, forward on the same deck, where he showed them his torch. Both tanks rested on a two-wheeled dolly, secured by leather straps, with the hoses wrapped neatly around the top of the tanks and the regulator.

Bailey began opening cabinet doors and bench drawers.

"What are you looking for?" Mike asked.

"Anything that might spark an idea. Somehow we need to link the motor to the rudder shaft."

As they talked, Dmitry began rolling the welding rig toward the door. Its weight kept it on the deck. All was well as long as the engineer could keep his footing and control the direction.

"You keep looking. I'll go help him," Mike said. He picked up a pair of dark welding goggles and some heavy gloves, and then chased after Dmitry.

When Mike re-entered the steering gear room, the engineer was lashing the welding rig to the safety rails. When he finished, Dmitry stood looking up at the broken braces, a puzzled expression on his face.

Mike studied the situation for a few minutes, and then gestured he could reach and hold a damaged strut steady while Dmitry cut it. One hand for the ship and one for the sailor, like in the days of old when sailors worked aloft in the rigging, he thought.

The engineer nodded.

Mike stepped up onto the catwalk's bottom safety rail, hoisted his right leg over the top rail, and then locked his foot behind the left leg. He grabbed a brace hanging down from the overhead and signaled he was ready with a wave of his free hand.

Dmitry ignited his torch and adjuster the regulator so that a thin blue flame roared from the torch. He positioned himself as Mike had done and began to cut the dangling brace.

Forty-five minutes later, they had enough of the debris cut out of the way to begin the next step. The pieces they had removed lay on the catwalk, clattering with each roll of the ship.

Bailey joined them. "We're out of luck, Chief. I can't find anything long enough, or strong enough to clamp onto the motor and rudder shafts, but nice job of cleaning up the place."

Spying a long piece of angle iron, Bailey picked it up and eyed it for straightness. "Hey, this might work," he said.

The ship rolled and water covered the starboard end of the catwalk.

"What are you thinking?" Mike asked.

"What if we took a couple of pieces of this angle iron and welded them together for strength."

"I thought you were looking for a shaft, something cylindrical."

"I was, but since I couldn't find anything strong enough, maybe a double thickness of this angle iron welded to the rudder and motor shafts would hold. It wouldn't be pretty, but it might turn the rudder."

"Welding the angle iron to the two shafts will be tough," Bailey continued. "Look up there; we have to hold the new piece in place while welding it to the motor shaft. Then we have to connect the other end to the rudder shaft, down there, and it must be straight or the motor bearings will burn up."

"Hey, it only has to last until the tug gets here, or the storm passes," Mike said.

"You're right. Let's do it," Bailey said.

Water continued sloshing into the steering gear room through the jagged holes in the hull *Boyington's* five-inch shell had made.

"Let's get a pump going before the water in the pit gets any deeper," Mike said. He communicated the need with words and gestures that Dmitry eventually understood.

The engineer motioned for the Americans to follow.

Ten minutes later, they were back, bruised and battered from carrying an archaic, cast iron water pump and hoses through the ever-shifting passageways. Dmitry primed the pump, and then with a mighty pull on the starter rope, the motor came to life in a cloud of choking blue exhaust smoke. The out-flow hose belched seawater. Mike fed the hose through the shell's exit hole, in the starboard hull, and the level of water began to fall. They lashed pump and hoses in place, then returned to the original problem.

Bailey picked up two pieces of three-inch angle iron and eyed each for straightness. Selecting one, he discarded the other and searched for a replacement. Finding a suitable piece, he leaned over the catwalk and pushed it against the motor shaft.

Dmitry caught on and scratched a cut-mark with a knife blade about five feet from the top. He then grabbed his torch, cut the two selected pieces to length, and welded them together.

"Now the tricky part—how do we get up to the motor and down to the rudder. There's no place to stand," Bailey said. He gestured as he talked, hoping to communicate the problem to the Russian.

Dmitry nodded his head, turned, and walked out.

"Has he got an idea or just quit?" Mike asked.

After a few minutes, Dmitry struggled back through the door with a long, wooden plank, close in dimension to an American two-by-eight.

Removing a fire axe from the bulkhead, Dmitry indicated his intentions. Bailey slid the plank over the edge of the catwalk and stood on it for stabilization. Dmitry leaned over the rail to anchor his body against the ever-rolling ship, took axe in hand, and crudely hacked a point at the end of the plank. He and Bailey lifted the pointed end onto the top safety rail and steered it toward the shell hole in the port side of the hull as Mike pushed it.

The three men rammed it in forcefully into the hole, then Dmitry lashed the end to the top safety rail, producing a platform over the pit to stand on.

Bailey climbed onto the plank and tentatively stood, grasping a bar that hung from the overhead. "This isn't going to work," he said. "We've got to get some kind of rail to lean against so we can have both hands free." He climbed back down to the catwalk.

With a series of gestures, they conveyed the problem to Dmitry. He turned to the door that led forward to this shop. When he returned, he carried a ten-foot section of one and a half inch iron steam pipe.

Having surmounted the language barrier, the three-man team welded a piece of angle iron vertically to the catwalk rails, then extended the steam pipe horizontally, parallel to the plank, across the chasm to the hull. Dmitry welded the pipe to the new vertical bar, four feet above the edge of the plank, and to the hull, above the hole where they had jammed the plank. They had their safety rail.

Starting again, Bailey climbed out on the plank, and holding onto the pipe, easily walked out to the motor and returned. "Perfect," he declared. Mike handed him the angle iron bar they had made, and he returned to a point beneath the steering motor shaft and lashed himself to the new handrail.

Dmitry followed, holding on to the rail with one hand and dragging the torch and hoses behind. Sweat dripped from his dirt stained face as he, too, lashed himself to the pipe.

Bailey, wearing welder's gloves and a mask, hoisted the heavy angle-iron bar into place with a muffled grunt. The plank bowed a few inches under the weight of the two men.

Dmitry lowered his welder's mask and went to work. After five minutes of stretching, straining, and cursing the burns that flying sparks and bits of hot metal inflicted on their bodies, they had welded the angle iron bar to the steering motor shaft. They climbed back to the safety of the catwalk, breathing heavily. Bailey rubbed his aching hands together.

Mike then lowered the end of the plank to the catwalk and lashed it in place. The other end still ran through the shell hole in the hull. He sat on the plank and worked his way out past the bar that hung down from the motor. His heart rate increased with each roll the ship made. Gripping the plank with both hands and balancing himself carefully, he placed his right foot against the bar and waited for Dmitry to get into place.

The Russian slid out on the plank, face down, locked his legs around the board, and hung with his upper body over the edge to reach the junction of the bar and rudder shaft with the torch.

Bailey stood on the plank to keep it from shifting, held the catwalk rail with one hand, and grasped Dmitry's belt with the other to keep the Russian from falling off the board into the watery pit below.

Mike, sweating profusely, pushed hard against the bar with his foot, forcing it firmly against the rudder shaft. He felt the heat from the bar, building and working its way through his shoe.

Dmitry ignored the constant splashes of grimy water against his welding mask and arms as the sparks flew. Finally, he pulled himself up. The torch made a loud pop when he extinguished the flame. They had finished the task, but would it work?

The three men worked themselves back onto the safety of the catwalk, and Dmitry stumbled off to replace the motor's fuses that had blown when the shell hit.

Mike wiped his sweaty palms on his trousers as he fought to maintain equilibrium.

Metal debris continued rattling about on the catwalk.

Dmitry returned after a few minutes, called the bridge, and told them to try the helm.

The three men stood back as the motor above them groaned. Creaking noises screeched over the roar of the sea. They held their breath and watched, expecting the bar to bend, or a weld to break. Neither event occurred as the jury-rigged bar turned the rudder shaft. Mike felt the ship slowly turning into the wind, the increased pitching and yawing, and a gradual diminishing of the dangerous rolls.

Three astonished men all took deep breaths, then exchanged handshakes and back slaps over their success.

The Americans began picking up the scrap metal as Dmitry pulled the torch rig away.

They met in the shop. Mike and Bailey stowed the old iron braces and started to leave, but Dmitry stopped them. He pulled a flask from his hip pocket and offered it to the Americans.

Stafford shook his head, but Bailey accepted and took a drink.

He choked then took him a minute to catch his breath. "Straight vodka," he whispered hoarsely.

Dmitry laughed at him and took a long gulp.

Stafford looked at the two men, smiled, and shook his head.

They all shook hands again. Dmitry waved for Mike and Bailey to follow and led them through the engine room and a series of interior ladders and passageways, back up to the bridge.

They met Padgett, Foss, Sergi, and Boris on the bridge.

Sergi grabbed Bailey, gave him a bear hug, and kissed both cheeks.

Bailey felt his face flush as he stepped back. "Guess he likes our work," he said.

"I think he just likes you," Foss suggested. "We better get outta here before taps, or you could be in serious trouble."

"Can we get our radios back?" Padgett asked.

"Yes, and if weather good, you go to ship when tug come," Sergi said. He then turned to the cabinet on the after bulkhead, retrieved the two walkie-talkies, and returned them to Stafford and Padgett. "You get guns when you leave."

"Fair enough. May I call my ship now?" Padgett asked.

"Yes, you call pirate captain," Sergi said. He smiled for the first time since the incident began.

CHAPTER 21

Freedom

Three-Hundred Miles Southeast of Nassau, Bahamas Islands

1730, Monday 29 October 1962

October 29, 1962—3:30 P.M.: U Thant, Secretary-General of the United Nations, briefs Adlai Stevenson, John McCloy, and Charles Yost on his meeting with Vasily Kuznetsov earlier in the day. U Thant tries to convince the Americans that the quarantine should now be suspended, but McCloy and Stevenson disagree, linking the end of the quarantine to the actual removal of offensive weapons from Cuba. They do agree, however, that the quarantine could be suspended for the duration of U Thant's visit to Cuba, scheduled to begin on October 30. (Summary of Meeting between U.S. Negotiators and U Thant on U Thant's Meeting with Kuznetsov)[1]

At 1800 local, Admiral Dennison, CINCLANT, announced that the low-level photoreconnaissance missions flown during the day all were successfully completed. However, one plane was fired on by a 37mm weapon as the pilot was on his way out near San Julian. Admiral Dennison also reported that the Soviet freighter Belovodsk had reached the quarantine line and was lying to.[4]

The Atlantic storm slowly diminished over the course of the afternoon. Gradually, the sun broke through the cloud cover, lifting Captain Ellingham's mood.

The walkie-talkie lying next to his bridge chair crackled, and Padgett's voice came through, loud and clear. "Boyington, Starboard One, do you copy, over."

The captain held the radio to his ear. "Ellingham here—go."

"Sir, they are going to set us free as soon as the tug gets here. Do you have an ETA yet?"

"It's on schedule to arrive around 2000, about two and a half hours from now unless it hits bad weather. Is everyone okay?"

"Yes, Sir. We're all ready for some good navy chow, but otherwise everyone's okay. The chief and Bailey jury-rigged the rudder so they can steer, at least for now."

"I thought they had you locked up."

"They did for a while, but the master got drunk, and the first mate released us. We were afraid the ship would capsize when she started taking some heavy rolls, so we offered to help with repairs."

"Oh. Well, good job. The old girl certainly took a few serious rolls at the peak of the storm. I wondered how they managed to turn her into the wind. I'll have the whaleboat ready to bring you home when the tug arrives, or sooner if you can sweet-talk your way into an early release."

"Yes, Sir, I'll try."

"We'll have steak dinners waiting for you."

"Sounds fantastic, Sir, Starboard One out."

The ocean-going tugboat *Santa María Soledad*, flying the flag of the Dominican Republic, arrived at 2130, delayed by the weather. The waves had diminished to three or four-feet. After several tries, working by moonlight and several of *Svetlana's* inadequate spotlights, a towline finally connected the freighter to the tug.

A smiling Ensign Padgett and the starboard boarding party stood at *Svetlana's* gangway as *Boyington's* motor whaleboat hit the water and started toward *Svetlana*.

Sergi and Dmitry shook hands with each of the Americans.

Boris, the bosun, extended his hand to Foss.

Mike saw Foss make a fist and his jaw lock. "Don't even think about it, Foss, if you want to leave this ship alive," Mike whispered.

Foss looked at Mike, then back at Boris. He relaxed his fist and shook hands.

Sergi handed the pistol belts back to Stafford and Padgett. "I hope you not feeling bad with us," he said. "Our master has bad temper sometimes when not drunk. It always bad when he drunk, but then he sleeps."

"Have a safe voyage to Caracas, but stay away from Cuba," Padgett said.

"No Cuba for us," Sergi said.

The whaleboat maneuvered up to the Jacob's ladder, and the Americans began descending in reverse rank order, junior man first.

The whaleboat plied its way across to the *Boyington*, its occupants hanging on with both hands as the bow come out of the water at the crest of each wave, then smashed into the trough.

"Were you going to punch that Russian, Foss?" Stafford asked.

"Damn straight, then I seen you didn't have your pistol back yet."

"That's not the best reason for pulling back, but I'm glad you did. If you had punched him and survived, and if we escaped afterwards, you'd have spent the rest of your life in the brig," Stafford said.

"Yeah, but think about how good it would've felt when that Russian bastard's nose crunched under my fist."

"Foss, you're hopeless," Mike said.

Most of *Boyington's* off-watch crew lined the port rails to welcome the boarding party back. The boat falls screeched as the gipsy turned, winching the whaleboat up from the sea. The captain and XO led the cheering as the party climbed out of the boat onto the 0-1 level. The ship's two senior officers shook each man's hand as they stepped aboard.

"First, on behalf of the entire crew, I want to welcome you men back and thank you for the job you did. We thank the good Lord that no one got hurt, and you're back on board unharmed. Now, go below, get some hot chow, and try to relax. Later, I'll need a full report covering how the Russians treated you, what you saw, and so forth. Mister Padgett, please coordinate that with the XO."

"Aye, aye, Sir," Padgett said.

"Okay, men, get below," Ellingham said.

Commander Kaestner briefed the captain as the mid watch assumed the duty. "Bosun Foss got to see everything in *Svetlana's* cargo holds when he volunteered to help out during the storm. It's all here in the report. He saw thirty two-and-a-half ton army trucks and two dozen armored personnel carriers. They also had crates lashed down on the weather decks, but the storm prevented him from opening them. However, that doesn't matter. The vehicles alone were reason enough to turn them back."

Ellingham leaned back in his desk chair, staring at the overhead. "What do you suppose went through that captain's mind letting our people board?"

"From what Mister Padgett said, he obviously isn't a real stable fellow. He no doubt thought he could bluff his way through. When that didn't work, he resorted to taking the team hostage. I'm guessing he never dreamed we would put a five inch shell in his steering gear."

"I'd bet he's been soaking his brain in vodka for years. The action he took could have put his ship and crew on the bottom and triggered World War III. What an idiot."

"Yes, Sir. Well, I'm glad that adventure is over."

"So am I. It's going to feel good, getting back to our ASW station. Is the final report ready to be sent?"

"Yes, Sir. All it needs is your signature."

"Okay, I'll drop it off at radio central. Let's hope for a little less excitement tomorrow."

CHAPTER 22

The Morning After

Two-Hundred Miles North of Caicos Passage

0800, Tuesday, 30 October 1962

On 30 October 1962, after thirty-five hours of tracking, the U.S.S. Charles P. Cecil (DDR 835), supported by ASW aircraft, forced Soviet submarine B-36 to the surface. Cecil transmitted a Russian text message:"Do you need help?" to which B-36 responded: "We do not need any help. Asking you not to interfere with my actions." Cecil followed the submarine on the surface until Friday, 02 November. (Deck Log Book of the U.S.S. Cecil; for Wednesday, 31 October 1962-Friday, 02 November 1962). Subsequently, CINCLANTFLT sent a message of congratulations to the Cecil: "Your persistent and expert holding of contact until exhaustion . . . has been followed with pride and admiration. Well done." [2]

The U.S.S. Blandy (DD 943) spotted a Soviet submarine on the surface at 0015 and pursued it after it submerged at 0128. Blandy continued tracking it, finally forcing it to surface seventeen hours later. It proved to be B-130.[2]

(B-130 was the third of the four Soviet reconnaissance submarines dispatched under Operation Kama, forced to surface. Author's note).

———————

The members of the starboard boarding party received permission from the captain to ignore reveille and sleep as long as they wished. Mike wandered into the chiefs' mess a little past eight, poured himself a cup of coffee, sat down at the nearest table, and stared mindlessly at the blank, gray bulkhead.

The chiefs' mess cook entered. "Can I get you something for breakfast, Chief Stafford?"

"No thanks, Charlie. A cup of your fabulous coffee is enough for now."

"Okay. We have blueberry pancakes and bacon this morning. Let me know if you change your mind."

"That's tempting. Let me think about it."

"Hey, Chief. What were things like over on that Russian ship?"

"Well, for one thing, they have a lot more room than we do on this ship. They get plenty of food, but their diet is quite different. Yesterday morning, we had fish pie for breakfast."

"Fish pie for breakfast, you gotta be kidding me."

"I'm not, but since they didn't offer anything else, most of us ate it and enjoyed it.

"Well, I'm glad all you guys got back okay. The whole crew got worried when the captain told us you were hostages."

"Thanks, Charlie. It's great to be back. I'm finished thinking now. Bring on some of those pancakes."

"You got it, Chief."

Charlie departed, and Chief Jones walked in, his coffee cup leading the way.

"Well, if it ain't sleeping beauty."

"And a good morning to you too, Bosun Jones."

"Did you get some breakfast?"

"Not yet. The Russians fed us so well I'm starting on a diet today."

"They made 'em eat fish for breakfast," Charlie said. He slid a tray heaped with pancakes and bacon, all covered in blueberry sauce onto the table in front of Mike.

"I guess that diet is gonna start later," Jones said. He turned toward the mess cook. "Charlie, fish for breakfast ain't bad. Most POW's don't get nothing for breakfast, or sometimes nothing for days."

"We weren't exactly POWs," Mike said. "We were more hostages of a drunken lunatic. The first mate, who spoke a little English, took care of us in spite of the crazy master. I'm glad it's over, and no one got hurt."

"That rusty ol' tub starting taking some serious rolls, looked like an easy twenty-five or thirty degrees from here," Jones said.

"Yeah, about then the master passed out drunk, and the first mate set us free. Bailey and I helped their engineer jury-rig the rudder so they had steering. Otherwise, it may well have capsized."

"Ol' Zarna did one hell of a job, shooting up their rudder, didn't he?"

"Yeah, he sure did. It was a perfect shot. I'm just glad he used a training round and not a high explosive shell, or I wouldn't be sitting here talking to you. That shot went straight through the steering gear room and took out the bearings and supports between the rudder and the steering motor."

Chief Ford entered as the two men talked. "How you feeling this morning, Mike?"

"Great, Ken, how you doing?"

"Scuttlebutt has it that you and Bailey saved that Russian scow from capsizing. Any truth to that rumor?"

"Maybe a little. They couldn't steer, and the Russians weren't doing anything to help themselves. We offered to help, and they gave us a free hand. Their engineer got busy, and between the three of us, we jury-rigged the rudder so at least they could get the ship turned into the wind. Things settled down a little after that."

Charlie, the mess cook, came up to the table still shaking his head. "The Russians made 'em eat fish for breakfast. I can't believe it."

"That's better than no breakfast," Ford said.

"Did Foss behave himself?" Jones asked.

"He did okay, but came close to punching the Russian bosun in the nose before we got outta there."

"What got that started?"

"I'm not sure, but with Foss it doesn't take much. He may have gotten in the first punch, but the Russian stood a few inches taller, had twenty or thirty pounds on him, and looked like he could handle himself. Foss may have gotten his ass kicked."

"Might have done him some good. He doesn't lose many fights."

"If he had taken a swing, we might still be there. They had the guns and outnumbered us at least six-to-one."

"Thank goodness everyone got back okay," Ford said.

"Since this is the morning for sea stories, Mike, tell ol' Ken about your visit to Cuba last year. But, before you start, do you guys know how to tell the difference between a fairy tale and a sea story?" Jones asked.

"No, Paul, how can you tell the difference between a fairy tale and a sea story?" Ford asked.

"Well, fairy tales always start out 'Once upon a time . . .' and sea stories always start out 'This is no shit . . .' " Jones slapped his knee and nearly fell off his chair laughing. Mike and Ken laughed too, but more at Jones than his joke.

Mike began, "This is no shit. Back during the Bay of Pigs invasion—"

Jones went into another fit of laughter.

"Ignore him, and tell your story, Mike," Ford said.

"Right. Well, the *Jaffey* had orders to provide fire support for the exiles' landing. Captain Schmidt sent me ashore with one of my strikers and a Cuban exile officer to direct *Jaffey's* gunfire, but the next morning when daylight came, the ship had left. Eventually, we made radio contact, and they said they had orders to leave the AOR, the exile brigade's area of responsibility.

"None of us could believe it. They abandoned us, knowing the exiles were already losing the fight. I couldn't understand the situation at the time. Later I learned that neither the navy nor Captain Schmidt had a choice. They were following orders—someone in the White House lost his nerve, and that scared us the most."

"Damn, man! What did you do?" Ford asked.

"On the first day, it became clear things weren't going well for the exiles. When I learned we were on our own and the navy wasn't coming back, I knew the exiles didn't have a chance. We hung in there with them for nearly three days, but there wasn't any hope. Most of their supplies never made it ashore. One entire battalion didn't even land, and they were eventually outnumbered a hundred to one by the Cuban Army and militia troops. It was a disaster."

Mike paused for a sip of coffee and lit a cigarette.

"My striker, a tough and resourceful kid from the south side of Chicago, 'found' a jeep as the exile front lines began to collapse. We took off without a clue of where we were going or how we could escape detection by Castro's forces that were swarming all over the place."

Jones lit another Camel from the butt of the one he had been smoking. "So, go on, what did you do?"

"We managed to escape the battlefield. After a week or so of running, we met some nice anti-Castro folks that really stuck their necks out for us. They helped us get on a train and we then rode most of the way to Gitmo."

"Mike, this story would make one hell of a great book. You should write one. It would make you rich. So how did you get on the base?" Jones asked.

"I've been shooting my mouth off too much already. When I did make it onto the base, some fellows from the Office of Naval Intelligence, the ONI, met me and put me through the proverbial wringer. Because of the security classification, I had to sign papers agreeing never to disclose parts of the story. I've told you as much as I can."

"What bullshit. I've never met a spook I liked," Jones said.

"Generally, I agree, however I met this beautiful blonde agent and married her."

"You kidding me? That gorgeous woman you showed me a picture of—she was a spook?" Jones said.

"Afraid so, but she came to her senses and resigned her commission."

"Well, if I ever meet a spook that looks like her, I may change my mind about 'em too. Listen, buddy, I gotta go check on things up forward. Seriously though, Mike, if you do write a book and make a million, remember I came up with the idea, so think about slipping me a few bucks, okay."

"Sure, Paul, if I make a million dollars, I'll give you half. How would that be?"

"Wow! That would be terrific, ol' Pal."

Jones left the compartment smiling from ear-to-ear.

Mike stood and looked at the grinning Ken Ford.

"You made yourself a friend for life," Ford said.

"Probably did."

Mike left the compartment and started to walk around the ship, checking on his men and their work. He found everything in good order, so he wandered up to the bridge. Captain Ellingham sat in his command chair looking out over the now much calmer Atlantic. When he saw Mike, he waved him over.

"How you feeling, Chief?"

"Great, Sir. Thanks for giving the boarding party holiday routine. We all appreciate that and are especially grateful for the meal you set out for us last night."

"Think nothing of it. You guys are the heroes of the cruise. Mister Padgett is writing you and Bailey up for medals."

"What?"

"You heard me. He and I both believe the quick thinking and skill you two exhibited saved the *Svetlana* from sinking, and taking the boarding party and the Russians with her."

"Well, thank you, Sir, but we were more concerned about saving our own skin at the time."

"That may be, but in the process you saved a ship, its Russian crew, and five other American sailors."

"All I can say is thank you, Sir. I think anyone would have done the same thing, but thank you."

"Chief, most men wouldn't have thought of what to do, and that's the difference. You do realize, the navy is going to have a hard time letting you go back into retirement after this thing is over, don't you?"

"I don't even want to think about that, Sir."

"I understand. But I want you to know I appreciate everything you've done on this ship, and I understand why Captain Schmidt praised you so highly. Keep up the great job you're doing. Even if you go back into retirement, you will have set a great example for the younger men, and maybe a couple of older ones, too."

"Thank you, Sir."

Mike left the bridge, humbled.

CHAPTER 23

More Trouble on the Mess Deck

Two-Hundred and Fifty Miles Northwest of Turks Island Passage

Wednesday, October 31 1962

(UN Secretary General) U Thant meets with Fidel Castro, Dorticós, and Roa for the second time during his stay in Cuba. Castro agrees to send the body of Rudolf Anderson, the pilot of the downed U-2, back to the United States. Castro claims that Anderson's plane "was brought down by Cuban antiaircraft guns, manned only by Cubans, inside Cuban territory." Complaining about continued U.S. aerial reconnaissance, he warns that "the Cuban people can no longer tolerate such daily provocations," and that Cuba will "destroy any plane any time which intruded into Cuban airspace." U Thant is unable to obtain Castro's approval for any form of inspection of the Soviet missile withdrawal. (Summary of U Thant's Meeting with President

Dorticos, Premier Castro and Foreign Minister Roa of Cuba, 10:00 A.M. October 31, 1962)[1]

A t noon the loudspeakers blared: "Now dinner for the crew." The routine morning ended, and a queue of hungry sailors had already formed on the starboard weather deck. The physically demanding task of the morning's refueling had stimulated the appetite of many.

Thirty minutes later, with a third of the crew not yet fed, the scullery broke down again. Tempers flared.

The master-at-arms and his assistant took immediate control of the situation, to prevent a repeat of the last such occasion. The chief commissary man responded with an improvised, tray-less meal as the electricians perspired freely in the hot, humid scullery compartment, trouble shooting the non-functioning machine.

Bosun Paul Jones stood at the starboard door, controlling the number of sailors entering the mess deck when Mike walked up to him. "Same problem?"

"Same problem, but a different trouble this time," Jones said. "Waller, the leading electrician, sent his skinny striker under the machine again to see if another wire on the control panel broke off, but everything the kid could see there was okay. They're starting over and going through the infernal contraption by the numbers. They ain't found nothing yet."

"Well, at least we have good order and discipline this time."

"Yeah, thank God for small favors. If that little shit Unger is responsible for this breakdown, I'll be amazed. I thought we had a full proof plan to protect the machine."

As Paul and Mike talked, and the chow line slowly diminished, Waller approached the pair. "Found the trouble, and it's definitely sabotage. Someone tied a string to an internal electrical plug on the drive motor so he could pull it out while working, put the scullery out of business, and appear innocent. But there was a screw up. He intended for the string to come clear out of the machine, but it broke off and got stuck inside; he couldn't get it out unnoticed. I'll bet a month's pay Unger did it. He was the only person in there when the machine quit working."

"Don't lose the string, Moses," Jones said.

"I can go you one better. Because of the way the string is connected to the plug, and the force involved, it broke the plug. We're replacing it now, and I have the broken plug with the string attached. I think it will be exhibit number one at someone's court martial."

"Good job. Let's go brief the XO, then I'll come back to the MAA shack, bag it, and lock it up," Jones said.

"Way to go, Moses," Mike said. "I doubt we'll have any more scullery trouble on this cruise."

"Chief, I don't expect to have another equipment failure like this for the rest of my career," Waller said.

Jones and Waller entered the pilothouse, where the XO was absorbed in the details of a navigation chart.

"Sir, did you hear we had another breakdown in the scullery?" Jones asked.

"Yes, I did, Chief. Is it fixed yet?"

"The electricians will have it running in a few minutes, Sir, but we got a bigger problem. Tell him, Waller."

The electrician pulled the broken plug and string from his pocket and dangled it in the air.

"What's that?" Kaestner asked.

"It's the cause of the breakdown, Sir." Waller said.

"And it's evidence for a court martial. Evidence of sabotage," Jones added.

"That's a very serious charge, Chief. Do you have a suspect?"

"Sir, Seaman Apprentice Unger was the only person in the scullery when the breakdown occurred." Jones said. "He had a motive. Chief Stafford put him in the scullery as a disciplinary measure. He's been a problem since he came aboard, and Mister Quinn asked the chief to try to straighten him out. I'd say Unger tried lashing back at the entire crew."

"There's no doubt about it being sabotage, Sir," Waller said. "Someone clearly looped the string around the plug and ran the string outside the cabinet, so that a quick jerk would disable the scullery machine. Whoever did it timed the act to cause the most trouble and allow him to appear innocent, just like two days ago. He wanted to cause a breakdown at chow time to piss off the crew."

"All right. . . . Chief, you interview Unger and see what he has to say, and I'll brief the captain. Let me know as soon as you've talked to him," Kaestner said.

When Jones returned to the mess deck, the scullery was up and running. Unger was ensconced in the scullery room, scrubbing away the last of the dinner trays.

The bosun went to the scullery window. "Come see me in the MAA shack when you're done, Unger."

"What's up, Chief?"

"Come see me when you're done."

"Okay, Chief."

Twenty minutes later Unger appeared at the open door of the MAA shack, wiping his hands on his wet, stained apron. Jones sat at his desk in the tiny office, reading a report. Unger knocked on the open door.

"Come in, Unger. Shut the door, and have a seat."

The sailor maneuvered the only other chair around so he could close the door of the tiny office. The two men sat facing one another, not more than two feet apart.

"What's this about, Chief?"

"This," Jones said. He picked up the broken plug with the string still attached, and swung it back and forth before Unger's eyes as if trying to hypnotize him.

Unger's face paled. "What's that?"

"It's the reason the scullery machine quit working today."

"Well, I'm glad it's fixed. It would've been bad for the ship if they couldn't fix it, wouldn't it?"

"Yes, it would have. But, it's going to be a lot worse for the person who caused the trouble."

"Well, I don't know nothing about that."

"Unger, you were the only person in that room today before the machine broke down."

"You don't know that. Someone else could have been in there earlier."

"Who? The door stayed locked all night, until I opened it up for you this morning. Then you were the only person in there until the machine broke down."

"Chief, I don't know nothing about it. Someone else made it break so I would get in trouble."

"Who do you think did it?"

"Probably Zarna?"

"Zarna? Gunner's Mate First Class Nick Zarna. Zarna, my assistant MAA—you're saying he got in the scullery today and broke the machine?"

218

"It could have been him. He could have come in here, got the key, and unlocked the scullery last night."

"Why would he want to get in the scullery at night?"

"To break the machine."

"And why would First Class Petty Officer Zarna want to break the scullery machine?"

"So he could get me in trouble."

"Tell me more, why would Zarna want to get you in trouble?"

"He doesn't like me and has been giving me a hard time since I came aboard."

"Unger, you have been written up six times, by four different petty officers since you came aboard three months ago. Does anyone like you?"

"Zarna made them do it. He hates me, and so does that new chief."

"You mean Chief Gunner's Mate Stafford?

"Yeah."

"Chief Stafford has only been aboard a little over a week, and you're saying he already hates you?"

"Yeah, him and Zarna and Mister Quinn too."

"You got a real fan club there, son. Sounds like you've pissed off everyone in your chain of command."

"Well, I didn't do nothing wrong, and I shouldn't be working in the scullery anyway. Chief Stafford just put me in there because he wanted to get his friend Harris back in the division. It's not even my turn to be on mess cooking."

"It sounds like the whole world is against you, Unger."

"Well, maybe just everyone in second division. And I didn't pull no plug out. One of them others did it."

"I haven't said a word about pulling a plug out."

"What?"

"How do you happen to know anything about a plug being removed? I didn't say what happened to the machine. I didn't say why it stopped working."

"It's got a string on it, like someone fixed it so they could pull it out with the machine still running."

"Oh . . . and when did you put the string on it, Unger?"

"I didn't do it."

"You pulled the string, Unger. You were the only person in the scullery when it happened, and fifty witnesses saw you in there alone."

"No. They all hate me. They did it, one of them. I think Zarna did it."

Speaking fast and loud, Jones leaned into the sailor's face. "Unger, you sabotaged the machine on Friday, and you did it again today. I know it, and you know it. You're in serious trouble, son. You're looking at a dishonorable discharge after you serve hard time in the brig. With a dishonorable discharge, you'll never be able to get a decent job. You've played one too many tricks, Unger. You've screwed yourself big time."

The blood drained from the young man's face, and he began to shake.

"No, it wasn't me. I didn't it."

Jones became even louder. "You did it, Unger, and it's time to be a man and face up to it. If you come clean and write up a confession, the judge may go easy on you at your court martial."

"Court martial? It's not my fault. They made me do it."

"So you're admitting you sabotaged the scullery machine."

"Chief, I can't go to the brig. It was a joke. Zarna bet me I couldn't do it." A tear rolled down Unger's pale cheek.

"It's time to knock off the bullshit and write up your story, Unger. It has to be the truth. If you lie and try to throw the blame on someone else, it will come back and bite you in the ass. So tell the truth." Jones's voice dropped to a near whisper. "It's the only way to go now, son."

Jones slid a report form and pen across the tiny desk. "Go out and sit down at one of the mess deck tables, and write down what you did to that machine—both times. Give it back to me when you're done. Tell the truth, Unger, only the truth. No bullshit. Every lie you tell will add more years to your brig time."

Both men left the office. Unger sat down at the first table he came to and stared at the blank form, his hands shaking. Tears fell on the paper, causing the paper to pucker. Jones exited the mess deck through the starboard door, lit a cigarette, and headed aft.

Thirty minutes later, Jones stood leaning on the stern lifelines, smoking while fixating on the sparkling sunlight reflecting off the crests of *Boyington's* wake. He didn't hear Unger approach.

"Here it is, Chief. I don't spell too good, but see if you can read it."

Jones turned and took the paper. "Don't worry about spelling. You're doing the right thing."

When he finished reading the confession, he looked the young man in the eye. "Seaman Apprentice David T. Unger, I place you under arrest for the willful damage and destruction of United States Navy property. Until a higher authority amends my order, you will report to the master-at-arms office whenever the bosun passes the word for restricted men and prisoners at large—PALs—to muster. Understood?"

"Yes, Chief. Understood."

"Okay, I'll set up an appointment with the XO. Until then, go about your normal duties, but stay out of trouble and don't forget to muster whenever PALs are called."

"Aye, aye, Chief."

Jones walked away, paper in hand. Unger sat down on an air vent and stared off at the horizon, his body shaking.

The executive officer looked up from his desk when Jones knocked on the open cabin door.

"I got a written confession from Unger, Sir."

"Okay, let's look it over," Kaestner said.

222

The XO leaned his elbows on the desk and supported his head, as he read the report and confession. Jones stood behind him, rereading the documents over the officer's shoulder.

Kaestner turned around in his chair. "I looked this up in the UCMJ after we talked earlier. We'll charge him with two violations of Article 109. I want to talk to the captain before I see Unger. I'll get back to you later. Good job, Chief."

"Thank you, Sir."

Later that afternoon, Jones and Unger met with the XO in his cabin. The seaman stood at attention, staring over the officer's head.

"Seaman Apprentice Unger, I have reviewed the charges against you and your written statement in regard to those charges," Kaestner said. "I am referring your case to the captain for disposition under the applicable articles of the Uniform Code of Military Justice. Until then, you will remain under arrest and a prisoner-at-large. The MAA will notify you of the date and time for your appearance before the commanding officer. The uniform will be dress white alpha. Do you understand?"

"Aye, aye, Sir."

"Very well, you're dismissed."

Unger made an about-face and departed.

"I can't imagine what went through that kid's mind that caused him to pull a stupid trick like this," Kaestner said.

"I don't know either, Sir. It's like he sees himself as an innocent victim. I think his problem is so deep that our normal disciplinary methods won't touch it. We can't have a guy like that in the crew, Sir, especially when the shells may start flying any day now."

"Okay, Chief. Keep a close eye on him until we can arrange to transfer him."

"Yes, Sir," Jones said.

That evening, Stafford, Ford, and Jones sat together in the chiefs' mess eating supper. Jones related Unger's confession and the details of case.

"I feel bad for the kid," Mike said. "He got himself into a hole, but just kept digging."

"We get all kinds, Mike. Some make it, and others don't. We give them our best shot, but if they don't have the right makings inside, they fail. Don't beat yourself up," Ford said.

"You're right, Ken. Look at Gibbs, the other screw-up from second division. We got his attention, and he's doing great in the deck gang," Jones said.

"That's good to hear," Mike said. "Have you had a chance to check him out in some confined space like we talked about? Have you seen any signs of claustrophobia?"

"Oh, yes, it's real. Foss tried to get him to paint the fan room in the first division compartment, and you know how tight they are. Gibbs tried, but panicked so severely once he got inside, it scared Foss, and that guy's fearless. He thought the kid had gone nuts, but once he got him back out into the big open compartment, he calmed down," Jones said.

"We need to get him to the medics and see if there's anything they can do for him. Life on a destroyer isn't in his future if that problem can't be resolved. I'll talk to the corpsman tomorrow and see what he recommends," Mike said.

CHAPTER 24

Rescue at Sea

One-Hundred and Twenty Miles Northeast of Turks Island Passage

0400, Thursday, 01 November 1962

November 1, 1962—1:00 A.M.: Adlai Stevenson reports to Washington that he has received preliminary reports from U Thant and Indar Jit Rikhye on their visit to Cuba. The U.N. officials report that relations between Cuba and the Soviet Union are, in Rikhye's words, "unbelievably bad." Rikhye states that although they have not had "definitive" discussions about the IL-28 bombers, "Russians repeated...that they were determined to take out all equipment which the president has regarded as offensive and this would include the IL-28's...." (Document 61, State Department Cable on Secretary General U Thant's Meetings with Castro, 11/1/62; Report by Rikhye on Impressions from United Nations visit to Cuba, 11/1/62)[1]

The U.S.S. Keppler (DD 765) assumed escort duties of B-130 (relieving Blandy). The Keppler and the submarine cruised at 7 knots on course 060. The sub's destination appeared to be the Soviet auxiliary ship, Terek. Keppler contacted the sub, but it declined assistance.[2]

The ASW Task Group, spread out over forty-two square miles of unseasonably calm and moonlit ocean, continued its primary mission. The carrier *Sibuyan Sea* was conducting night flight operations, launching and recovering S2F Tracker aircraft. At 0400, the morning watch assumed the duty throughout the task group.

On *Boyington's* bridge, Lieutenant Engle, the OOD, sat in the captain's elevated chair lost in his thoughts. The JOOD, Lieutenant Junior Grade Hal White, entered the pilothouse carrying a fresh cup of coffee as the 1JV talker called out a change of orders for the ship. "Sir, we're ordered to relieve *Browning* on plane guard."

Engle slid off the captain's comfortable bridge chair, entered the pilothouse, and walked over to the radar repeater. He stared down at the yellow images that represented ships of the formation. "Come about hard to starboard, steer two-six-zero, turns for two-five knots."

The ship began a sharp right turn as it increased speed and departed the screening formation.

White, caught off balance by the turn, tipped his mug spilling coffee on his fingers. He uttered an oath, then wiped his hand with a handkerchief.

"Did you get burned, Sir?" the quartermaster asked.

"Nothing serious. Hey, we're heading for plane guard duty. I always enjoy watching the landings close up, especially at night."

"Yes, Sir, so do I. It beats the usual monotony."

Lieutenant Engle made two more direction and speed changes before the destroyer's course aligned with the carrier's stern. He carefully reduced the ship's speed so that it would exactly match that of the huge ship when they reached the plane guard station, five-hundred yards off the carrier's port quarter.

He called the captain. "Sir, this is the OOD. DESRON Forty-Two ordered us to replace *Browning* on plane guard. The carrier's steering zero-eight-zero, and we're about five minutes to station. They're launching now and will begin recovery ops at daybreak, about ninety minutes from now."

"Very well, carry on. I'll be up after breakfast."

Engle moved back to the radar repeater to check the positions of the other destroyers and his own, in relation to the carrier. Due to their proximity to the carrier and the need to react immediately in an emergency, plane guard duty required a constant, high degree of concentration by all bridge personnel, especially him. His adrenaline level rose.

The lieutenant, now back in the captain's chair, watched the rescue helicopter flying alongside the carrier, maintaining a speed to match the ship's, about one-hundred feet above the water. *Sibuyan Sea's* flight deck sat sixty feet above the water, so the rescue pilot chose the perfect spot to observe the steam catapults shooting planes off into the black sky.

At dawn, the carrier began recovery operations, landing the S2F Trackers that had been in the air patrolling for submarines for the past six hours. The planes were landing at five-minute intervals.

Captain Ellingham entered the pilothouse at 0610.

Lieutenant Engle slid out of the captain's chair and greeted the skipper with a smile. "Good morning, Sir."

"Everything under control, Mister Engle?"

"Yes, Sir. So far, so good. They have four more birds to land."

"Okay, I'm going to check on things in CIC," Ellingham said.

Just as he stepped over the coaming into the passageway, one of the aircraft roared over the *Boyington* so low that several of the bridge crew ducked, their reflexes triggered by the unusually loud roar of plane's engines.

The plane's approach was dangerously low. The pilot fought for altitude, but over-corrected, ending up inches too high to catch the carrier's arresting cables with his tail hook. Directly ahead, on the bow of the flight deck sat a dozen parked aircraft. He pulled back on the yoke attempting to gain enough altitude to fly over them, but in his panic, he pulled up too sharply. The aircraft nosed up and wing-stalled. He shoved the yoke forward and hard to port to break the stall and avoid crashing on the flight deck. The starboard wing rose high in the air as the nose dropped.

He fought furiously, but couldn't right the aircraft. Several sailors standing on the port side of the flight deck dived for cover. The plane blew past them, heading toward the ocean. The pilot continued to fight, pulling back on the yoke with all his strength. The plane hit the water at a shallow angle, but slammed the occupants like a speeding automobile crashing into the back of a semi-trailer.

On *Boyington's* bridge, witnesses to the unfolding tragedy stood helpless. The OOD shouted, "Helm, hard left rudder, all ahead flank. Bosun, sound the alarm and call away the rescue party. Prepare to launch the motor whaleboat."

Answering the rudder, the ship rolled hard to starboard and shuddered to gain speed. The alarm blared throughout the ship.

The captain stopped in the passageway and turned back. The sudden change in course and speed caused him to lose balance temporarily. He regained equilibrium, reentered the pilothouse, and quickly assessed the situation.

He ran to the starboard open bridge and saw his ship rapidly approaching the spot where the broken aircraft floated, but the ship had swung too far left of the spot. "Conn, come about to starboard and get us next to the crash site."

The alarm continued screaming in the background as the bosun shouted into the 1-MC microphone, "Now all hands man rescue stations. Motor whaleboat crew, man your stations, and prepare to launch. This is not a drill. I repeat . . . all hands man rescue stations. Motor whaleboat crew stand-by to launch."

The ship coasted to within forty yards of the floating aircraft. "All back one-third," the OOD ordered. The din and clamor nearly drown out his orders. Vibrations caused by the reversed rotation of the screws coursed through the hull. The ship's forward motion quickly slowed.

"All stop," Engle ordered. He timed his command to halt the ship's drift directly opposite the crash site.

Having more planes to land, the carrier continued on course leaving the rescue mission to *Boyington*. Another destroyer would move into the plane guard slot.

On the 0-1 level, Bosun Jones shouted orders at the launch crew. With the davits still locked in place, the winch operator lowered the whaleboat to the level of the 0-1 deck and halted. The boat crew and rescue party boarded and rapidly prepared for their mission, checking their equipment and donning life jackets.

With the party on board, BM3 Garcia, the coxswain, gave Jones a thumbs-up signal. The chief boatswain roared, "Away the whaleboat."

"Hold it, Boats," Mike Stafford shouted as he came running across the torpedo deck from the starboard ladder. He didn't wait for Jones to react, leaping into the whaleboat as the davits began swinging the boat outboard.

Jones stood next to the winch operator. "Don't stop. Get that damn boat in the water."

The launching process continued. The davits swung the boat out over the water, and then the winch again began paying out the cables. Bosun Garcia started the engine as the boat dropped slowly toward the water. Blue exhaust smoke belched out briefly engulfing the boat in a dense cloud.

The whaleboat splashed into the water, and the crew immediately released the boat-falls. Garcia engaged the screw, slammed the throttle to max RPMs, and the boat leaped forward, causing several sailors to lose their balance and topple backward off their seats.

Mike held tightly to the gunwale as the boat rose and fell in the rolling sea. With his free hand, he began removing his khakis.

Moments later an explosion in the floating aircraft stunned him. The airplane's tail rose, then fell back. Mike knew that in minutes the plane and its four-man flight crew would slip below the surface. The odor of burning aviation fuel permeated the air. Flames shot skyward from the wings above the engines. The whaleboat shook as it slammed to the bottom of a trough and threw salt spray over the passengers.

Coxswain Garcia steered around the floating wreckage to approach from the windward side and avoid the flames, smoke, and heat from the burning plane.

Above them, the rescue helicopter circled with a high power search light aimed at the crash site. The pilot saw the whaleboat approaching, and some of the aircrew escaping from the rear of the aircraft. He increased altitude, to reduce the chopper's downdraft that now fanned the flames exacerbating the rescue effort.

Mike spotted two of the plane's crew in the water with their survival vests inflated and assumed the other two crewmen were still in the plane. As Garcia maneuvered toward the men in the water, sailors in the whaleboat cast lines to them.

Standing on a seat, Mike dove into the black water. He surfaced fifteen feet away and began swimming with powerful strokes toward the plane.

Now closer to the plane, he saw the copilot frantically struggling to open the emergency escape window. Flames danced in the cockpit behind the airman. The sinking plane floated low in the water, enabling Mike to swim directly up to the window. He saw that the top of the window frame had sprung slightly away from the fuselage, but it had jammed, and the copilot couldn't get the leverage necessary to force the lower section open. Mike reached up, grabbing the top of the window frame with both hands. He braced his feet against the fuselage and pulled with all his strength. The frame tore loose, throwing him back into the water. When he resurfaced, he saw the copilot swing his body into the opening, inflate his vest, and jump into the water.

Mike yelled, "Did the pilot get out?"

"He's dead."

"Are you positive?"

"Affirmative, a metal rod impaled him, right through the chest."

"Okay, let's get away from here. Are you hurt—can you swim?" Stafford asked.

"Yeah, I can swim, but not well, my leg's cut up."

Sailors in the whaleboat recovered the other two air crewmen. Garcia then turned the boat toward Mike and the copilot who were clinging to each other. Minutes later, the boat crew had them aboard. The hospital corpsman cut away the leg of the copilot's flight suit and attended to a deep gash the aviator had along his right thigh.

As Garcia turned the whaleboat back toward *Boyington*, the aircraft's tail rose out of the water, and it nosed down, sinking beneath the surface in slow motion. All that remained of the warplane were patches of burning avgas and oil floating on the surface at the wreck site and a small patch of flotsam. The rescue team and three surviving aircrew watched in stunned silence as they pulled away from the scene.

The captain, executive officer, and scores of *Boyington's* crew lined the port rails as the whaleboat rounded the ship and came along side.

Mike hastened to pull his pants on as the bosuns winched the boat back aboard. Cheers rang out as the airmen, with lots of helping hands, disembarked from the whaleboat. They rang out again when the rescue party stepped onto the destroyer's deck. Mike carried his shoes and shirt.

The ship's chief hospital corpsman led a procession of sailors who helped the two ambulatory flyers move below to sickbay. Two sailors carried the injured copilot in a wire stretcher.

Ellingham grabbed Mike's bare, wet shoulder as he shook his hand. "You did an incredibly brave thing there, Chief. I think that flyer owes you his life."

"I don't know, Sir. He nearly had the hatch open by the time I got there."

"We'll get his side of things later. Did everyone get out?"

"No, Sir. The copilot said the pilot died when they hit the water."

"Oh, shit, we especially don't need that kind of loss right now. At least we were here for the others. We'll talk later. I want to check on the survivors, and let the *Sibuyan Sea* know who made it and their status."

Mike turned toward the chiefs' compartment as Ellingham headed for sickbay.

In the background, Bosun Jones cussed at a slow moving sailor hosing saltwater off the whaleboat's hull. A corpsman striker replenished the whaleboat's first aid kit, while a seaman cleaned the copilot's blood off a seat and the deck. Another sailor refueled the boat's fuel tank.

On the bridge, the OOD gave orders to rejoin the task group. The floating oil and avgas that continued to burn on the ocean surface, created a memorial at the crash spot, as *Boyington* got underway again.

CHAPTER 25

Back to Business

One-Hundred and Twenty Miles Northeast of Turks Island Passage

Thursday, 01 November 1962

Reconnaissance flights over Cuba resumed with the launch of six sorties. All six returned safely. Their photographs revealed that all known MRBM sites in Cuba either were in the process or were completely dismantled. The missiles and launch equipment were gone, and the launch pads bulldozed. However, the present location of the missiles was unknown. Construction activity at the IRBM sites had stopped and the installations partially destroyed.[4]

However, assembly of the IL-28 bomber aircraft continued. One appeared to be completed, and two more were finished except for engine cowlings. Three others lacked only engines, while 21 remained in their crates.[4]

Based on a review of all information available, the Chief of Naval Operations' Submarine Contact Evaluation Board estimated that at least four and possibly as many as seven Soviet submarines were operating in the Southwestern Atlantic. The Navy had thus far photographed five Soviet "F" class submarines in the Atlantic. The Board considered that two of these were the same submarine; however, should this not be the case, an additional positive submarine existed.[4]

T he tragic loss of the aircraft and pilot morphed into history. Leaders on the carrier directed their efforts at refocusing the various crews on the mission. Three more planes remained aloft, running low on fuel. The *Sibuyan Sea* sailors had to quickly regroup and resume landing operations to recover the remaining planes.

Deep in the vast interior of the carrier, the S2F squadron commander sat in his cabin and began writing a letter to the widow of the pilot who had died in the crash, one of the worse tasks a commander ever faces. As he searched for the right words, he fully understood his personal grief paled in comparison to that of the poor widow his letter would reach. In his twenty-two years of service, he had only had to write one other such letter. Experience certainly didn't make the effort easier.

The navy would classify the pilot's death as a non-combat accident at sea.

Back on board *Boyington*, Mike emerged from the shower, dressed, and entered the mess compartment for breakfast. He filled a coffee mug, and then joined Ken Ford at his table.

"Mike, you sure pulled one heck of a brave stunt. What possessed you to jump into the whaleboat and join the rescue crew?" Ken asked.

"I don't know, Ken. It might have been a flash back to an event that occurred about ten years ago, back during the Korean War."

Bosun Jones entered the messing compartment. "What kinda lies you two telling this morning?"

Ken ignored the interruption. "So what happened over there?"

Mike began. "This is no shit . . ."

Jones laughed. "Okay, I gotta hear this."

"Quit beating that dead horse, Mike, and tell the story," Ken said.

Mike began again, "Captain Schmidt and I were on the destroyer *Mayfield*, with the invasion of Wonsan about to commence. We received orders to clear mines from the harbor, unusual duty for a destroyer, but there weren't any minesweepers to do the job.

"Long story made short, sonar located a commie mine. Like all young fools who consider themselves indestructible, I volunteered to dive down and unhook it so we could destroy it with gunfire.

"The whaleboat crew took me out to the spot, I dove down and unfastened the anchor chain, and the mine floated to the surface. The coxswain was circling around waiting on me, and lost sight of the mine.

I had surfaced, but the height of the waves kept me hidden most of the time. High winds were sweeping across the harbor, keeping the sea rough and the air cold.

"A strong gust sent the floating mine into the whaleboat, and blew it and its crew into the next world. Some shrapnel cut up my shoulder, but Captain Schmidt maneuvered the *Mayfield* in and the crew pulled me out of the harbor before I lost too much blood. I was air-evaced to the carrier where they saved my arm for sure, and probably my life.

"Somehow, subconsciously I suppose, I must have connected those events with today's crash and had to try to save those airmen before an explosion got them too. A minor explosion occurred, and a fire roared in the plane's cabin, but nothing like that North Korean mine, thank God."

"Wow, you never mentioned anything about that experience before," Ford said. "It's a good thing for that flyer that a spirit from the past moved you to dive in and pull him free, just minutes before the plane sank."

A loud whopping sound caught their attention, and they all looked up.

"Sounds like a chopper—I'll bet it's here to pick up the fly-boys," Ford said.

"Yeah, let's go say good-by," Mike said.

Out on the main deck, Mike, Ken, and Paul walked toward the fantail, looking up at the huge Sea King ASW helicopter hovering sixty or seventy feet above *Boyington's* fantail. A winch line lowered from a hoist on the chopper's side. The flyers were together in a group, two standing, and the third lying in a long mesh basket-like stretcher.

Mike walked up to the stretcher and kneeled down. "Hi, I'm Mike Stafford."

"You're the guy that got me out of the plane, right?" the copilot said.

"Well, I just helped a little. I think you were getting ready to chew your way through the aluminum as I arrived."

"Chief Stafford, I'm Lieutenant JG Joe Worthington, and I definitely owe you a beer."

As they talked, the winch pulled the first airman up to the helicopter and descended for the next man.

"Sorry about your pilot. Guess there wasn't anything any of us could have done."

Worthington's eyes moistened. "What a great guy—I've known him since college. We've been flying together for two years. He's got a terrific wife, back at Cecil Field . . . no kids, fortunately."

"Oh, you aren't from Quonset Point?"

"No, the Sibuyan Sea is, of course, but my squadron is home ported in Jacksonville, rough duty."

"Yes Sir, I'm sure it is. Well, the sling is coming down for you now. Hope that leg is okay. Maybe we can have a beer in Havana when this goat rope is over."

"That sounds like a plan, Chief. Take care, and thanks again."

Mike came to attention and saluted.

Worthington returned the salute as the hoist lifted the stretcher off the deck and into the air.

"Come on, Mike. We got a breakfast to finish," Ford said.

As they turned, a nearby loud speaker blared. The bosun piped the call for attention then announced, "Now hear this. Now hear this. All hands muster at quarters."

"So much for breakfast," Stafford said.

The three separated, heading for their respective muster stations.

The excitement of the plane crash and the rescue died, and the normal routine resumed. The bridge and CIC watch remained on high alert as flight operations continued.

At 1000, the radio tuned to the tactical net crackled to life. "Siena, this is Adeline Alpha, over."

Lieutenant Junior Grade Rudolph, the CIC officer, snatched up the handset. "Adeline Alpha, this is Siena, over."

"Siena, Adeline Alpha. Proceed to ASW screening station four and relieve Brewmeister, over."

"Roger, Adeline Alpha, understand Siena relieves Brewmeister at station four, Siena out."

Rudolph turned to the DRT. "Get course and speed to station four." He then passed the word to the bridge. "Bridge, CIC. DESRON

Forty-Two ordered us to relieve *Keffer* at station four. I'll have a course shortly."

"Roger, CIC, bridge out." Lieutenant Quinn, the OOD, breathed a sigh of relief. Flight operations had been busy since his watch began at 0800. He looked at the radar repeater, saw what he had to do, and worked out course and speed to station four in his head.

When CIC rang again, the course they suggested matched the one he had calculated. "Helm, come about to port, steer three-four-five, make turns for two oh knots."

The helmsman repeated the order as Quinn rang the captain.

"Ellingham."

"Sir, Quinn here. We're heading for ASW station four. Estimated time to station is twenty-one minutes."

"Okay, Pat. Let me know when we're there."

"Aye, aye, Sir."

Quinn stepped out on the open bridge and watched as the ship's wake of foaming white water curved to the north. *Keffer* came up fast behind the carrier and slid into the plane-guard station.

That afternoon, Seaman Apprentice Unger stood in the wardroom facing Captain Ellingham. Lieutenant Commander Kaestner stood one-step behind the captain and to his right. Chief Jones stood to Kaestner's left. The three wore work khakis.

Unger, in dress whites, faced the captain. Behind him stood Ensign Padgett and Chief Stafford, his division officer and leading petty officer, respectively.

Chief Jones called the group to attention.

The muffled brush of waves washing against the destroyer's sides made the only audible sound save an occasional soft metallic groan emanating from deep within the bowels of the ship.

The captain spoke, "Seaman Apprentice David T. Unger, serial number 381 07 86, U.S. Navy, you are officially charged with two violations of the Uniform Code of Military Justice, Section 908, Article 109: Military property of the United States, loss, damage, destruction or wrongful disposition.

"These two charges relate to your sabotage of the scullery machine aboard the U.S.S. *Boyington*, DD 953, on or about 27 and 31 October 1962, as you have confessed to in writing. That confession has been appended to Master at Arm's report Number 62-13, of 31 October 1962.

"Lieutenant Commander John R. Kaestner, Executive Officer of this command, has investigated the charges and attested to their correctness. The Judge Advocate General of the United States Second Fleet has further reviewed the charges.

"Seaman Apprentice Unger, I hereby remand you to the custody of the master-at-arms of this vessel as a prisoner at large, pending court martial by the Commander, ASW Task Force, United States Second

Fleet. You will abide by all restrictions imposed on you by the MAA. Do you understand my orders?"

"Aye, aye, Sir."

"You are dismissed."

Unger executed an about-face. Looking at Ensign Padgett and Chief Stafford, he took a deep breath. "I'm sorry for the stupid things I done," he whispered.

"Yes, they were stupid. And now it's time to pay the piper," Padgett said.

"Yes, Sir."

Unger followed Stafford out of the wardroom. "What do you think they'll do to me, Chief?"

"It's hard to say. The court martial will decide, but I've never been good at predicting their decisions. The charges are serious, and the timing will definitely go against you. Trying to sabotage your ship when we're on a wartime footing wasn't real bright."

Unger turned, his head dropped, and he walked away slowly.

The evening movie, *Ben Hur*, starring Charlton Heston, began at 1900 on the mess deck. The film, though a bit dated, remained popular with the crew and drew a substantial audience.

Forty-five minutes into second reel, the loudspeaker interrupted. "Attention all hands, this is the captain speaking. We have received orders to evaluate a submarine contact detected by a patrol plane. The last known contact location is two and a half hours away. I anticipate going to general-quarters, condition one antisubmarine, at 2400, so get some rest, and be prepared. That is all."

Under condition-one ASW, only sailors assigned to those weapons and systems needed to battle a submarine responded. All but one gun crew and most of the other sailors went about their normal business. In this instance, it meant they could stay in their racks when the alarm sounded.

After the captain's announcement, many in the audience rose and departed.

The noticeable increase in the ship's speed underscored the captain's message. The off-duty sailors involved with anti-submarine warfare turned-in, hoping for a few hours sleep before trouble started.

At 2350, the loud speakers boomed: "Now hear this. General-quarters, general-quarters. Set Condition-One Antisubmarine. Set Material Condition Zulu. This is not a drill, general-quarters." The alarm bell continued to ring as sailors assigned to the first watch of ASW-One ran to their battle stations. *Boyington* raced toward her foe, fully prepared for battle.

CHAPTER 26

Lost: One Submarine and One Sailor

Two-Hundred and Fifty Miles Northeast of Turks Island Passage

Friday, 02 November 1962

November 2, 1962—10:00 A.M.: At a meeting of the ExComm, Kennedy confirms that the United States will press for the removal of the IL-28 bombers currently stationed in Cuba. In other matters, Kennedy states that the quarantine must continue to be maintained but only by hailing all vessels entering the quarantine zone. He reconfirms orders to U.S. Navy vessels not to board Soviet Bloc ships. (Document 63, NSC ExComm Nov 2, 1962, 10:00 A.M., Meeting no. 17)[1]

For the next five days, the naval quarantine was characterized by continued surveillance of merchant ships entering and leaving Cuban ports and aerial reconnaissance of the dismantling of missile sites.

Throughout this period, there also were repeated submarine contacts and surfacing.[4]

Anavy P2V Neptune, call sign Top Hat Two, flying out of Cecil Field Naval Air Station, Jacksonville, Florida, had detected a submarine inside the Walnut Line. Flag Plot at headquarters, U.S. Navy, designated the contact as C-32. *Boyington* sailed over seventy miles to investigate, arriving shortly after midnight.

"Siena, this is Top Hat Two, I dropped an array of passive sonobuoys, but have lost contact with Charlie three-two. I'm going to broaden my search pattern."

"Roger Top Hat Two, we are twenty minutes south and closing. Siena out," Lieutenant Caruthers, the mid-watch OOD, responded.

Boyington proceeded toward the submarine's datum, the last known position, as her air search radar tracked the Neptune crisscrossing the area at twelve-hundred feet, listening for a report from the sonar buoys.

The destroyer reached the datum and began cruising in ever widening circles, pinging with her powerful sonar. The search continued for hours.

Top Hat One relieved its sister aircraft at 0200 and dropped another pattern of sonobuoys. At 0312, the aircraft received a sonar hit. The pilot immediately radioed the submarine's location to Siena.

The OOD called out the heading. As the helm responded, he called the Captain. "It's the OOD, Sir, Top Hat has a contact. We're heading there now. The estimated time to target is twenty-three minutes."

"Okay, I'm on my way up," Ellingham said.

Shortly thereafter, SO2 Berlinski, the sonar operator gained a contact. The bridge 1JS telephone talker relayed the report. "Sir, sonar contact heading zero-two-seven; range one two oh double-oh; depth one five zero."

"Conn, all ahead flank, steer zero-two-seven." Caruthers ordered.

As the ship surged forward, Ellingham entered the pilothouse. "The Captain's on the bridge," the boatswain announced.

"How we doing, Mister Caruthers?" Ellingham asked.

"Sonar's locked on the contact, Sir. It's running, but we'll catch up with it in fifteen or twenty minutes, depending on what kind of underwater speed they can generate."

"Very well, let's catch this one." Ellingham walked over to the ASW attack director. He quickly assessed the situation, and then exited out to the port side open bridge.

The sonar talker called out an update. "Sir, the sub's diving on the same heading. Range eight oh double-oh; depth two double-oh."

Five minutes passed. "Sir, sonar, has lost the contact. They say it must have found the thermocline and ducked under it," the 1JS talker reported.

Seaman Apprentice Maxwell, the 1JS circuit telephone talker on his first cruise, felt a surge of importance as he observed the OOD's reaction to the information he passed. He moved over next to Seaman Kildare, the talker on the 1JV circuit. "What's this 'thermocline' thing I just reported?"

Seaman Kildare, a two-year veteran of bridge watches, puffed up his chest and smiled. "Oh, that's a layer of water where there's a big temperature change. It separates the warmer water from the colder water below and messes with the sonar. Submariners can hide under it. It kinda makes them invisible."

"Cool, I never even heard the word before. I hope I pronounced it right."

"You did. If you hear any other words you don't know, just ask me. I've been standing these watches for a long time."

Maxwell watched Lieutenant Caruthers pace the pilothouse deck. The officer displayed frustration that the sub had managed to slip away.

"Maxwell, tell sonar to keep pinging. I'll slow down to reduce the screw noise. Helm, steady as she goes, turns for five knots," Caruthers ordered.

Maxwell passed the word to sonar, then again turned to his fellow telephone talker. "Hey Kildare, what's 'screw noise'," he whispered.

"The noise our propellers make when they churn up the water. Man, you don't know anything, do you?"

"You said I could ask."

"Yeah, well keep your voice down or the OOD will jump all over us. He's already pissed off."

⁂

Caruthers snatched up a radio handset and called the patrol plane. "Top Hat One, Siena, we've lost contact—you picking up anything?"

"Negative, Siena. All the buoys are quiet."

"Roger, Siena out."

Boyington began a new grid search pattern centered on the revised datum, hoping to reestablish contact. She turned in ever widening circles with her sonar pinging at full power, trying to locate the illusive submarine.

At 0500, neither the Neptune nor the destroyer had regained contact with the sub. The OOD called DESRON Forty-Two to update the situation. "Adeline Alpha, this is Siena. We lost Charlie three-two at 0352. Top Hat One has broken off and is returning to station. Our fuel is at twenty percent."

"Siena, Adeline Alpha, continue searching until relieved by Silver Spur, then rendezvous with Checkbook for refueling, Adeline Alpha out."

"Silver spur" was the call sign for the U.S.S. *Browning.*

The OOD hung up the handset. "This would be one hell of a place to run out of fuel," he said to the quartermaster. "Where'd the skipper go?"

"Back to his cabin."

He picked up the sound powered telephone, turned the selector dial to the captain's cabin, and cranked.

"Sir, it's the OOD. The DESRON Forty-Two duty officer ordered us to stay on station until relieved by *Browning*."

"Do they understand our fuel situation?" Ellingham asked.

"Yes, Sir, I made that clear to them."

"Okay, have the oil king sound the bunkers every half hour and keep our speed under fifteen knots. I am not going let them strand us out here with dry tanks."

"Aye, aye, Sir."

At a quarter past six, the sun burst over the horizon with a brilliant red-orange corona, foretelling bad weather to come. On the positive side, however, the *Browning* arrived on station, relieving the thirsty *Boyington*. The OOD immediately shaped a course for the *Sibuyan Sea*.

The destroyer approached the aircraft carrier to refuel, but today's meeting between the two ships had an additional purpose. The first connection between them would permit the transfer of fuel. The second, a steel cable, high-line, from the destroyer's 0-1 level to the carrier would allow a bosun's chair to glide across the turbulent water between the two ships on a pulley, pulled by sailors on the carrier.

The passenger, Seaman Apprentice David T. Unger, would make a one-way trip across the gap between the two ships. A marine sergeant from *Sibuyan Sea's* master-at-arms force stood ready to greet him and escort him to the ship's brig where he would sit until events permitted a court martial to convene.

A written confession had sealed his guilt. The only unanswered question being the punishment, and that issue would have to wait. The misbehavior of an eighteen-year-old seaman, after all, represented a low priority. An unknown number of Soviet submarines still prowled the depths of the Atlantic, waiting for orders to launch a torpedo at the carrier with its four-thousand-man crew and eighty-five aircraft.

As the *Sibuyan Sea* and *Boyington* captains carefully guided their respective ships during the hazardous refueling and personnel transfer operation, a third captain observed the operation from a position nearly a mile to the north.

"Down periscope. They are refueling that destroyer that nearly caught us. Dive to one-hundred meters and steer zero-one-zero."

"Diving to one-hundred meters, Comrade Captain," the planesman responded.

"Coming about to zero-one-zero, Comrade Captain," the helmsman called out.

"Sonar, what do you have?"

"Nothing, Comrade Captain. They cannot use their sonars when in such close proximity. I am listening and will know the minute they begin to search."

"Very well. We must be careful not to divulge our presence, so use only passive techniques until we put some distance between us and the destroyer."

"Aye, Aye, Sir."

"Comrade Captain, we are approaching one-hundred meters," the planesman reported.

"Sonar, where is the thermocline?"

"About ten meters below us, Comrade Captain."

"Right. Steady as she goes. Turns for five knots."

CHAPTER 27

Score One for the Home Team
Three-Hundred Miles Northeast of Turks Island Passage

Saturday, 03 November 1962

The nineteenth meeting of the ExComm focuses on inspection questions and the issue of the IL-28 bombers. Adlai Stevenson, who attends the meeting with John McCloy and Charles Yost, brings the group up to date on the slow-moving talks in New York. President Kennedy states his belief that the United States should announce that it considers the IL-28s to be offensive weapons to be withdrawn from Cuba, but he agrees that the public announcement of this position should be delayed until the next day. (Summary Record of NSC Executive Committee Meeting No. 19, November 3, 1962, 4:30 p.m.)[1]

The sea was choppy when *Boyington* turned north after receiving orders to pursue yet another submarine contact. The P2V

Neptune, that made initial contact with the sub, continued tracking it with aerial launched sonar buoys.

CNO Flag Plot designated the contact as C-33. However, based on its maneuver patterns, the sonar technicians on the P2V, call sign Top Hat One, were convinced the sub was the same one that had slipped from their grasp yesterday.

The destroyer's mission, as with all submarine contacts since the crisis began, remained to locate the vessel and signal it to surface for identification purposes. This action, designed to send a clear message to the Soviets of the U.S. Navy's anti-submarine capability, had apparently worked. The number of new submarine contacts had steadily decreased recently.

At 0510, *Boyington's* sonar operator reported a contact within a mile of the position reported by the aircraft.

Mister White, the officer of the deck, immediately dialed the captain's cabin. "Sir, it's the OOD. We have a submarine contact, bearing, three-one-eight, true; range eight oh-double-oh; depth, three double-oh."

"Stay on it, I'll be right up," the captain responded.

Ellingham entered the pilothouse minutes later. "I have the deck. Mister White, take the conn. Bosun, call general quarters, set condition ASW-One."

White immediately advised the helm that he had the conn and received acknowledgement from the helmsman. Mister Padgett, the JOOD, who had been conning the ship, stepped aside.

"Mister Padgett, notify DESRON Forty-Two we have acquired the contact," Ellingham said.

The boatswain's mate of the watch pressed the 1MC talk button with one hand, raised the pipe to his lips with the other, and blew the call *All Hands*. "Now hear this. General quarters, General quarters. Set condition ASW-One. Set material condition Zulu. This is not a drill."

The alarm bell clanged throughout the ship, urging haste.

Crewmen hurried to their ASW battle stations and prepared for an engagement with the submarine.

Fifteen minutes passed. Sonar reported the contact: bearing, three-one-eight, true; range, two oh double-oh; depth three double-oh; contact making five knots.

Boyington slowed, as she grew within a nautical mile of the sub's position. Ellingham's tight jaw revealed the tension he felt. Others on the bridge began to mirror the captain's concern.

Lieutenant Engle entered the pilothouse from CIC and approached the skipper. "Sir, the commodore says, 'Stay on top of this contact, and don't let it out of your grip.' He's requesting an S2F to help us."

"What? Does he think that we let it go on purpose yesterday?"

"No, Sir. I'd guess he's as frustrated as we are."

"You're right. I have a problem with this business of being halfway at war. I wish one of these SOBs would take a shot at us so we could sink 'em and go home. I'm tired of playing hide and seek."

"Yes, Sir. I think most of the men feel the same way."

"When's that plane supposed to arrive?"

"Around zero six hundred," Engle said.

"This could turn out to be a grueling day, assuming 'we don't let it out of our grip.' We don't know how much longer they can stay submerged."

Ellingham turned to the exec, "Let's try sending that NOTAM signal and see what happens."

The XO grabbed a notebook from the quartermasters table and rang sonar on the sound powered telephone. He addressed the sonar officer. "Mister Sherwood, we want to try signaling the sub using the NOTAM procedure." Kaestner flipped a page in the notebook. "Here it is: transmit the signal 'IDKCA' on 8kc."

After a five minute wait, sonar advised the sub had not answered nor had they changed course.

Half an hour later, the S2F Tracker arrived and began flying a pattern over the submerged submarine with the magnetic anomaly detection probe extended from its tail. It quickly verified the sub's presence. Top Hat One loitered at five thousand feet, monitoring the sub's movements with signals from the sonar buoys they had dropped.

Boyington circled the sub continuously in four-mile wide circles, maintaining sonar contact. On occasion, the sub would slow, but maintained the same course, never exceeding five knots.

The morning crept on, and the ASW crew grew fidgety after hours of inactivity at their GQ posts.

At 0800, CIC advised the bridge that Top Hat One reported the contact diving and turning to starboard with a heading of three-four-five, true; depth three-five-oh.

Seconds later, Sonarman Second Class Griffin, five decks below the pilothouse, in the icy-cold sonar control room, observed the same maneuver by the sub and advised the bridge.

Ellingham rushed to the ASW attack director. "Conn, come about to starboard, steer three-four-five." He then moved out onto the wing of the open bridge.

Fifteen minutes passed, and the sub stayed on course. "Sir, sonar says we're on top of the contact," the 1JS talker announced.

"Sonar, transmit the NOTAM signal again," Ellingham ordered.

Minutes passed while silence reigned on the bridge.

"Sonar, any response to the signal?" the Captain asked.

"Negative, Sir. But she's turning to starboard."

Ellingham moved back to the ASW attack director and watched the sub change course. "Maybe she's going to come around to zero-nine-zero as the NOTAM directed. Conn, come about to starboard, steer three-six-zero, turns for five knots."

Boyington slowed and turned with the submarine. The captain continued to monitor the attack director and make incremental changes in course and speed to stay with the sub.

The two vessels cruised on parallel courses for another ten minutes, but the sub did not attempt to surface and stayed at a depth of three-hundred and fifty feet, making five knots.

"Sonar, send that 'IDKCA' signal one more time. Gunnery, prepare to drop signal grenades," the captain said.

Ellingham waited.

No response—finally, he shrugged. "Gunnery, drop four signal grenades."

After a brief pause, gunnery reported, "Grenades away."

Three-hundred and fifty feet below *Boyington*, another captain shouldered an immense burden of responsibility.

"Comrade Captain," the sonarman said. "The Americans are sending that signal again. I copied it down this time. They keep sending 'IDKCA.' I don't know if it is an English word or what it means."

"Captain Lieutenant," the Russian captain addressed his executive officer. "Look through our message book. Headquarters sent something out a few weeks ago about signals the Americans might use. I can't remember what they were abo—"

A series of explosions interrupted the captain and stunned the submarine crew.

"Battle stations, they are attacking us. Helm, hard to starboard, all ahead full. Emergency dive, take us down to one-hundred and fifty meters. We have to get below the thermocline quickly," the captain shouted.

"Sir, sonar says the sub is running. They're turning to starboard again and diving," the 1JS talker reported.

Ellingham ran to the attack director.

"Captain, Top Hat One reports the sub is turning and picking up speed," the 1JV talker said.

"Mister Padgett, notify DESRON Forty-Two of the situation," Ellingham ordered. "Conn, come about to starboard, steer zero-zero-five, turns for one oh knots."

Five minutes passed. No one on the bridge spoke.

"Captain, sonar is losing contact with the sub."

The XO turned to Ellingham, "What the hell is wrong with those guys? Why won't they surface and identify themselves?"

"They may not know what's going on. They might even think we're at war and come up shooting," the captain said, "and if they do, they're in for a big surprise because we're going to hit them and hit them hard."

The Soviet submarine crossed below the thermocline layer and continued turning until it circled around behind *Boyington*, gaining the added protection of the destroyer's noisy wake.

"Comrade Captain Petrov, I found the message. It says when the Americans send the signal 'IDKCA,' they want us to surface on an easterly course and identify ourselves," the exec said.

"Identify ourselves or give them a better target?"

"The message says they might drop harmless explosive devices. Maybe they aren't attacking us."

"I'm not taking any chances. Rig for silent running. I'm going to stay right under their screws. They will never find us."

An hour passed, and neither the Boyington nor either of two the aircraft regained contact.

An angry Captain Ellingham picked up the radiotelephone handset. "Adeline Alpha this is Siena actual, over."

"Go ahead Siena, Adeline Alpha actual."

"Adeline Alpha, Siena. We can't find Charlie thirty-three. Over."

"What about the Neptune?"

"They lost it too and are heading home."

"Keep searching. I'll send help," Adeline Alpha out.

Ellingham hung up the handset with a noticeable degree of frustration. He paused, "Bosun, secure from ASW-One."

With that, he left the bridge and headed for CIC, where he joined Mister Engle at the DRT. "Where's the sub's last confirmed location?"

Engle pointed to the last of a series of small dots on the paper that indicated the locations reported by sonar. "Right here, Sir."

"Okay, get me a course to this location, and we'll start a circular search pattern." Ellingham drew a bull's eye target on the DRT chart, several inches south of the last known location, and left.

Back on the bridge, the captain again waited.

Engle entered the bridge minutes later with the course written on a scrap of paper. "Here it is, Sir. Also, Adeline Alpha just called to advise *Negley* is on her way to join us."

An irritated captain called out the new course and speed.

Top Hat Three arrived on station to resume the search. The S2F Trackers also continued assisting in the hunt by flying a grid pattern over a ten square-mile area.

"Comrade Captain, the destroyer is turning and increasing speed. We won't be able to keep up with her. We'll lose our cover," the sonar operator said.

"Let them go. They don't know where we are now and they're leaving. We'll sit here and wait them out. All stop."

Boyington reached the point Ellingham had designated and began circling with a two-mile radius.

Two hours later *Negley* arrived and joined in the search. Ellingham increased the radius to four miles.

The watch changed, and the bosun announced dinner for the crew. Seated on the bridge in his command chair, Ellingham ate a sandwich without tasting it.

Five and a half hours passed. The two destroyers had broadened their search to a six-mile radius and continued the search.

––––––––––––––––––

On the submarine, the temperature in most compartments exceeded ninety degrees Fahrenheit, and the atmosphere approached an unbreathable state.

In an attempt to remain as silent as possible, most of the crew had nothing to do other than sit or recline in their sweat soaked bunks. Since there were more men that bunks, patience neared the breaking point. Boredom made minutes feel like hours.

The sailors scratched at the always-present red skin rashes exacerbated by a lack of bathing, clean clothes, fresh air, proper diet, and medication.

"Captain Petrov, conditions are horrible. I don't know how much longer the crew can endure."

"Is it the crew that may not endure or you, Comrade Captain Lieutenant? I haven't heard any complaints from the crew."

"Sir, they are good men and will die before complaining, but my job is to look after them, and I'm telling you they are nearing the breaking point.

"In my opinion, the Americans were signaling us to surface for identification in accordance with the message our headquarters sent. If they intended to sink us, they could have done so hours ago, Sir."

The captain's feet and legs ached, and his head throbbed. He had been standing at his central command post for over twelve hours without a break. Sweat dripped down his arms and legs. His sweat soaked shoes squished as if he had been wading in the surf.

"Perhaps you're right, Comrade. Helmsman, steer zero-nine-zero. Planesman, take her up to fifty meters."

The 1JS talker broke the silence that had blanketed the bridge. "Captain, sonar has a contact: bearing, zero-nine-zero, true; range, two five double-oh; depth, two double-oh and decreasing; speed, five knots."

The pilothouse became a beehive of activity with Ellingham shouting orders. "CIC, get me a course to intercept. Bosun, sound GQ, set ASW Condition One."

The Bosun made the announcement, then flipped the switch for the alarm bell. Its clanging resounded throughout the ship.

CIC provided the course. The captain ordered a turn and flank speed.

Boyington and her crew sparked to life. They had flushed the quarry, and the hunt resumed.

Ten miles away, similar activities took place on *Negley*.

Twenty minutes passed, then sonar reported. "We're directly over her now, Sir."

"Sonar, send that NOTAM signal again. Gunnery, prepare to drop four more grenades, but wrap each one up tight with a roll of toilet paper this time so they'll sink deeper before exploding. Maybe they didn't hear them before."

The sub stopped its assent.

It took ten minutes for the gunners to obtain four rolls of toilet paper and wrap the grenades.

Finally, the 1JV talker reported, "Sir, Gunnery says the gift wrapped grenades are ready."

"Grenades away."

Another three minutes passed. "Sir, sonar reports the grenades went off," the 1JS talker said.

"Comrade Captain, they are sending that signal again, 'IDKCA.' Look, here is the message. It says they will send this signal and drop—"

Four distinct, close-by explosions interrupted the executive officer's explanation.

"All right, Captain Lieutenant, we will surface, but you better pray to that God you are always talking about that a war hasn't started or we will soon join him, whomever, and wherever he is."

When they finally reached a depth of eighteen meters, Captain Petrov climbed the ladder to the navigation deck. In his weakened state, turning the wheel to open the hatch required most of his strength. He managed to break the seal, and seawater showered down on him. What normally would have been an irritant, actually felt refreshing. He climbed up onto the deck and raised the periscope.

Searching aft, he spotted a blurry ship and adjusted the optics. An American destroyer, hull number 953, came into focus. It was gracefully cutting through the waves about a thousand meters off his port quarter. Continuing around to starboard, he found another destroyer three-thousand meters astern and closing.

As he examined the ship that had forced him to surface, the executive officer climbed up to the open bridge hatch and spun it open. Both officers received another saltwater shower.

Petrov lowered the periscope and followed the exec up to the open bridge. He relished the clean, fresh air, breathing in deeply. The sky was clear, the sun, a bright orange sphere, teetered on the western horizon with halos of apricot and russet, a deep pink shelf stretched off to the southwest. Basking in the serene open air, for a moment he completely forgot the warship rapidly approaching his port side. It flashed a signal lamp at him, breaking the spell he had succumbed to.

"Signalman to the cockpit on the double," he shouted.

Finally, over fourteen hours after the encounter began, *Boyington's* lookouts reported a submarine sail breaking the surface on course zero-nine-zero. The destroyer closed to one-thousand yards off the submarine's port quarter. The boat continued to surface.

Ellingham stood on the starboard bridge wing focusing his binoculars. The rapidly fading daylight was still sufficient to illuminate the sub's open bridge. He could see two Soviet sailors, probably officers, looking back at him through their binoculars. "I guess those buggers have had enough. I'm sure conditions down there are horrible after all this time."

"Yes, Sir," Mister Engle said. "You know it has to be hot inside that boat, and the air must be putrid."

The captain called for the signalman. "Kessler, use your lamp and our new codes to ask the sub crew to identify themselves."

"Aye, aye, Sir." The signalman ran aft to the big signal lamp and pivoted it around toward the sub. After consulting the codebook, he flashed a series of long and short bursts of light.

A Russian sailor copied the letters, then looking in his codebook determined the Americans were asking who they were. He informed his captain and received permission to reply. He flashed back the coded response, U.S.S.R. Naval Vessel B-115.

Kessler advised Captain Ellingham.

"Very well, ask them if they need assistance."

Another exchange of coded phrases produced the answer, "No, thank you," and a question for the Americans. "What ship?"

With the captain's permission, Kessler answered, "U.S.S. *Boyington*."

"Kessler, find the code notifying them we're moving in close for photographs," Ellingham said.

Ellingham waited for the sub to confirm their understanding. "Conn, come alongside the sub. Keep a separation of at least one-hundred feet, and let's get some pictures before the sun sets."

Quartermaster Gandolfi steadied himself on the signal bridge, and using a camera equipped with a zoom lens, snapped a dozen pictures of the surfaced prey. He then gave the bridge a thumbs-up signal.

"Conn, take us back out to a thousand yards and position us off the sub's port quarter," the OOD ordered. "CIC, update the commodore—mission accomplished. Bosun, secure from ASW One."

Negley pulled up to the sub's starboard quarter and settled in at a range of one-thousand yards.

Boyington dropped back to the sub's port quarter and gradually increased the separation.

Ten-minutes later, Mister Engle entered the pilothouse and walked over to the captain's chair. "Sir, the commodore is ordering Negley to escort the Russians out of the quarantine area. He wants us free to chase and photograph freighters departing Cuba."

"Okay. Keep me posted." Ellingham said.

At 2100, Negley cruising along the sub's starboard side took over escort duties while Boyington turned south, headed for the carrier to refuel and prepare for the next mission. Her weary off-watch crew showered and turned in for a few hours sleep. All were tired, but proud they had forced an enemy submarine to the surface after a continuous fourteen-hour duel.

While neither side had fired a shot, the Soviets had to realize they would all be dead if they had tried to attack or escape the iron jaws of the American blockade. They also had to realize their covert spying mission lay in a shambles, a total failure. The cruise home would be, without doubt, an unpleasant one, at least for this captain.

———

Negley ordered the submarine to come about to zero three zero and followed her north until they crossed the Walnut Line where they parted company. The final radar contact indicated the sub continued on a heading toward mother Russia.

CHAPTER 28

Photo Op

Atlantic Ocean

Three-Hundred Miles Northeast of Mona Passage

Monday, 05 November 1962

On 5 November, the Russians began loading and shipping their medium range ballistic missiles and bombers from the Cuban port at Mariel, back to the Soviet Union. They failed to follow their own departure schedule, but the vast number of U.S. Navy ships and aircraft patrolling the area made it impossible for them to avoid inspections. Destroyers cruising alongside, along with low flying patrol planes and helicopters carefully observed and photographed every ship leaving. By agreement, freighters carried all offensive missiles and aircraft on the weather decks, open for inspection. The Navy tracked and observed the ships from the Cuban ports, until they passed the quarantine line, on their way back to the Soviet Union.[3]

B oyington's first interception of a missile-carrying Soviet freighter began as the bosun piped the evening meal. A P2V, Neptune patrol plane spotted the northbound *Sevastopol* leaving Cuba and vectored the destroyer to it. The freighter maintained a steady course and speed as the destroyer approached.

"Mister Frankel, get the photographer up on the 0-3 level. I want plenty of pictures of that freighter's deck cargo from both sides. We'll start with their starboard side. Call down when he's done, and I'll swing around to their port side," Captain Ellingham said.

Ensign Frankel, the JOOD, retreated to the signal bridge where the combat cameraman lingered. "Grab your gear, Slone. We're going up on the 0-3 level to get a better view."

The two climbed the ladder to the smaller, but higher, deck. Slone, a nineteen-year-old photographer's mate third class lugged two large bags of equipment. Not part of the crew, Second Fleet had assigned him temporarily to photograph the Soviet missiles as they departed Cuba on their way back to Russia. He had arrived, via a highline transfer from the carrier, at the last refueling.

"The captain wants lots of pictures. Do you have plenty of film?" Frankel asked.

"Oh, yes, Sir. I can take hundreds of pictures. What all do you want photographed?"

274

"The obvious thing is the missiles on the open deck, but get the ship's name and homeport with a stern shot and any sign of activity that you see. We're going to pass by their starboard side slowly, and then slip around to the port side. We'll be within about three-hundred feet of the freighter."

"Yes, Sir, I'll get a wide angle picture as we approach, then switch lenses for close up shots of the missiles."

"Okay, let me know when you're done, and I'll have the ship reposition so you can see the freighter's port side."

Sloan snapped away as *Boyington* cruised alongside the freighter. Several Russian seamen came out and posed with the missiles. Sloan photographed them, too.

After forty-five minutes of close sailing and picture taking, the Americans waved good-by to the cooperative Russians and sailed off.

The film would eventually find its way to the hands of navy intelligence specialists, air force photo analysts, and CIA experts. Those individuals faced a daunting, manpower-intensive task. They would endeavor to reconcile the numbers and descriptions of missiles photographed by the navy with the aerial reconnaissance photographs of the Cuban launch sites. That data would then be compared with the number of missiles and types, the Soviets claimed to have placed on Cuban soil. Their goal was to account for every single missile.

Three hours after leaving *Sevastopol*, CIC reported a radar contact, fifteen miles to the west, steering north by northeast at eighteen knots. The OOD reported the contact to the captain.

"Set a course to intercept at flank speed. Radio the TG and tell them what we're chasing. Give me the ETA on the contact when you get it," Ellingham ordered.

The task group gave the destroyer formal orders to intercept.

Boyington caught up with the contact an hour and fifteen minutes later. It proved to be another Soviet freighter, the *Ivan Volikov*. Like the *Sevastopol*, this one also carried a cargo of missiles on her open deck. Canvas shrouds concealed them from direct viewing, but the distinctive shape left little doubt as to what they were.

Ellingham entered the pilothouse.

"Captain's on the bridge," the bosun sang out.

Ellingham stepped out onto the port wing and focused his binoculars on the freighter. "Call them on the international frequency and tell them to uncover their cargo."

Mister Riley, the OOD, made the call.

"No response, Sir," Riley reported.

"Then send the code by signal lamp," Ellingham said.

As part of the agreement between the United States and the Soviet Union, both countries disseminated a list of codes to their fleets, which would facilitate communications. Captain Ellingham was calling for one of the five letter combinations that requested the Soviet vessel stay on her present course at twelve knots and undercover her cargo.

The signalman saw the Russians signal back with a long steady light, meaning message received, but nothing further happened.

Five minutes passed. "Send the same signal again, Mister Riley," Ellingham said.

Another acknowledgement flashed across the quarter mile separation between the ships, but nothing occurred in the way of compliance.

"Okay, stand-by," Ellingham said. He picked up the handset on the task group tactical frequency.

"Checkbook, this is Siena actual, over."

"Siena, Checkbook, go ahead."

"Checkbook, Siena actual: We intercepted the Soviet freighter *Ivan Volikov* and have flashed the code requesting they uncover their deck cargo twice. They acknowledged receiving it, but are not complying—request orders."

"Stand by, Siena."

Ten minutes passed. "Siena, this is Checkbook actual, over."

The CIC watch officer called the bridge. "Captain, the Admiral is on the tactical channel."

"Roger that," Ellingham responded. He reached for the tactical handset.

"Checkbook, this is Siena actual, over."

"Siena, I have notified TF 135 of your situation. They will work the issue through the State Department. Someone didn't get the word, apparently. In the mean time, I'll have Adeline Alpha send some help over to keep you company, and let them know we're serious. Checkbook out."

"Roger, Checkbook, Siena out."

"Mister Riley, the admiral has bumped the issue up the chain. It will be several hours at best before anything is resolved. He's going to have the commodore send another ship over to indicate to the Russians that we are serious about our request.

"It's too dark to get any good photos now anyway, so let's put a half mile between us and plan on getting our pictures in the morning. When help shows up, have them cover *Ivan's* port side. We'll stay over here to starboard. I'm going below to get some chow."

"Aye, aye, Sir."

The *Keffer* arrived on station at 0130 and took up position one-half mile off the freighter's port side. The three ships cruised through the night at eighteen knots.

Ellingham entered the pilothouse at dawn. "Any developments, Mister Engle?" he asked the OOD.

"Negative, Sir, quiet watch so far."

"Good. Have you heard anything from *Keffer*?"

"They checked-in with the mid-watch, but have been quiet since then."

"Okay, let's flash the magic phrase and see if the Russians want to play now," the captain said.

Engle stepped out on the open bridge and called to the duty signalman. "Kessler, fire up your lamp and send the code that directs them to uncover their cargo."

After a brief delay, the freighter signaled back with a different coded phrase.

Signalman First Class Kessler copied the letters then checked the codebook. He entered the pilothouse, "Mister Engle, their response means, 'I will stay on course at twelve knots and uncover my cargo'"

"Very well. Bosun, pass the word for the photographer to report to the bridge."

Lieutenant Commander Kaestner entered the pilothouse.

"Good morning, XO. Today is going to be a grand one. The sky is clear, and the Russian has decided to show us his wares," Ellingham said. "Let's get the photographer up on the 0-3 level and have Mister Frankel coordinate the picture taking like he did yesterday."

"Aye, aye, Sir," Kaestner said.

It took the Russian sailors over an hour to untie and remove the canvas covers. When they finished, the sun reflected off four sixty-foot long, four-foot diameter, medium range ballistic missiles, known in NATO as the Soviet SS-4 Sandal. The photographer snapped away, capturing pictures from various angles. Mission accomplished.

Signalman Kessler flashed a message of thanks, and the two American destroyers turned west to rejoin the *Sibuyan Sea* and take on fuel.

During the next two weeks U.S. Navy ships, primarily destroyers, would photograph over a dozen Soviet freighters, carrying strategic offensive weapons from Cuba back to the Soviet Union.

Around the globe, people of all nations began to relax as the two most powerful nations slowly sheathed their weapons. Cooler heads had prevailed, avoiding a nuclear cataclysm.

CHAPTER 29

Liberty Call

San Juan, Puerto Rico

Friday, 9 November 1962

At 0700 local, the U.S.S. Blandy (DD 943) intercepted the Soviet freighter Dvinogorsk and asked her to roll back the coverings on the missiles. The Soviet vessel complied. Blandy reported that there was a large cylindrical object beneath, encased in a watertight seal.[4]

At 0800 local, the U.S.S. Newport News (CA 148) and U.S.S. Leary (DD 879) intercepted the freighter Labinsk. Newport News went alongside and hailed the Soviet vessel on 500KC. "How many missiles on board?" The reply was, "All on deck. See for yourself." In response to a request to uncover the missiles, sailors rolled back the canvas on one. It had the same cylindrical shape and size as Blandy observed on the Dvinogorsk; Newport News reported this one as mounted on a wheeled vehicle.[4]

Ellingham requested and received permission to make a port call, as international tensions lessened. The following day, *Boyington* tied up in San Juan, **Puerto Rico** for three days of rest and replenishment. However, plenty of work accompanied the R & R. It began with the loading of stores. By 0800, a line of three delivery trucks formed on the pier. Immediately after quarters, a work party of forty men began carrying crates of produce, bags of potatoes, boxes of canned goods, and a myriad of other non-food items aboard.

Engineers connected hoses from fuel barges, and Navy Standard Fuel Oil began flowing into the ship's bunkers, fore and aft. Water hoses and a telephone line all had to be connected, and electricians had to shift the ship's electrical load to shore power. More importantly from the crew's prospective, the mailbags had arrived. Letters were quickly sorted, and distributed.

Once the storerooms and fuel tanks reached capacity, routine maintenance began. The sides always needed paint, so the bosuns with paint rollers on six-foot poles stretched from small barges floating alongside to reach areas of the hull inaccessible at sea. Tasks that had to take place in port, such as preventative maintenance on radar, sonar, communications, navigation, and propulsion gear, received top priority.

Work progressed in spite of three absent crewmen. Seaman Apprentice Unger sat in the *Sibuyan Sea's* brig awaiting court martial. Seaman Apprentice Gibbs had departed for the U.S. Navy Hospital at

Portsmouth, Virginia, for a psychiatric evaluation of his alleged claustrophobic condition. With far less associated drama, Fireman Jason Evans visited the dentist, hoping for relief from a painful toothache.

Liberty call sounded for section two at 1100, granting twelve hours of temporary freedom for one-third of the enlisted crew. Most of those entitled to depart had done so by 1115. Section three would have to wait until 1100 on Saturday. Sunday would see the sailors of section one going ashore for their respite. Come Monday, ship and crew would be back on their way to the Walnut Line.

With the magnificent Caribe Hilton Hotel glistening in the noonday sun, a dozen of *Boyington's* sailors surveyed the beach. An impossible azure sky stretched to the horizon free of clouds, and the beach beckoned them, spread out like a smooth, white carpet.

The sailors, however, ignored those wonders of Mother Nature as they surveyed another of her gifts, a bevy of beautiful, copper-toned women lying on brightly colored beach towels or sitting under large, pastel umbrellas, sipping cool drinks.

After over two weeks at sea, living with the imminent threat of global war and death, the men were ready to let off a full head of steam and had found the starting place. Two of their number would find dinner dates. One would meet his future wife, and most would return to the ship intoxicated to some degree no later than 2300, or face disciplinary action.

Many of the older crewmen sought a less physically demanding pastime at the gambling tables or went sightseeing in the grand old city.

Married men, like chiefs Mike Stafford and Ken Ford, sought out a place where they could place long distance calls to their wives. Their search took them to the nearby U.S. Coast Guard Station. They flipped a coin to determine the first to use the only available pay telephone. Mike won.

"Hello," a soft, sweet voice answered.

"Sandy, remember me?"

"I'm not sure. Say a few more words."

"I love you and miss you."

"You sound a little like my long lost husband."

"I can only afford three minutes on this call, so say the words I want to hear."

"I love you, Mike, and I miss you. Maria misses you, and Goober has given up hope that you'll ever return. He finally left his post at the front window yesterday."

"Kiss them both for me. I miss you all so much."

"I'll kiss Maria, but Goober will have to wait for your return to get his. How much longer will you be gone?"

"I don't know, but things seem to be cooling off. You may well know more about what's happening than I do."

"The people on TV seem to think the crisis has nearly ended."

"They may be right. Our mission now is taking pictures of Soviet ships hauling their missiles back home."

"So you may be coming home soon?"

"Honey, I'm not going to promise anything, but I don't think it's going to last too much longer, maybe a couple more weeks."

"Oh, Mike, I hope so. It already seems like you've been gone for months."

"Sandy, I love you and Maria, and can't wait to get home, but we better say goodbye now or I'll have to get a bank loan to pay for the call."

"Okay, sweetheart. I love you and miss you terribly. Be safe and hurry home."

"I love you too. Goodbye."

Ken made his call while Mike stood in the shade of an ancient Banyan tree, smoking a Lucky Strike and thinking about his family and their future.

Later, the two men walked through Old San Juan, both somewhat morose after their telephone calls. They made their way to the northern tip of the harbor where they toured Castillo de San Felipe del Morro, like genuine tourists.

Afterwards, they began the trek back toward the port and their ship. The long walk had stimulated their appetites, so they found a small café and enjoyed a delicious traditional Caribbean dinner accompanied by a frosty pitcher of white sangria.

They rested their tired feet by completing the final leg of trip to the pier in a horse drawn carriage, arriving long before the curfew hour.

———————

San Juan, like any port in the world, offered plenty of trouble for those who sought it. Unfortunately, that formed the starting point for many, Boatswain's Mate First Class Foss being one individual so inclined.

After five hours of hard drinking, he staggered out of a bar with an attractive young lady who promised to take him to a cockfight, his idea of immersing himself in the local culture.

———————

Liberty ended at 2300 for *Boyington's* crew. At 2315, Ensign Frankel, the OOD, opened the liberty card box and withdrew the cards that had been deposited as the sailors in section two returned to the ship.

He handed the stack of cards to the petty officer of the watch. "Here, Griffin, run these against the list of men who drew their cards and went ashore."

Ten minutes later, Griffin looked up from the small shelf that served as a desk for the quarterdeck watch standers. "Sir, I've checked the cards twice, and BM1 Foss's isn't here. He hasn't returned."

"Damn—Jackson, run up to first division and see if anyone has seen Foss or knows where he might be," Frankel said.

Seaman Jackson, the quarterdeck messenger, returned with ominous news. Several of Foss's mates in first division had seen him ashore earlier in the afternoon, but none had seen him since then.

Mister Frankel called Lieutenant (JG) Anderson, Foss's division officer, and reported the bosun apparently now AWOL.

Mister Anderson called Lieutenant Quinn, the head of the gunnery department, and briefed him on the situation. Anderson then began a personal search of the ship, hoping to find Foss onboard.

Lieutenant Quinn sent for Chief Boatswain's Mate Jones, the leading petty officer of the gunnery department.

Jones reported to Quinn's cabin. "What's up, Sir?"

"It seems Foss may be AWOL. He hasn't turned in his liberty card, and no one in the division has seen him for six or seven hours."

"Oh, shit. That knucklehead could be anywhere. I better go ashore and start looking for him. I'd like to take Chief Stafford along to help me search, Sir."

"Okay, call back to the quarterdeck every hour or so in case he shows up here."

"Aye, aye, Sir."

Jones returned to the chiefs' quarters and found Mike, already in his rack. "Mike, you asleep?"

"Would've been, what do you want?"

"Foss is AWOL. Mister Quinn wants us to go find him."

"Us? This sounds like a first division problem to me."

"Come on, Mike, be a buddy. You know I'd help you if one of your motley gunners jumped ship."

"Yeah, okay, give me a couple of minutes to get dressed."

"A good man you are. I'll meet you on the quarterdeck."

Fifteen minutes later, Mike walked up to Jones aft of the quarterdeck, leaning on the lifeline and smoking a cigarette.

"I checked with Bosun Dalton, he and Foss are buddies and usually hang out together. He said Foss left the Chicago Bar around sixteen hundred with one of the local girls, but hasn't seen him since. He couldn't describe the woman," Jones said.

"Great, he could be laying in a back alley somewhere, or floating in the harbor by now," Mike said.

"Yeah, or maybe he's found the love of his life and can't leave her. I know that feeling all too well. Let's check with the Shore Patrol first, then if we have to, the Armed Forces Police, although I hate those bastards."

They walked to the head of the pier and hailed a cab.

Twenty-five minutes later, Jones led the way in to the headquarters of the San Juan Shore Patrol and approached the petty officer behind the counter. "We're from the *Boyington* and seem to have a bosun AWOL. Have you guys picked up a BM1, name of Foss?"

The SP checked his logbook. "Sorry, Chief, not yet. Do you have any idea what part of town he visited?"

"One of our crew saw him leave the Chicago Bar around sixteen hundred," Jones said.

"Okay, I'll radio our truck in Old San Juan and have them drive by the bar and look around."

"Where's the Armed Forces Police office?" Mike asked.

"It's farther on downtown. I'll call 'em and see if they have anything on Foss. Hang on."

Jones looked at Stafford. "If that SOB costs me a night's sleep, he'll be paying for it the rest of the cruise."

The SP returned. "AFP doesn't have anything on a BM1 Foss. I gave them his name and the ship in case they turn something up on him. When you sailing?"

"Monday morning. Thanks for your help," Jones said.

Back on the street, Mike said, "What next Sherlock?"

"I reckon we ought to go check out the Chicago Bar."

"This could turn into a real fun night," Mike said.

"Yeah, whoopee. Just what I wanted to do after a hard day's work. That stupid SOBs gonna catch hell when I get hold of him," Jones promised.

They again caught a cab and headed to Old San Juan.

CHAPTER 30

Wine, Women, and Song
San Juan, Puerto Rico

Saturday, 10 November 1962

A helicopter from the U.S.S. Newport News (CA 148) using a MK3 neutron detector over the freighter Bratsk reported active reactions, but that the results were inconclusive. The Wasp Group was directed to conduct a second flight using the detector over the Bratsk and obtain more conclusive data.[4]

Of the four submarines that secretly left for Cuba on 1 October, the U.S. Navy detected and closely tracked three: 1) B-36, commanded by Aleksei Dubivko, and identified by the U.S. Navy as C-26, 2) B-59, commanded by Valentin Savitsky, and identified as C-19, and 3) B-130, commanded by Nikolai Shumkov, and identified as C-18. Only submarine B-4, commanded by Captain Rurik Ketov, escaped intensive U.S. monitoring (although U.S. patrol aircraft may have spotted it). In a major defeat of the Soviet mission, these three submarines came to the surface under thorough U.S. Navy scrutiny.[1]

Stafford and Jones found the Chicago Bar filled with patrons, but they were all civilians. The music blared, and the humid air hung like a wet sheet, as Little Eva sang about the delights of *Loco-Motion*. Several women dressed in very tight and colorful skirts danced nearby. They immediately gained Jones's full attention until Mike spoiled the moment with a reminder of their mission.

Jones shook his head and turned to the bartender. "We lost one of our shipmates today. Big husky guy, dressed in whites. He's got Betty Grable tattooed on his left forearm and some nude red-head on the other arm." One of our friends saw him here around four o'clock this afternoon. Said the guy left with a woman."

"Sorry, *Señor*, there were many sailors in here earlier today. I do not remember one as you describe."

"Okay, thanks," Jones said.

As they stepped back outside the bar, a gray shore patrol panel truck came bouncing down the cobble stone street and stopped in front of the bar. An engineman first class, wearing an SP brassard, rounded the front of the truck. He stuck out his hand. "Name's Sellers. Gotta a call on a missing bosun . . . he one of yours, Chief?"

Jones shook his hand. "I'm Paul Jones from the *Boyington*. Yeah, probably—we're looking for a BM1, name of Foss."

"Right, that's the name we got. Did you check out the bar?"

"We talked to the bartender, but didn't learn nothing."

"Okay, stick around while we walk through the place. Maybe someone we know will be there and can help."

Sellers's partner slid out from behind the steering wheel, slipped his baton into the holder on his pistol belt, and followed the engineman into the bar.

Jones leaned against the truck and lit a cigarette.

"This could turn into a long night," Mike said.

Jones stared at the entrance door of the Chicago Bar. "Or maybe not," he replied.

Two young women stepped out of the bar. One made eye contact with Jones and smiled. "You look lonely, sailorman," she said.

"I am, but that problem will have to wait. I've lost one of my sailors."

"You should take more care where you put them. My name is Juanita, and my lovely and lonely friend is Lucía." She stepped closer. "And what is your name, sailorman?"

"I'm Paul, Juanita, and my friend here is Mike."

She extended her hand, and Jones gallantly kissed it.

"Oh, Paul, you make my heart go boom-boom. You like me, yes?" She turned around on one heel to display her tight red dress from every angle as Lucía moved in close to Mike.

"You're a real doll, Juanita, but we're on duty now. Maybe if you could help us find our man we could party later."

"You look like nice man, Paul. I help you now, and we party later." She looked at Stafford. "Mister Mike . . . you like to party with Lucía?"

Jones signaled Mike with a nod.

"Oh sure, I'm a regular party animal."

"I love to party with animal-man," Lucía said. She slipped her arm around Mike and leaned her head on his shoulder. The overpowering scent of her perfume made his eyes water.

Jones turned back toward Juanita. "Okay, as I said, one of my men is missing. He came in here this afternoon, but left around four o'clock. Were you and Lucía here then?"

"Maybe . . . we come and go."

"The guy we're looking for is real big." Jones raised his hand to indicate Foss's height. "He would have been wearing a white uniform, not khaki like ours. His name is Foss."

"*Si*, I know this Foss. He come here often. He spend lot of time and money here today. But I do not like him. We go out once last summer. He mean when he drinks too much. Always fighting, even with other sailormans."

"Did you go with him today?"

"He say he buy me lunch, but then only want to go to bed. He get mad—say I eat too much. I leave him at *el restaurante*."

"Did you see him again?"

"*Si*, he come back to bar later and want to go out with Lucía, but she say no."

"What did he do then?"

"He drink lots more *cerveza*, then leave with Bianca."

"Do you know where they went?"

The bar door opened, and the two SPs came back out.

"Evening, Ladies," Petty Officer Sellers, said.

"These women saw Foss drinking in here today. They said he left with a woman called Bianca."

Jones turned back to Juanita. "So, do you know where Foss and Bianca went?"

"He want to see bull fight, but there is no bull fight. She tell him there is cockfight. I think they go there."

"Do you know where the cockfight is?" Mike asked.

"No, sorry. I do not like that . . . cockfighting."

"Thank you for your help, Juanita. You are a nice lady," Jones said. He discreetly pressed a five-dollar bill into her hand.

Juanita kissed him on the cheek. "You go find Foss and lock him up, then come back to see me, okay, Paul?"

"Sure, Juanita. Thank you."

The women set off down the narrow, dark street. All four men closely monitored their departure until they disappeared in the shadows.

Sellers broke the silence. "Chief, your man may be in serious trouble."

"Nothing new for him," Jones said.

Sellers's wore a deadly serious expression. "I've heard that some guys who went off with that woman, Bianca, were never seen again. Rumor has it the merchant marine lost a seaman last month. He was in her company before he disappeared.

"Tell you what, we'll drop you off at your ship, and then see if we can get the local cops interested enough to check out some of the spots around here where we aren't welcome."

"I appreciate that, Sellers. Foss is one of those guys that does one hell of a job at sea, but is allergic to land or something. Seems like every time he goes ashore, he ends up in a jam," Jones said.

"Yeah, I get to meet a lot of guys like that," Sellers said.

After a short ride to the waterfront, Jones and Stafford thanked the two shore patrolmen for their help, exited the truck, and walked down the pier toward the *Boyington*.

"What do you think, Paul?" Mike asked.

"Doesn't sound good, does it?"

Chief Commissaryman Baker had OOD duty. Jones and Stafford rendered quarterdeck courtesies and boarded. The clock on the bulkhead above the little desk indicated 0150.

"Did Foss show up yet?" Jones asked.

"No, haven't seen or heard anything on him. Mister Quinn is pissed, keeps calling down here. You guys find out anything?"

"Nah. I think the lad's in a world of hurt somewhere," Jones said.

"Too bad. He's up for chief again this year, isn't he?" Baker asked.

"Yeah, unless someone kidnapped him and is holding him for ransom, he can kiss that goodbye," Stafford said.

Jones and Mike found Lieutenant Quinn sitting on the wardroom couch, staring mindlessly at the fifteen-inch, black and white television. A Spanish language drama took place on screen, but Quinn had the sound turned off.

"Any luck, Chief?"

"A little, but the news ain't good. We learned Foss spent the day drinking, and then went off into Old San Juan with a woman to see a cockfight."

"Great, most of that part of town is off-limits, isn't it?"

"Yes, Sir. There's some real bad neighborhoods up there. The SPs ain't allowed to go in unless accompanied by the local cops."

"Great—so what do we do now?"

"We talked with the SP night patrol team. They're going to report the situation to the locals and see if they'll check out some of the areas where illegal activities occur. The AFP is on the lookout for Foss too."

"Okay, will the SPs call us with an update at some point?"

"Yes, Sir. If we haven't heard anything by morning, I'll go back over after quarters and see what info I can scare up."

"Okay, Chief, thanks. I guess that's all we can do tonight. See me first thing in the morning," Quinn said.

CHAPTER 31

Luna Street, Old San Juan
San Juan, Puerto Rico

0830, Saturday, 10 November 1962

There was a great deal of pressure on the Navy from the White House to complete the missile count. The President wanted to announce to the nation that removal of the missiles was complete and the operation concluded. However, one ship, the Kurchatov—eluded surveillance.[4]

D ivision officers announced Foss's disappearance to the crew at quarters with a harsh admonishment to stay out of all off-limits establishments and the restricted areas of the city. The XO posted a map listing the forbidden places and areas on the bulletin board, next to the Watch, Quarters, and Station Bill. The captain put out the word that any crewmember found in one of the off-limits places or areas would automatically receive a captain's mast, and the punishment would be harsh.

Quarters ended, and the workday commenced. Mister Quinn and Chief Jones received a summons to meet with the XO in the chart room.

"What's the latest on Foss?" Kaestner asked. His expression and tone of voice signaled more than a little dissatisfaction with the situation.

"Sir, we haven't heard anything new this morning. Chief Jones is going over to Shore Patrol Headquarters to see what he can find out," Quinn said.

"Okay, but I want you to go, too. We don't have much time, considering the size of this city. Call me if you get anything less than complete cooperation. I want answers today. Understand?"

"Aye, aye, Sir," Quinn said.

When they reached the main deck, Quinn turned toward Jones. "You ready to go now?"

"Yes, Sir."

"Okay, let's do it."

Half an hour later, they entered Shore Patrol headquarters. "We're from the *Boyington*," Quinn said. "Do you have any information on our missing man, BM1 Foss?"

"One moment, Sir. Let me get the watch officer," the desk petty officer said.

He returned minutes later, following an officer.

"Good morning, I'm Lieutenant Banyan. How can I help?"

"Patrick Quinn. Glad to meet you. This is Chief Boatswain's Mate Jones. We're from the *Boyington* and have an AWOL case pending, BM1 Foss."

"Right. I know about him. We got the report sometime early this morning."

"Yes, Sir," Jones said. "I made that report here in the office and met with EN1 Sellers later at the Chicago Bar in Old San Juan."

"The bottom line is we don't know any more now than we did last night. Sellers met with officers from the San Juan Police Department after talking with you and convinced them to check out the known trouble spots. They made their rounds, but didn't turn up any sailors," Banyan said.

"Did you learn anything more about the woman, Bianca, he supposedly went off with?" Jones said.

"Just a minute, let me get the report." Banyan walked over to a desk and rifled through a short stack of papers. "Here it is . . . no, the cops know who she is, but they haven't found her."

"We sail Monday morning so we've got to find this guy ASAP," Quinn said.

"I understand, Lieutenant. We're looking, AFP is looking, the locals have his description, and they're looking, too. Maybe he doesn't want us to find him. Maybe he's in love. There are a multitude of possibilities with every AWOL case."

"Is there anything we can do to help? I could get a dozen Shore Patrol volunteers, maybe more, from the ship to assist you," Quinn said.

"I appreciate the offer, Lieutenant Quinn, but if he has gone into the old city we need the locals, who know their way around, to do the searching. I'll pass your offer along to the commander. We have your quarterdeck telephone number and will call if anything develops."

"Okay, thanks for your help," Quinn said. The two left the SP office.

"Any ideas, Chief?"

"I'd like to go over by the Chicago Bar and see if anyone is up and about yet."

"Sounds good to me. I don't want to face the XO without something more than we have so far," Quinn said.

Jones hailed a cab.

The front door of the Chicago Bar stood open, but the lights were low, and no music disturbed the denizens who required several shots of rum to lubricate the start of their day.

Jones got the bartender's attention and ordered two coffees.

When the bartender returned, he said, "Hope this is okay. Not many of our customers ask for coffee."

Jones took a sip. "It's fine. Maybe you can help us. We're looking for a girl, name of Bianca."

"Too early for her. Come back tonight, *Señor.*"

"Any idea where she is now. Do you know where she lives?"

"No."

Quinn laid a ten-dollar bill on the bar. "Think real hard. She left here yesterday afternoon with one of our sailors."

The bartender waved his hand across the bar, and the sawbuck magically disappeared. "You may want to take a walk down Calle Luna," the bartender said.

The men downed their coffee and turned to depart.

"Señors, su café. Fifty cents, *por favor."*

"Fifty cents. Outrageous," Jones said. He flipped a half dollar to the bartender and stormed out.

"Cheap bastard couldn't have taken the coffee money outta the ten spot you gave him," Jones said. "Quarter a cup, and it wasn't even fresh. I can't believe it."

The two sailors violated the navy's off-limits order regarding Luna Street and found another dark, musty bar open for business.

"We're looking for a woman," Quinn said to the bartender.

"It is too early, *Señor.* Come back tonight, and the place be full of the most beautiful women in all of Puerto Rico, maybe the whole world."

"I mean we're trying to locate a particular woman. Her name is Bianca, and the bartender at the Chicago Bar thinks she lives around here. Do you know a woman by that name?"

"Bianca, Bianca . . . no, I no remember anyone by that name."

Quinn pulled out another ten-dollar bill and laid it on the bar.

"You know, there is a *señorita* . . . yes-yes, now I recall. Turn right and go about half way down the block on this side of the street. Enter the yellow door, go up the stairs, and ask for her."

"Thank you," Quinn said.

————

Lieutenant Quinn turned to Jones as they exited the bar. "Payday is five days away, and I'm now flat broke, so this better be good."

They found the yellow door without any difficulty and pushed it open. It revealed a dark stairway, littered with beer cans, bottles, and cigarette butts. The stairs squeaked ominously as they made their way up, Quinn following Jones. At the top, the stairs opened onto a long, narrow, hallway vacant except for scattered litter. Stagnate air discouraged deep breathing. A low wattage light bulb dangled from the ceiling half way down the hall. No doors on either side were open. The men stared at each other.

Jones summoned the voice he had used to shout orders over the roaring sea for the past twenty-five years. "Bianca, you here?"

Silence greeted his hail.

He shouted again, "Bianca, *venga aqui.*"

Minutes passed, then a door squeaked open, and a gorgeous woman with a riotous mane of glistening black hair appeared. Barefoot, in a thin blouse and cut-offs, she appeared to have just awakened.

"I'm impressed," Quinn said.

"She is beautiful."

"No, I mean that you speak Spanish."

"Oh, thanks, Sir, but I only know enough to get in trouble."

They walked toward the woman. "¿Bianca, *habla usted inglés?*" Jones asked.

"Un poco inglés."

"She speaks a little English," Jones translated.

"Do you know a man named Foss?" Quinn asked.

"No intiendo."

"She doesn't understand. Let me try, Sir. ¿Bianca, *conocere Foss?*"

"Sí."

"Dónde está Foss?"

"Se fue de aquí anoche," Bianca said.

"She knows him and said he left here last night."

"Ask her where he went," Quinn said.

Jones asked in Spanish, and then translated her reply. "She said she doesn't know where the bastard went, and if she ever sees him again she is going to kill him."

Bianca pulled open her blouse, exposing her ample, but badly bruised breasts. "I see Foss, I kill heem." To emphasize her point, she drew a small caliber, chrome plated handgun from a hip pocket and fired two rounds into the ceiling. Plaster rained down on the two men.

"Sir, I don't think she has anything else to tell us regarding his whereabouts, and it might be best to shove off now. She seems upset," Jones said.

"Good suggestion. Follow me," Quinn said.

"Muchas gracias, Bianca. Adiós," Jones said. He broke into a fast walk toward the stairs, trying to catch up with Lieutenant Quinn.

When they reached the street, Jones hailed a cab.

"When we get back to the ship, I'll call that SP lieutenant, Banyan, and tell him where Bianca lives. Maybe the local cops can learn something more from her. At least we know Foss was still alive as recently as last night or early this morning when he left her place," Quinn said.

"Yes, Sir. Of course, someone could've put a shiv between his ribs before he reached the end of Calle Luna."

"There's that, too," Quinn said.

Jones sat down with Mike and Ken in the chiefs' mess and lit a Camel.

"Any luck this morning?" Mike asked.

"A little. We found Bianca, Foss's Friday night date. Apparently, there ain't any wedding bells in their future. She plans to kill him if she sees him again."

"What a shame. Another budding romance gone bad," Ford said.

"She demonstrated her intentions by firing her pistol into the ceiling of the apartment."

306

"Whoa," Mike said. "She really picked up on his faults right away."

"Yeah, he got a little rough with her. She showed us her bruises."

"Too bad. The man definitely has a problem controlling his anger," Ford said.

"The charges are racking up on the lad. So far, we got him on AWOL and violation of an off-limits order. If the cops find him before Bianca does, he may be looking at assault and battery, too," Jones said.

"Yeah, but he better hope the cops find him before she does. I guess his chances of making chief are gone now," Ford said.

"He'll be lucky to keep two of his three chevrons," Jones added.

"Speaking of disciplinary action," Mike said. "I heard Unger had his court martial and got busted to E-1 with three years hard labor, forfeiture of pay, and a dishonorable discharge when he gets out of the brig."

"Hell of a way to start adult life. I hope he survives and comes out a better man," Ford said.

"If he'd sabotaged something other than the scullery, like maybe one of the guns, he could've got life in Leavenworth, and if the war had started, he'd be looking at a death sentence," Jones said.

"Three years hard labor won't be fun. Those marine brig guards have some definite ideas about what that sentence means. It will make him or break him . . . no middle ground," Ford said.

"Yeah, too bad, but we gave him a chance," Jones said.

"Getting back to Foss, what's next, Paul?" Mike asked.

"Mister Quinn offered the SPs a dozen petty officers to help search for him, but they said that if he's in Old Town, it's up to the San Juan police to get him. The Shore Patrol isn't welcome in the neighborhood they think he went into. It's out of our hands now," Jones said.

CHAPTER 32

Hell Hath no Fury . . .
San Juan, Puerto Rico

Sunday, 11 November 1962

The low-level Cuba reconnaissance flights for the day returned without incident. On previous and succeeding days, Navy and Air Force aircraft alternately flew these sorties. Additionally, the U.S. continued high-altitude U-2 photographic missions. Although scheduled daily, frequent cancellations, or a reduction of the number of sorties, of these missions occurred.[4]

The U.S.S. Blandy (DD 943) intercepted the Kurchatov...bringing the total of missiles that were visually sighted and photographed to forty-two.[4]

A re-inspection of Bratsk and Polzunov with the Naval Research Laboratory neutron-sensing device produced negative results, and the remaining re-inspection schedule was canceled.[4]

Mike's internal alarm clock sounded. He woke quickly and rolled out of his rack onto the deck to begin his morning ritual of thirty push-ups. After a cold shower and a shave, he dressed in work khakis and headed to the chiefs' mess for a hot breakfast.

Bosun Paul Jones had arrived earlier and hoisted the last bite of chipped beef on toast with baked beans.

"What's up, Paul?"

"My blood pressure."

"Yeah? Did one of your ex-wives or former girlfriends show up with a summons?"

"Nothing that simple. The SPs brought John Dalton back this morning at 0200. He got tanked up and caused a disturbance up on Luna Street last night. When the fight started, a bartender called the cops. They took him downtown and locked him up. The bastards know our liberty ends at 2300, so they held him until 0100 just to make him AWOL, and then called the shore patrol to come get him.

"With Foss gone, Dalton's now the number-two man in the division. Drunk and on report—what the hell did I do to deserve a crew like these knuckle-heads?" Jones said.

"Who knows? Might be the phase of the moon of something," Mike suggested.

"Yeah, well the doc is trying to bring him around. Had him puffing oxygen and gave him some kinda shot. Hopefully he'll be functional by Monday when we shove off. I'm so damn mad at the stupid SOB, I may take him down in the anchor chain locker and beat the shit outta him."

"He's not worth losing a stripe over, Paul. Any overnight news on Foss?" Mike asked.

"Nah, not a word. I'm worried about the idiot. He's been in plenty of scrapes over the ten years I've known him, but this time everything feels different somehow."

"He's still got almost twenty-four hours to come to his senses. I bet he shows up as they're pulling the brow away," Stafford said.

"Yeah, this ship's his only home, and I think the crew's his only family."

Jones looked up from his now empty mess tray. "Hey, Charlie, you got any more of those beans?"

"Chief, if I give you any more, somebody else ain't gonna his full share," the mess cook said.

"You'd be doing 'somebody' a favor, Charlie, but for the benefit of the guys that have to work around the bosun all day, cut him off," Mike said.

The passageway door opened, and the quarterdeck messenger entered. "Chief Jones, the OOD wants to see you right now. Some woman is trying to get hold of you."

"I knew it. How many ex-wives do you have on this island?" Mike asked. He spoke to Jones's back—the bosun already flying out of the compartment.

Jones arrived on the quarterdeck breathing hard.

"There you are," the OOD said.

"Yes, Sir. Who's looking for me?"

"Some woman showed up at the Shore Patrol office downtown asking for you. The only name they gave me was 'Juanita'. You know who she is?"

"Yes, Sir. She might know something about Foss. Any message?"

"Only that she wants to see you."

"Is she there now?"

"I think so. Let me call them back."

Jones stepped off the quarterdeck and lit a cigarette.

"Chief, she's still there. You want to talk to her or what?" the OOD called out.

"Tell them I'm on my way, and have her wait right there."

Jones rushed back to the chiefs' quarters to change out of his work khakis. He stopped by the gunnery office to tell Mister Quinn about the call, and then double-timed down to pier to find a taxi.

At the Shore Patrol Office, Juanita paced the floor in front of the counter, wearing a low cut, tight, coral print dress. Her long black hair swished to the opposite shoulder each time she changed direction. A trail of cigarette smoke followed her. The duty petty officer had his eyes locked on her, obviously enjoying the visual treat, unusual for the morning shift.

When Juanita saw Jones enter, she ran to him and took his hand. "Paul, we talk outside." They left the building and walked down the sidewalk.

"I hear some things about Foss last night," she said. She paused and took a deep breath. "Me and Lucía go to a bar on Calle Sol last night and see Bianca there. She sits with some men I know are dangerous . . . bad, bad men."

"Go on, Juanita. What'd you hear?"

"Foss may be bad hurt or dead. They tell Bianca, Foss he lose lots of monies at the cockfight and not pay them. That is not a good thing when dealing with these men, you know."

"Yes, yes, go on. What else did they say?"

"They say, Foss no pay in cash, he pay in blood."

"Did they say where the cockfight took place?"

"No, but I know there are always fights in the old city. But these men are so bad, the *policía* don't go there."

"Do you think Bianca knows where Foss is?"

"Bianca, she hate Foss, want him dead. I think she tell Foss to bet on wrong cock, make him lose monies."

"Okay, did you hear anything else?"

"No, that is what I hear. I no like Foss or Bianca, but I like you and know it important you find Foss."

"I like you too, Juanita. But I gotta a big problem if I can't find Foss today. I better go see Bianca."

Juanita grabbed Jones's sleeve and held tightly. "No, no, Paul, that bad idea. Very bad idea. She have men hurt you."

"Yeah, you might be right. I'll see if the Shore Patrol or the police can help."

"Paul, you no say my name to *policía*, please."

"No, Juanita, you've been great. I won't tell anyone your name."

"Okay, you come see me again tonight."

"I'll try. Right now, I gotta find Foss. Thanks for what you did, telling me, and everything. Where you gonna be tonight?"

"Bar Caribe, on Calle San Francisco. You know it."

"I'll find it."

She stood on her toes and kissed his cheek. Paul gave her a hug and turned to leave.

"Bring your friend, Mike. My girlfriend Lucía, she like him."

"I'll try, but don't count on it," Paul said. He hailed a taxi and rode back to the ship, trying to decide on a course of action.

In the gunnery office, Jones told Lieutenant Quinn what he had learned.

"We need to go see the XO. We're running out of time," Quinn said. He turned and made several calls, trying to locate Commander Kaestner.

"He's up on the bridge. Let's go," Quinn said.

When they walked into the pilothouse, Kaestner looked up from the log book on the quartermaster's table, and he wasn't smiling. "Hope you have some good news for me, Mister Quinn."

"Mixed bag, Sir. Bosun Jones has learned Foss got into debt with some local hoodlums and couldn't pay. They may have collected in blood."

"How'd you learn that, Chief?" Kaestner said.

"Well, Sir, there's this woman. . . ."

"Never mind, Chief. What can we do to find Foss?" Kaestner asked.

"Short of calling in the Marines, I don't think we can do anything. The local police need to get off their ass and sweep through old town. Dead or alive, I think that's where he is," Jones said.

"Okay, let me see if the ol' man's free."

Ten minutes later, Kaestner, Quinn, and Jones faced Captain Ellingham in his office. "So how solid is this information?" the skipper asked.

"As good as we're ever gonna get, Sir," the XO said.

Mister Quinn spoke, "Sir, yesterday, Chief Jones and I found the woman Foss went out with the night he disappeared. Her name is Bianca. There is no doubt she wanted to see Foss harmed, and not without reason, but that's another story. I believe she has the means to make that happen."

"Captain, this Bianca may have given Foss some false betting information on a cockfight to get him in trouble with the local mafia," Jones said. "When he couldn't pay up, they most likely did something to him. The trouble is we know he went into the restricted area of old town. It's restricted because it's so dangerous the cops are afraid to go in there, and the shore patrol isn't allowed to go there unless accompanied by the local cops."

Lieutenant Commander Kaestner summed things up. "Sir, this is beyond us. I've talked to the Shore Patrol commander, and like the chief said, their standing orders forbid them from entering the area where Foss disappeared without police protection. If anything further is going to happen, we need to bump this up and over into the civilian chain of command. Maybe the mayor or governor needs to be involved. It may take the feds to sort it all out."

"Okay, men. The ball's in my court now. Let me see what I can do, but it sounds like we've lost Foss. We're sailing tomorrow at 0800 with or without him," Ellingham said.

CHAPTER 33

Saving the LouisaMaría II
San Juan, Puerto Rico

0600, Monday, 12 November 1962

At a special White House Executive Committee, Mr. John McCloy said the Soviet negotiators were pushing hard for a lifting of the quarantine and a formal pledge that the U.S. would not invade Cuba.[4]

Before the meeting adjourned, the Executive Committee adopted Secretary of State Rusk's position that when the IL-28 bombers were on the way out of Cuba, the negotiators would discuss the possibility of lifting the quarantine, and, when an acceptable arrangement was reached for inspecting ships carrying materials to Cuba, the U.S. would consider a guarantee against invasion.[4]

The bosun's pipe shattered the tranquility of the berthing compartments. "Reveille, reveille, all hands heave to, and trice up, the smoking lamp is lighted in all authorized spaces. Sweepers, start your brooms. . . ." The bosun droned on with his monotone routine announcements. During the next two hours, over three-hundred sailors would fully prepare themselves and the ship for departure. Bosun Foss, however, wouldn't grace their ranks.

The number one hawser splashed into the harbor at 0800, and *Boyington* backed out of her dock. Minutes later, she sailed past the redoubt of Morro Castle and cut into the waves of the Atlantic, heading north to rejoin the ASW Task Group.

Morale of the crew had improved. Everyone had the opportunity to go ashore, and the vast majority had done so. Now, the time had arrived to go back to work.

Finally, it seemed, the missile crisis had begun winding down. Significant numbers of U.S. Navy ships and planes were returning to their homeports and air stations. Soviet ships continued departing from Cuban ports. As they left, destroyers or cruisers intercepted them on the high sea and photographed their deadly cargo of ballistic missiles.

Shortly after the bosun passed the word to secure the Special Sea and Anchor Detail, and the normal steering watch had taken up their positions, Lieutenant Commander Kaestner entered the pilothouse and approached the captain. "Sir, have you heard anything back on the Foss situation?"

The captain motioned for Kaestner to follow him. The two men walked out on the open bridge where they could talk privately.

"Yes, after our talk yesterday morning, I called the commander at Roosevelt Roads Naval Air Station. He's the senior naval officer on the island. A couple of hours later, he advised that he had contacted the Mayor's office but didn't get much help, so he turned it over to the FBI. They took the matter quite seriously. We did our part, now it's wait-and-see time," Ellingham said.

"Good. I bet they'll shake up the local cops."

"No doubt. Well, we have a beautiful, sunny day to photograph a Soviet ship and their missiles. I hope we can find one."

"It may not be a long wait, Sir. CIC is monitoring some radio chatter about a Soviet ship in the Caicos Passage now."

"Maybe we'll get lucky. Let's bear a little more to the west and see if we can improve our odds."

"Aye, aye, Sir. I'll see what CIC has now and get us a new course," Kaestner said. "One more thing, Sir, we need to schedule a captain's mast for bosun Dalton on his AWOL and disturbing the peace charges."

"Right, let's do it tomorrow, before we get busy again," Ellingham said.

Chiefs Stafford and Jones sat around a table in the chiefs' mess after their noon meal.

"Any word on Foss yet?" Mike asked.

"Yeah, the XO told me the navy turned it over to the FBI," Jones said.

319

"Hey, that's serious business. Kinda says the locals couldn't or wouldn't handle it."

"That's because they couldn't or wouldn't. Serves the bastards right. After listening to some stories the Shore Patrol told, and a few things Juanita said, I think some of 'em are dirty. You can't make me believe every cop in San Juan is afraid of the scum that run the cockfights and all the other crap that goes on around that town," Jones said.

Mike stood to refill his coffee mug. "I don't doubt you're right, Paul. It usually works out where someone in authority is getting rich off of all the crime."

"Thing is, if two or three hoods tried to jump Foss, they'd get an ass kicking, unless they shot or stabbed him. He is the toughest, meanest sonabitch I've ever known in my life. He lives to fight—should've gone into the ring professionally. Course, professional boxers have to follow rules, and Foss ain't too keen on rules when he's fighting or drinking."

"I'd guess his navy career is over, and his retirement's gone. Getting the FBI on your trail for being AWOL and now missing movement won't go over real well with the honchos. Hell of a thing after eighteen years' service."

"You're right about that, Mike. If he comes back, or they catch him, he's looking at brig time where he'll no doubt get into more trouble."

Chief Ken Ford entered the compartment with his big *Blandy* mug and headed for the coffee urn. "What's up, guys?"

"Jones just told me the FBI is hunting for Foss," Mike said.

"Whoa. Who smacked that bee hive?"

"Captain Ellingham lit a fire under someone's ass," Jones said.

"Well, I hope they find him," Ford said.

"What's happening with Dalton, Paul?" Mike asked.

"He's gotta AWOL charge against him, and a captain's mast in the near future. The skipper is so pissed over the Foss thing I think he'll throw the book at Dalton."

"That'll put you in a bind, won't it?"

"Sure as God made seaweed, it will," Jones said.

"Okay, time for me to get busy and earn my pay." Mike stood, stretched, and left.

───────

At 1600, *Boyington's* radio tuned to the international distress frequency squawked an SOS call from a Dominican costal freighter, reporting engine failure, and taking on water. The coordinates provided indicated it could be nearly a two-hour cruise to reach the stricken vessel.

Captain Ellingham ordered the OOD to proceed at flank speed. He picked up the 1-MC microphone. "Attention all hands, this is the captain speaking. We are responding to an SOS call and should reach the troubled vessel within a couple of hours. When we get within radar range, I'll call for rescue teams, so be ready to respond. That is all."

Captain Ellingham stepped into the dimly lit CIC. "Is there anything new on the distress channel?"

"No, Sir," Mister White, the CIC watch officer, said. "Last thing we heard, they still couldn't get their engine started. Their generator is dead, of course, and their emergency radio battery is dying so we may lose communications with them soon."

"Okay, let me know the minute you hear anything from them. Let the commodore know where we're going."

Ellingham returned to the bridge and called the engineering office. "Mister Caruthers, this ship we're on the way to assist has no power and is in danger of sinking. Get a party of enginemen and machinists ready to board her. They'll need a couple of handy billies too. The boat's taking on water."

"Yes, Sir. Any idea if they have hoses for our pumps?"

"No, and we're losing radio contact with them so I can't ask. Take a set of hoses for each pump, and you won't have to worry about connection problems. Get your party organized and up on the 0-1 level by 1730."

"Aye, aye, Sir."

CIC reported radar contact, but no radio response at 1745.

Boyington plowed on through the gently rolling sea at flank speed of over thirty knots, heading north by northwest. The bosuns completed preparations to launch the motor whaleboat as the ship's medic, Chief Hospital Corpsman Robert Shay, and his striker checked their medical bag and supplies maintained in the boat. Engineers were assembling their tools and equipment on the torpedo deck.

At 1815, the 0-3 lookout reported a visual sighting.

"Steer, three-three-zero; turns for one-five knots," the OOD ordered. The ship slowed.

Minutes later the destroyer circled around and drifted to a stop next to the stricken vessel. The stern plate identified her as the *LouisaMaría II* out of San Pedro de Macoris, Dominican Republic.

"Bosun, get the megaphone and hail her," Ellingham ordered.

Dalton walked out on the open bridge and looked down at the sixty-five foot coastal freighter. Four Caribbean sailors looked up hopefully. He lifted the megaphone, "Ahoy the LouisaMaria. Do you speak English?"

"Yes, mon, some English. *Habla usted español?*"

"Tell them, *'Poco español,'* Mister Quinn said.

Ellingham looked at Quinn. "You speak Spanish?"

Quinn smiled, *"Poco.* Bosun Jones has been teaching me."

"Okay, Dalton, give the megaphone to Mister Quinn. Mister Quinn, tell them we're going to send a boat over with some sailors to help them," Ellingham said.

Quinn tried, but it took several exchanges until the Dominicans understood his Spanglish.

"Is the whaleboat ready?" Ellingham asked.

"Yes, Sir. It's all loaded and ready to go," the XO said.

"Away the whaleboat," Ellingham ordered.

On the 0-1 level, Bosun Jones repeated the captain's order. A deck hand started the winch and the steel cables slowly unwound, lowering the boat to the sea.

When the boat splashed into the water, a seaman released the boat falls, and Coxswain Garcia turned the boat toward the small freighter.

On the freighter, sailors lowered a five-step Jacob's ladder over the side. Chief Jones and Machinist's Mate Bill Bailey scrambled up to the main deck.

"Where you taking on water?" Jones asked in Spanish.

One of the Dominicans took him aft and raised a hatch. Seawater stood two-feet deep in the engine room.

"Get the handy billies over here on the double," Jones shouted.

Engineman Second Class Howard Magee heaved the pumps up from the whaleboat, and Bailey carried them, one at a time on the rolling deck, to the after hatch.

Magee threw the hoses up onto the ship's narrow deck and then climbed aboard.

Ten minutes later, both pumps were humming, and water gushed over the side from the exhaust hoses. The engineers sat on the fantail smoking as they waited for the pumps to finish their job.

Chief Jones and Electronics Technician Third Class Fred Fenster followed the master to the pilothouse to check on the vessel's radiotelephone. Since the ship's generator wasn't working, they had powered the radio with a car battery, borrowed from the 1953 Chevrolet, tied down on the main deck, forward of the bridge. That battery had since died.

"The only hope is to get the generator running," Fenster said. "We don't have any batteries on the *Boyington* that can provide enough current for this old radio."

"What about the boat batteries?" Jones asked.

"Boat batteries?"

"Yeah, the whaleboat and the gig both have electric starters. They use six-volt storage batteries like this one," Jones said.

"Oh, yeah. The electricians maintain the boat batteries. The only ones I take care of are dry-cells for the portable radios," Fenster said.

"Good thing they sent a bosun along to keep you geniuses out of trouble."

"Right, Chief. Next time the radar goes out, I'll call a bosun."

"Don't push your luck, kid," Jones said. You gotta get back to the ship, and a bosun is in charge of the whaleboat."

Fenster offered a weak smile.

Once the pumps cleared the engine room, Bailey and Magee followed the Dominican engineer down into the dark, filthy space. Jones stayed on deck at the hatch to avoid the grease, oil, and dirty water and to translate as needed.

Using battle lanterns they brought along, the two Americans began inspecting the equipment. Bailey noticed the water level rising in the bilge and pointed.

After translation, they learned the ship always leaked, but a pump usually kept water to a minimum. Today, the pump broke down, the engine room flooded, and they lost all power.

"Oh, my," Magee groaned. "Where do we start?"

"The pump, its priority number one, but let's get one of the handy billies restarted first." Bailey said.

Magee shouted up to Chief Jones to restart a handy billy. Once it began drawing water from the bilge, they removed the ship's pump and took it up on deck to begin repairs.

"I can handle this, why don't you go below and see what it's gonna take get the engine running," Bailey said.

"Okay. Wish I'd brought a clothespin," Magee said.

"A what?" Bailey said.

"A clothespin, you know, to pinch off my nose so I don't have to smell that stinking engine room."

"Sorry, man. Let's hurry up and fix this thing and get the hell outta here," Bailey said.

"Right." Magee climbed back down into the engine room and joined the Dominican wiping off the engine with oily rags.

The sun sank into the sea, and *Boyington's* signalmen tried to illuminate the *LouisaMaría II* with their big signal lamps. The whaleboat made several trips between the two ships delivering tools, more battle lantern batteries, sandwiches, and coffee.

Chief Machinist Mate Chantre rode over on the second trip to oversee engine repairs. The condition of the ship and its engine stunned him.

After a frustrating half-hour repairing the pump on the rolling deck, with a lantern as his primary light source, Bailey had it back together and ready to install. He lowered it down the into the engine room.

"Fixed already?" Magee asked.

"I hope. A bunch of crud had the impeller jammed. You would think they would have a filter on the intake side, but no."

"Give us a hand here, Bailey. We're trying to replace the fuel injector," Chantre said.

An hour later, the men stood back and crossed their fingers. The Dominican engineer pushed the start button. The engine coughed and sputtered several times, then came to life.

Cheers echoed all over the *LouisaMaría II* and across the water on the *Boyington*.

Three tired, oil soaked American sailors crawled out of the engine room hatch.

LouisaMaría's bare-footed master danced for joy on the forecastle, while a Rastafarian crewman pounded out a rhythm on an overturned bucket. The odor of marijuana floated over the rusty freighter.

"Grab your gear men, and let's make like gators and drag ass outta here," Chief Chantre said.

As the men lowered their tools and pumps into the whaleboat, the master danced aft to thank them for saving his ship.

He offered a bottle of rum to show his gratitude, but Chief Jones graciously declined, citing navy policy.

The master thought prohibiting rum a strange policy, so he pulled a bag of pot from the pocket of his cut-off jeans and offered it.

Jones again extended his regrets. He shook hands with the master and engineer and bid them fair winds and following seas.

The Rastaman resumed his drumming as the whaleboat pulled away.

———

Coxswain Garcia spun the whaleboat's wheel and headed back to the *Boyington,* where hot showers and clean racks awaited a tired repair crew.

The OOD set a course to rendezvous with the task group and ordered turns for twenty knots.

The *LouisaMaría II* sailed off into the dark of night, leaving a tantalizing aroma and the fading sound of Rasta music floating on the gentle breeze.

CHAPTER 34

Dalton

Three-Hundred and Fifty Miles Northeast of Mona Passage

Tuesday, 13 November 1962

The Walnut Line was still intact, but the Navy was only pursuing trailing actions. Admiral Anderson, the Chief of Naval Operations, felt the U.S. should advise the Soviets that we still intended to enforce the quarantine by search and force when necessary, until they honored the agreement to remove their strategic bombers from Cuba.[4]

The President and Secretary of Defense were concerned about the ability of the Navy to use force without sinking a Soviet ship or inflicting casualties and were reluctant to grant permission for the use of force.[4]

Admiral Anderson informed the SECDEF of the procedures the Navy would follow should it be necessary to use force. If a ship failed to stop after hailing and it became necessary to use force, the interdicting ship would initiate an escalating sequence of actions. The first warning would be firing a powder charge with no projectile in the breach. The next warning, a shot fired of across the bow of the reluctant ship. The final step would be firing a short range, three or five-inch, non-explosive shell to destroy the ship's rudder and propeller. The admiral considered it highly unlikely that any merchant captain would attempt to proceed after this sequence.[4]

By mid-morning Tuesday, *Boyington* had rejoined the task group and resumed quarantine patrol activities. Destroyers were trailing and photographing Cuba bound vessels, but the president had ordered a suspension of all searches. There had not been any recent submarine contacts. Photographing the last of the departing Soviet Bloc freighters and their cargos of ballistic missiles seemed to be the final mission.

At 1300, Commander Ellingham convened a Captain's Mast for Bosun Dalton on the mess deck. All off-watch crewmen were required to attend.

Lieutenant Commander Kaestner and Assistant Master at Arms, Gunner's Mate First Class Zarna, stood side-by-side near the forward bulkhead, facing the ship's company.

Zarna called out, "Attention on deck."

Captain Ellingham entered and stood in front of the XO and Zarna, facing the crew.

Dalton, in dress whites, stepped forward, came to the position of attention, and faced the captain. Lieutenant Junior Grade Anderson, his division officer, and Chief Boatswain's Mate Jones, his division petty officer, fell-in behind Dalton and stood at attention.

The captain began, "Boatswain's Mate Second Class John H. Dalton, serial number 443 21 96, U.S. Navy, you are officially charged with two violations of the Uniform Code of Military Justice: First, Section 886, Article 86: Absence without Leave. On or about 10 November 1962, you failed to return to your duty station, the U.S.S. *Boyington*, DD 953, by 2300 local, the prescribed expiration of liberty. Second, Section 934, Article 134: Disorderly conduct, drunkenness. On or about 10 November 1962, you engaged in drunken, disorderly conduct, namely, brawling in the public street. This behavior resulted in your arrest and incarceration by the San Juan, Puerto Rico Police Department.

"Do you understand these charges?" Ellingham asked.

"Yes, Sir," Dalton mumbled.

"Do you wish to appeal these charges?"

"No, Sir."

"Boatswain's Mate Second Class John H. Dalton, I sentence you to thirty-day's restriction without suspension from duty; detention of one-half month's pay for one month; and, reduction to pay grade to E-4, Boatswain's Mate Third Class.

"You are remanded into the custody of the master-at-arms and forbidden to leave this vessel prior to 2400 Wednesday, 12 December

1962. You will abide by all restrictions imposed on you by the MAA, including the requirement to muster, with the prisoners-at-large and restricted members. Do you understand my orders?"

"Aye, aye, Sir."

"Master-at-arms, take charge."

GM1 Zarna stepped up to Dalton's side and turned to face the captain. "Left face."

Both men pivoted to the left. "Forward march." The two passed in front of the ship's company and marched to the MAA office at the rear of the mess deck.

The compartment remained silent.

"Ship's Company . . . dismissed," Captain Ellingham's voice boomed.

At 1830, Captain Ellingham sat in his cabin looking down at a carefully prepared and arranged dinner plate. He sliced off a bite of baked ham. As he raised it to his mouth, the sound powered telephone squawked.

"Sir, it's the OOD. The commodore has ordered us to intercept and photograph the Soviet cargo ship *Volgoles*. She's about fifty miles northwest of our present position, reportedly heading north at eighteen knots."

"Sounds like an all night chase. What's our fuel situation?"

"Eighty percent at last sounding, Sir."

"Okay, stay at twenty knots. We'll get the pictures in the morning. Give the photographer a heads-up."

"Aye, aye, Sir. Enjoy your supper."

"I will, thank you," Ellingham said.

In the chiefs' mess, Stafford and Jones were also about to eat. "That looked like quite a muddle you got involved with last night," Mike said.

"Yeah, some of these islanders are a little crazy. I can't believe what they'll put to sea in. I think the only way they can live so close to death is to stay stoned or drunk, or both, all the time," Jones said.

"Where were they going?"

"The master told me they had picked up that car in Nassau and were taking it to Antigua for someone. The forward hold looked full too, but I don't know what kind of cargo they were carrying—thought it best not to ask."

"I wonder what would have happened to them if we hadn't come along when we did."

"They were only a few hours away from sinking. The stern had already dropped below the water line due to the flooded engine room."

"No wonder the master danced after you guys bailed his ass out."

"What a character. Happy as could be. What you never had you can't miss, and the most he has ever had is that fifty year old scow. The crewmen have far less, but they're happy too. Maybe I'll come down here after I retire and live that life. I wonder if Juanita would live with me on a tramp freighter."

"What about Roxie back in Newport?"

"Oh yeah, or her. Do you think she would go for a life at sea?"

"Doubt it, Paul. They're both city girls. They like the glamour of the night lights."

"Hey, what about Bianca, that me and Mister Quinn found when we went looking for Foss. There's a real tigress I'd like to tame."

"From everything I heard about her, you'd be outta your league with that one."

"Yeah, you're probably right, Mike. Guess I'll have to keep looking."

"Good plan."

———

At sunrise the following morning, the freighter *Volgoles* cruised within visual range of *Boyington*. Lieutenant Riley called the skipper, "Captain, it's the OOD. We're a mile astern of the Russian and ready to take pictures."

"Okay, you know the drill. I'll be up in a few minutes," Ellingham said.

Riley conned the destroyer alongside the Soviet ship's starboard side, and the signalmen flashed the requisite signal requesting a visual inspection of the missiles.

———

Photographer's Mate Third Class Sloan stood on the 0-3 level with his big camera bag at his side, and Mister Frankel, his minder, stood with him looking at the freighter through binoculars.

"Let's go up on the 0-4 level where we can get a better view," Frankel said.

Sloan looked up at the higher deck, and the forward fire control director that sat atop it. "That's an awfully small deck, Sir. Are you sure we need to go up there?"

"Definitely. Follow me," Frankel said.

They climbed the ladder to the highest deck on the ship. "Look how much better the view is from here," Frankel said. As he talked, he looked up at the radar antenna platforms high above them on the forward mast.

"Yes, Sir, but I feel the ship's roll more up here."

"As soon as they get the missiles uncovered, get busy with your camera, and we'll go back down."

"Okay. I hope I don't get sea sick again up here."

"It's all in your head, Sloan. Concentrate on your camera, and you'll be okay."

It took three-quarters of an hour for the Russian seamen to uncover the four big missiles. Sloan documented the process on film. After he photographed the cargo on the starboard side of *Volgoles,* the OOD maneuvered the destroyer around to the freighter's port side, and Sloan took more photos.

As the bosun piped the crew to breakfast, Sloan packed up his gear and descended the ladders to the signal bridge. He passed a signalman busy flashing a message of thanks to the Soviets for their cooperation and started for the ladder down to the torpedo deck.

Frankel patted the photographer on the back. "Good job, Sloan. Take special care of that film."

"Yes, Sir. I'm going to stow my gear and get some chow."

"Okay, see you later," Frankel said.

CHAPTER 35
Bad Weather
Fifty Miles North of Turks Island Passage

Wednesday, 14 November 1962

The final week of the naval quarantine began with all major decisions and actions now originating at the diplomatic level. The last obstacle to the successful removal of all Soviet offensive weapons in Cuba concerned the withdrawal of the IL-28 bombers. However, U.S. negotiators were confident that the USSR would acquiesce on this point. Quarantine forces continued to intercept, trail, and photograph ships approaching and leaving Cuba.[4]

The first sign of relaxation came on 14 November when the Chairman of the Joint Chiefs of Staff (CJCS) removed the worldwide communication MINIMIZE order which had been issued on 21 October. The Strategic Air Command, which had generated an awesome nuclear deterrent capability, received orders to reduce its airborne alert to the status held prior to 21 October.[4]

A n ominous sight greeted Captain Ellingham when he entered the pilothouse after breakfast. In the east, the sky splintered into striations of purple, magenta, and scarlet as the sun broke above the horizon. An old seafarer's cliché flashed through his mind: Red sky at night, sailor's delight, red sky in morn, sailor be warned.

Lieutenant Commander Kaestner walked out on the bridge minutes later.

"I don't like the look of that sky, XO. We get any weather bulletins?"

"Yes, Sir. I picked this up one in radio central a few minutes ago." He handed the message to the captain.

Ellingham read it quickly and handed it back. "Twenty to thirty knot winds, intermittent rain squalls, Beaufort Force Five. We've had it too easy lately, John. Ol' man Neptune is going to stir things up a bit today."

"Yes, Sir. I'll make a quick inspection of the ship and make sure we're ready."

"Good idea."

The morning passed slowly, as the seas increased, and visibility decreased. As noon approached, *Boyington* plowed through five to eight-foot waves at ten knots on routine patrol.

Bridge personnel and lookouts donned rain ponchos to protect themselves from the occasional squalls and the wind driven spray. Each thrust the bow made into the oncoming waves threw up a fresh sheet of foamy seawater, which flooded across the forecastle and blew aft, across the open bridge and signal deck.

***

As the mess cooks began serving the noon meal, Commander Kaestner's spirits were high. The ship's interior had begun to sparkle. Bosun Jones had called-off all weather-deck work and assigned his men to tasks in the interior spaces. Six first-division sailors scrubbed and touched up the paint in their berthing compartment in the forecastle. Others swabbed and waxed the passageway decks throughout the ship.

The XO met Jones in the forward athwartships passageway. "Bosun, your men are doing a great job. This is the best the passageways have looked in weeks."

"Thank you, Sir, but don't expect them to stay this way. With the beating the hull and weather decks are taking now, we're gonna be busy outside as soon as the weather breaks."

"I understand, but now that you're getting everything squared away, perhaps one man could be assigned to keep the interior passageways up to *Boyington* standards."

"Yes, Sir, I'll see what I can do. Anything else, Sir?"

"No, carry on."

"Aye, Aye, Sir." Jones headed aft, toward the chiefs' quarters, discontent obvious on his face.

***

As the bosun passed through the mess deck, a five-gallon can of Kool Aid sitting at the end of the serving line tipped over when the ship took a heavy roll. Within seconds, cherry Kool Aid covered the green asbestos tile deck as the rolling ship sloshed the sticky drink from side to side.

Jones grabbed two of his men as they deposited their trays in the scullery window. "On the double, get a couple of buckets and swabs, and soak this shit up. It's gonna get tracked all over the decks we just cleaned and waxed. Get the lead outta your ass. Move."

He grabbed a third man. "Get a couple of blankets and put one at each end of the mess desk so there's something for people to wipe their shoes on. Go on, double-time."

"Where am I gonna get two blankets, Chief?"

"Go down in the supply division berthing compartment, and grab 'em off of the first two racks you come to. Them guys always get the newest and best of everything, so they won't have no problem replacing 'em."

"Okay, Chief, if you say so."

"I say so. Get your ass in gear, go, go." The seaman ran off to carry out his orders.

Jones proceeded on to the chiefs' mess. Stafford and Ford were already eating. Jones sat down at their table with a sigh.

"What's up, Boats?" Ford asked.

"XO's on my ass to keep the passageways all spit and polish, and some knuckle head mess cook set a five gallon can of Kool Aid out and didn't secure it. Now the mess desk is covered in cherry slush, and all the work we did this morning on the decks is gonna be ruined."

"What's up with you, Ken?" Jones asked.

"Nothing. I just got up from my morning nap and came in here for a quiet dinner."

"Great. I always thought you guys had bunks down in them black holes you call engineering spaces."

As they talked, all three subconsciously raised and lowered one end of their compartmented food tray to keep their dinner from sliding off and splattering on the deck, or becoming part of their neighbor's meal.

"What's with this weather?" Mike asked.

"Some fricking hurricane is stirring things up in the Caribbean," Jones said. "This is just the outer edge of it, according to Quartermaster Gandolfi. Lots of water is breaking over the bow, so mount fifty-one may need some paint when the weather clears."

"I hope none of our mattresses, I mean machinery, down below get wet," Ford said.

"I knew it, you slacker," Jones said.

"You guys stay cool. I'm going to make my rounds to see if all the mounts are still there," Mike said.

"See you later," Ford said.

Jones grunted something and departed without eating.

Captain Ellingham entered the pilothouse and spotted the XO at the radar repeater. "I felt a course change, what's up?"

"The admiral is turning the task group northeast to try and get away from the worse of this weather. There's a hurricane working its way across the Caribbean, and we're catching the outer-bands. It's hitting Cuba now," Kaestner said.

"Okay, any damage yet?"

"None reported, Sir."

"How's the fuel?"

"Sixty percent. As soon as we find calmer seas, the carrier plans to refuel the squadron."

"Any idea how long that will be?"

"At least another five or six hours. Any longer, and they'll have to wait until morning to start. With these clouds it'll get dark early."

"Right, I'm going to take a walk around. Are you staying up here?"

"Yes, Sir, I will," Kaestner said.

Ellingham pulled on a poncho and stepped out onto the open bridge. The stiff breeze immediately struck him. He walked aft to the signal bridge and saw two men huddled out of the wind and rain at their station on the lee side. They greeted him.

Turning, he climbed the ladder to the 0-3 level. There he found the lone lookout, soaked and cold due to a complete lack of shelter.

"You seeing much out there?" the skipper asked.

"No, Sir. Visibility is five-hundred yards at best."

"Right, the radar's working okay, so why don't you go down to the pilothouse and finish your watch there. I don't think this weather is going to lift for a while."

"Thank you, Sir. I'll do that," the seaman said.

Ellingham descended to the 0-1 level and walked aft to mount fifty-two. As he looked over the fantail, all appeared to be in order. Waves washed over the main deck, but all watertight doors and hatches had been dogged shut. He returned to his cabin and changed out of his wet pants and shoes. Sitting down at his desk, he began clearing the paperwork that had accumulated.

Hour by hour, as they plowed north, the effects of the storm lessened.

The mess cooks, aided by two deck seamen, had swabbed up the Kool Aid and scrubbed the deck clean.

The chief commissaryman revised the menu for the evening meal to simplify preparation. The huge, steam heated coppers used for most cooking presented a safety hazard in foul weather. Grilled ham and cheese sandwiches replaced pork chops as the main course. Powdered mashed potatoes gave way to canned applesauce.

The Kool Aid can, now secured to one leg of a table by heavy line and proper navy knots met Chief Jones's exacting standards. He had personally inspected it.

At 1800, the task group rendezvoused with the fleet oiler U.S.S. Caloosahatchee (AO-98). She could refuel two ships simultaneously, so

343

the two destroyers lowest on fuel pulled alongside first, and operations began.

Once those two ships had their fill, the oiler captain curtailed operations due to the heavy seas and failing light. *Boyington* would have to wait until dawn.

The movie *Thunder Road*, starring Robert Mitchum, began on the mess deck at 1900.

CHAPTER 36

The Last Photograph

Three-Hundred Miles Northwest of Turks Island Passage

Thursday, 15 November 1962

Routine replacement and relief of surface units continued. However, there was no stand down of contingency forces, which had reached a peak of readiness for any eventuality. While the U.S. and USSR negotiators parried on the IL-28 question and tried to cope with Castro's intransigence, five large-hatch Russian ships left Soviet ports and were believed en route to Cuba. The Navy ordered a covert aerial inspection using a neutron sensor in an effort to detect the presence of nuclear cargo. Soviet submarine activity was nil, with only two possible contacts reported on the previous day.[4]

Up to this point in the quarantine operation, naval aircraft had flown 30,000 flight hours in 9,000 sorties for a total distance of six million miles. Sixty-eight aerial squadrons composed of 19,000 personnel, and eight aircraft carriers, whose combined crews totaled 25,000 personnel, had participated in the action.[4]

The ninety cruisers and destroyers involved had steamed for a total of 780,000 miles, and each of the carriers had covered a 10,000-mile track. Atlantic Fleet service ships had provided logistic support to an afloat population of 85,000 in 183 ships, which deployed over a 2,100-mile front.[4]

A t sunrise, *Boyington* cruised along *Caloosahatchee's* starboard side while *Sibuyan Sea* occupied her port side refueling stations. Each ship maintained a separation of approximately ninety feet from the oiler's sides and a speed of precisely twelve knots. The three helmsmen concentrated on their tasks, knowing the slightest error could end in a catastrophe. They endured the incredible stress as part of the job. The three ship's captains, who shouldered the ultimate responsibility, each had the utmost confidence in their quartermasters. However, they stayed on their respective bridges during the entire operation, sharing the tension.

Refueling began at first light. To expedite the process, two fuel hoses stretched across to the destroyer. The newly demoted BM3 Dalton honchoed the forward refueling station. At the after station, BM3 Bill Hudson ran the operation. The process would take approximately thirty minutes after the hoses were in place.

Once the oil king decreed the bunkers full, the hoses returned to the oiler, and the connections severed, Ellingham called for all-ahead flank, and the destroyer peeled away, hard to starboard. Another destroyer slipped into the space vacated by *Boyington,* and the refueling operation repeated.

Four destroyers would come and go in the time it would take to refuel the *Sibuyan Sea* that required not only NSFO, but also various grades of aviation fuel for her variety of aircraft.

When *Boyington* arrived on station, three miles northeast of the carrier, Ellingham had the speed reduced to twelve knots and waited for orders. The crew queued-up for breakfast and a routine day at sea began.

The destroyer rolled gently through moderate seas on a cloudy afternoon when orders arrived to intercept yet another Soviet freighter.

"Steer, three-one-zero; turns for two-five knots," the OOD ordered. The helmsman echoed the order with a "Sir" appended.

The contact had transited the Caicos Passage and set a course northeast, toward the Soviet Union's northern ports. They might intercept within one or two hours, depending on the freighter's speed and the sea state. Currently, conditions were moderate with waves of three to five feet. Visibility averaged three miles with threatening low, dark clouds.

Chief Mike Stafford stood at the port bulwark, protected from the wind and spray, smoking a Lucky Strike, when Sloan the photographer joined him.

"Got your camera loaded up for another session with the Russians?" Mike asked.

"The camera's ready, but I don't know if I am."

"How so?"

"I don't seem able to adjust to this constant motion. I've been seasick every day since I came aboard. Guess I should've joined the army."

"Some folks just take longer to adapt. Keep your belly full, even if you have to live on crackers. Stay outside as much as you can and concentrate on the horizon."

"Some of the guys have been telling me stuff like that, and it works for a while, then when I have to look through the camera lens and the ship is rolling, like now, the seasickness comes back."

"Sorry, I don't know any tricks to use with a camera. The good news is that this whole business is nearly over. I think we'll be heading home in a few days. Where are you stationed?"

"Norfolk. Where is this ship's homeport?"

"Newport, Rhode Island."

"I wonder how I'll get back to Norfolk."

"Don't worry, someone will figure out a way. If not, you may find you like Newport better anyway. I do."

"Never been there."

"Where you from?"

"Powell, Ohio, a little ways north of Columbus. Ever hear of it?"

348

"No."

"Well, it's a great little town, and I'd like to be there right now."

"Does that mean you're not going to make the navy a career?"

"Chief, I have twenty-one months and seventeen days to go, and then I'm outta here."

"Hang in there and try to find something about navy life you like. It will make time go by faster."

"Thanks, Chief. I'll try, but now I'm going to go eat a box of saltines and hope to get through the upcoming photo shoot."

"Good luck," Mike said.

Sloan disappeared through the watertight door. Mike lit another cigarette and turned back to the sea.

"Now station the special photographic detail," boomed the loud speakers.

On the bridge, Lieutenant Quinn took the deck and conn, QM1 Gandolfi relieved the helmsman. During the photographic mission, the ships cruised with less than a two-hundred foot separation, so the most experienced men assumed bridge duties. Ellingham was always present.

Mister Frankel met Sloan on the signal bridge, and both stared through the mist at the looming Soviet freighter.

"I've been thinking, if we climbed up to the air search radar antenna platform, we could get some fantastic shots, looking down on the freighter's deck," Frankel said.

Sloan looked up toward the top of the forward mast. "Are you saying we're going to climb up the mast?"

"Yeah, don't you think that would be great? You could get some shots that will make history, make you famous."

"I'd rather remain anonymous and alive."

"Oh, come on. The bosuns and electronic technicians go up there all the time. Five minutes, snap as many shots as you can, and we're done."

"I don't know, Sir. Last time I got sick on the 0-4 level, and that's nothing compared to that radar platform up near the top of the mast."

"I thought you'd like the idea. I made all the arrangements. The radar is off, the antenna is secured, and I got us some safety belts. Come on, grab your stuff, and let's go."

Sloan's face turned white with fear as he began the climb. Frankel followed him up the ladder.

"Don't look down, Sloan. Just keep climbing," Frankel said.

The higher they climbed on the mast, the greater the effect of the ship's rolling. Near the top, if they looked down at the extreme of each roll, they had a seagull's view of the ocean.

Finally, they reached the platform. "Push that hatch up, and climb through," Frankel ordered.

Sloan opened the hatch and shoved his camera bag through first, then slid through, and reclined on the platform deck with a white-knuckle grip on the low safety railing. Frankel followed.

"Hook your belt around the mast, and get your camera out. We'll be alongside the freighter in a couple of minutes."

"I don't think I can do this, Sir."

"Sure you can. Hook up."

Sloan hooked his belt, and then sat up and retrieved his camera.

Frankel plugged in a telephone headset and called the bridge. "We're on the SPS-6 platform, ready to shoot pictures."

The bridge talker called out the information to the OOD.

Ellingham spun around when he heard the report. "Who the hell told those two to go up there is weather like this?"

No one knew.

"Get them down immediately," the captain roared.

Frankel suddenly realized he had made a major blunder. "Get a couple of quick shots, Sloan, and we'll go back down."

Sloan obliged, then stowed the camera.

"Okay, now unhook your belt and get back down through the hatch. I'll bring the camera bag. Remember, slowly take one-step at a time, and don't look down."

Sloan began the process. He unhooked his belt, moved his legs to the side, and opened the hatch.

"You're doing great. Drop your legs through the hatch one at a time and get a footing on the ladder."

Sloan sat on the edge of the hatch and placed his feet on the top rung of the ladder.

"Okay, good job. Now start down, one-step at a time—don't hurry, make sure you have good footing before you put your weight on the lower leg."

"Y-Yes, Sir."

Sloan's head dropped through the hatch. Frankel put the camera bag's strap over his head and swung into position to descend through the hatch.

The ship took a hard roll hard to port, and the mast swung out over the water. Sloan's stomach revolted and he retched violently. His grip failed, and he dropped from the ladder falling silently. No one saw or heard the splash when his eighty-foot fall ended in the turbulent sea.

The ship rolled back to starboard as Frankel took his first steps down the ladder. He looked down and realized Sloan wasn't there. Stunned, it took a fraction of a second to realize what had happened. He screamed at the top of his lungs, "Man overboard."

He flew down the ladder, his legs a near blur of motion.

A signalman directly below heard him and ran forward to the bridge, repeating the cry.

Bosun Hudson grabbed the 1-MC microphone, "Man overboard, port side. Man overboard, this is not a drill."

The OOD shouted, "All back one-third. Muster the rescue detail and standby to launch the motor whaleboat."

He backed the ship to a spot near where he presumed Sloan had fallen. The fantail lookout carefully scanned the sea.

Frankel ran aft along the port side, main deck, shouting, "Man overboard." Sloan's camera bag remained around his neck and bounced against his hip with each stride he took.

Bosun Jones ran aft along weather deck and mounted the midships ladder, two steps at a time. Dalton and Garcia met him on the torpedo deck and raced to run-out the whaleboat davits. The chief corpsman arrived.

The whaleboat splashed into the water with the rescue party aboard and roared away.

The fantail lookout strained his eyes to spot a man as the waves created ever-changing frothy peaks and valleys. Two men raced to the top of mount fifty-two for a longer-range view. Every crewman, not on watch, lined the rails, looking for a swimmer.

Ensign Frankel paced rapidly in circles on the fantail, looking down, and mumbling to himself.

The Soviet freighter, unaware of what had happened, or what the Americans were doing, steamed away at twelve knots.

Coxswain Garcia skillfully maneuvered the whaleboat about in the rough sea. The waves continued running at four to five feet, high enough that the boat crew could not see a swimmer in an adjacent trough, if indeed one had been there.

Jones kept yelling, through a battery-powered megaphone. "Sloan, if you hear me, yell."

He didn't receive an answer.

───────────

The OOD radioed DESRON Forty-Two and explained what had happened. The squadron watch officer dispatched *Bartow* to catch the Russian and ordered the *Spenser* to help with the rescue.

Ellingham called Frankel to the bridge. He took him aside, away from the other watch standers. "Tell me what the hell happened up there."

Frankel recited the events.

"Why, in God's name, did you take that young man up the mast? I understand he's been seasick from the moment he stepped on board."

"Sir, he seemed to be doing okay, and I thought we could get better pictures from up there."

"And you weren't aware that no one climbs the mast without running a sign-off chit through CIC, radio central, engineering, and most importantly, the OOD?"

"I forgot about the chit, Sir. I told CIC, and they said the radars are always secured when we're close to another ship."

"You better pray we save that man. Get a tablet and write up the story you just told me. There will be an investigation when we get to back to port, even if we find the poor fellow."

"Yes, Sir."

"Dismissed."

Ensign Frankel came to attention, executed an about-face, and walked away.

Captain Ellingham, sitting in his elevated chair, stared blindly over the vast ocean, lost in thought and prayer.

Two helicopters from the *Sibuyan Sea* arrived and began flying search patterns.

An hour later, the *Spenser* arrived and joined in the search.

The sun sank below the horizon and the heavy cloud cover blocked the moonlight, leaving the ocean's surface in total darkness. Captain Ellingham ended the search for the night. He sent a message detailing the events to his commander, COMDESRON Forty-Two.

At first light the next morning, the *Boyington* circled the area at five knots, searching in ever widening circles. The sea had calmed over night. Waves were now capping at two feet. After four hours, the captain gave up any hope of recovering the body, and the ship departed. Ellingham declared Petty Officer Sloan officially lost at sea, and the search over.

PART III

THE BEGINNING OF THE END

CHAPTER 37

Winding Down

One-Hundred and Sixty Miles East of Nassau, Bahamas Islands

Friday, 16 November 1962

The Joint Chiefs' of Staff met with the President to discuss removal of the Soviet IL-28's bombers and the military implications of negotiating a no-invasion policy towards Cuba. They argued for removal of the IL-28's, preferably by negotiation, otherwise by blockade or direct military action. Further, they recommended the removal of Soviet personnel from Cuba as an immediate objective of negotiation with the USSR and a condition for granting a no-invasion pledge. In this regard, the JCS said that any such assurance to Castro should state U.S. obligations under the Rio Pact and link the assurance to Cuban good behavior and acceptance of aerial surveillance. The Chiefs opposed the seeking of a means for long-term verification and inspection against offensive weapons in Cuba in exchange for United Nations inspection of the Caribbean and a nuclear-free zone in Latin America.[4]

November 16, 1962—7:00 A.M.: The largest amphibious landing since WW II begins as part of an exercise at Onslow Beach, North Carolina. The two-day exercise, a full scale rehearsal for an invasion of Cuba, included six marine battalion landing teams, four by assault boats and two by helicopter assault carriers. (CINCLANT Historical Account of Cuban Crisis, 4/29/63, p.151; Summary of Items of Significant Interest Period 090701-100700 November 1962)[1]

Captain Ellingham sat in his elevated bridge chair, looking out over the serene ocean surface, thinking about the death of the young sailor. He had spent an hour this morning, composing a letter to the lad's family. Technically the responsibility for writing the letter of condolence rested with Sloan's commander, back in Norfolk. However, the unfortunate event had occurred on his ship, not in Norfolk, and he felt obliged to accomplish the task. The Norfolk commander would also offer his condolences.

The XO approached, and sensed the aura of despondency that surrounded the captain. "It wasn't your fault, Sir."

"Everything that happens on or to this ship and its crew, good or bad is my fault, John. That's what command is all about."

"I understand, Sir. I meant, don't take it personally."

"I know what you meant . . . thank you. I didn't mean to sound churlish. There wasn't any bad intent on anyone's part, just bad judgment. The navy will deal with that soon enough. But you're right, I need to move on, and so does the crew. How is Mister Frankel holding up?"

"Not too well. He's devastated—feels like he killed Sloan."

"I'll have a talk with him, but we may need to get him ashore. Where is he now?"

"In his cabin. I told him to take the day off."

"Okay. This operation is going to wrap up soon. I'm going to see if we can make a port call in Bermuda on the way home. I'd like to try to end the deployment on a high note if we can. The crew needs it after losing folks the way we have."

"Good idea, Sir. It's been a crazy month."

Ellingham rose, ending the informal meeting. Kaestner departed for CIC.

The captain went below to officer country and knocked on Frankel's cabin door.

The ensign answered in his skivvies, unshaven and disheveled.

"Sorry, Sir. The XO gave me the day off."

"I know. How are you holding up?"

"Not too good, Sir."

"May I come in?"

"Oh, yes, Sir. Of course, Sir. Sorry."

Ellingham entered and closed the door. Frankel offered him the only chair, and then sat on his rack.

"Mister Frankel, accidents happen. We will deal with the circumstances later, but for now, you, the rest of the crew, and I must keep going. We all have our jobs to do, responsibilities to meet.

"Death is a big part of our business. I fully understand your feelings, but you can't give in to them. You must compartmentalize what happened for now. You'll have to address the matter later, but as an officer, you must move on for now. We don't have the luxury of time and space that others not in the sea services do."

"Yes, Sir, I know all that, but . . . but, I still feel responsible. I, I don't know how I can live with the guilt."

"Box it up for now, Ensign. You have a duty to the men in your division and to the ship. That duty calls you now, and you must answer. If we had gone into combat last week, men would have died, good men, close friends, maybe. As an officer, you have to accept that and keep going. We don't have time to mourn while at sea.

"You and I are going to answer for what happened to Sloan. Now is not the time or place, however, and sitting in here isn't going to bring him back or make the memory go away."

"You, Sir?"

"Ensign, have you forgotten? The commander is responsible for everything that happens."

"Yes, Sir, I guess I did. Sorry."

"Okay, now get shaved and dressed. Duty calls. We'll deal with the accident later, after we get back to Newport."

"Yes, Sir. Thank you, Captain. I'll be back to work in a few minutes."

"Good. Feel free to come see me or Commander Kaestner anytime you need to talk." Ellingham stood and departed.

Stafford, Jones, and Ford sat for noon chow in the chiefs' mess.

"What's going to happen to Mister Frankel?" Ford asked.

"I saw him in the passageway right before chow call. He looked okay, kinda withdrawn maybe, didn't have anything to say, but he seemed functional," Mike said.

"Didn't have no business taking that kid up the mast. I think he's gonna get hammered," Jones said.

"Hold on, Paul. We don't know the whole story yet, do we?" Mike said.

"What story? He didn't get a chit signed off to go aloft. Damn boot ensign. Taking a shortcut like that got a sailor killed. I think he screwed up, big time," Jones said.

"You may well be right, but until he has his day in court, give him the benefit of doubt," Mike said.

"Yeah, you're right," Jones said. "It's just a frickin' shame."

"That it is," Mike said.

Ford stood. "You both may be right. Main thing we gotta do is keep the crew together, and let the navy handle the rest."

"Never knew you were such a philosophical guy, Ken," Jones said.

"And I never knew you to use a big word like 'philosophical,' Paul," Mike said.

"Screw you, Mike. I may sound stupid sometimes, but I ain't. My Mensa group considers me quite the erudite pedagogue."

"What!" Ken and Mike said in unison.

"Mensa, no way," Ford added.

"So's if'n there's anything else you'd care to know, simply elucidate your hypothesis, and I'll endeavor to formulate a construct to affirm or reject said supposition. Know what I'm saying?" Jones asked.

"No," Stafford said.

"Me neither," Ford said.

"Who the hell are you, and what have you done with our friend, Paul Jones?" Mike asked.

"Come on, guys, I'm just having you on," Jones said.

"So you're not a Mensa member?" Ford asked.

"Not anymore, the meetings got boring."

"I gotta go. The BS is getting too deep in here," Mike said. He rose and left.

"Where's Chief Stafford going? He only had three cups of coffee," Charlie, the mess cook, said.

"He said the conversation got too deep for him," Jones replied.

Charlie walked away, shaking his head.

The Atlantic Fleet destroyers had intercepted every freighter that the Soviet Union identified as returning ballistic missiles from Cuba to Russia. With each interception, the missiles had been uncovered and photographed. Intelligence analysts continued to meticulously comb through the photographs trying to verify that the number of missiles shipped equaled the number of weapons the Soviets claimed to have placed on the island. Some in the intelligence community remained skeptical, but the White House accepted the Soviet claim and declared an end to that phase of the crisis.

Since the end of October, no new submarine contacts occurred. The strategic bombers in Cuba were the only threat remaining. Russian technicians uncrated and assembled them non-stop right through the crisis. Negotiations over the planes, however, continued with every indication they too would soon reach a successful conclusion.

The Commander in Chief of the United States Atlantic Command ordered a gradual decrease in the size of the task force at sea.

Captain Ellingham took his seat at the head of the wardroom dinner table, while the other officers stood behind their chairs. "Gentlemen, please be seated." Once the others were comfortable, he continued, "I have some rather good news to share with you tonight. The ASW Task Group has been deactivated, and we are going to turn north and head home tonight at midnight."

The wardroom officers clapped and sounded off, "Here! Here!"

"This has been a difficult cruise, but the mission has been successful in spite of several serious setbacks. Under your leadership, we intercepted two freighters and inspected one, the *Svetlana*. That particular mission nearly became a disaster, but for the fast actions of Mister Padgett's boarding detail.

"We witnessed the horrible crash of an S2F aircraft and the tragic loss of the pilot, but rescued the crew. Along with those significant matters, we chased a couple of submarines, and forced one to the surface after a prolonged time at general quarters.

"Then, after the Soviet's capitulated, we photographed a number of missiles on their way home."

The captain paused and looked at each of the officers around the table.

"As I said, the voyage hasn't been without its problems," Ellingham continued. "One of our young seamen received a court martial for sabotage; a senior petty officer disappeared in San Juan and is still missing; we nearly lost a seaman during a refueling accident; and sadly, a petty officer fell to his death during the photographic mission."

No one turned to look in the direction of Ensign Frankel, who stared at the tabletop.

"These negatives and especially the tragic loss of Petty Officer Sloan, unfortunately, cast a shadow on an otherwise a successful mission. Nevertheless, we pressed on and did our job under rather stressful conditions and the constant threat of war. In sum, each of you and the entire crew can be proud of the ship and the part you played in its mission.

"Fortunately, our president and his staff forged a diplomatic solution, averting war. The world and our country are safer now than when the mission began."

The officers again clapped and in unison acclaimed, "Here! Here!"

"Commander Kaestner, would you like to add anything?"

"Yes, thank you, Sir. Gentlemen, I want to add my personal thanks for the splendid cooperation you gave me, especially during some of the more trying times. Teamwork always has an element of personal sacrifice, and not one of you ever failed to set aside your personal wants or desires when the ship, the crew, or the mission called. I thank you and salute you."

"Very well, let's have our prayer and eat," Ellingham said.

Mr. Caruthers led the prayer, and then the stewards entered and began serving.

⸻

At 0001, the watch changed and the on-coming OOD, Mister White, passed the order that would begin the cruise home: "Helm, come about to port and, steer three-five-zero; turns for two oh knots."

"Coming about to port; steer, three-five-zero, turns for two oh knots," The helmsman called out. He then added, "Heading home, Sir."

CHAPTER 38

Foss

Six-Hundred Miles Southwest of Bermuda

Saturday, 17 November 1962

As of this date, there had been no basic changes in force posture. Naval units were still at sea and ready. The Continental Air Defense Command's interceptor forces were at their wartime dispersal bases at 1/3rd alert and still were substantially augmented in the Southeast U.S., and particularly in Florida. SAC aircraft remained dispersed with 1/8th airborne and a total generated force of 1,456 planes and 355 ballistic missiles. Air forces committed to CINCLANT operations plans were ready for a daylight response for selective targets within Cuba within a two-to-twelve hour timetable. Contingency invasion forces were ready on a seven-day reaction basis, following a pre-assault air strike. The commanders of these forces reported that they could maintain their current status of readiness for about 30 more days without adverse effects.[4]

Three pilots reported a possible SAM missile launch from Cuba at 1100. The object produced a white trail of flame at high altitude, described as extremely brilliant. The flame became shorter and seemed to burn out with several red flashes. The object maintained a steady course and might have originated from the Matanzas SA-2 site, which was 50 miles distant from the reporting aircraft. There was no evidence of a deliberate attempt to shoot down U.S. aircraft, although several reconnaissance planes were over water in the vicinity at the time.[4]

The aircraft carrier *Sibuyan Sea* and Destroyer Squadron Forty-Two steamed north at twenty knots through mildly rolling seas. Morale peaked throughout the task group, knowing they would be home soon.

Aboard *Boyington*, Captain Ellingham and Lieutenant Commander Kaestner stood on the open bridge, watching the other ships of the squadron cut through the waves. The older destroyers had knife like bows that sliced into the waves. In rougher seas huge quantities of water washed over their decks. The newer ships, like *Bartow* and *Boyington* had flared bows, called hurricane bows, which prevented all but the heaviest seas from flooding the forward weather decks.

The radio room messenger approached. "Excuse me, Captain. Couple of messages for you."

Ellingham signed the log, took the papers, and read each message. "Bad news, John."

"We've been ordered back south?"

"No, not quite that bad. The commodore turned down my request for a port-call in Bermuda. He wants the squadron to sail into Newport as a unit. The CRUDESLANT band is going to welcome us home."

"At least the family men will be happy. That wasn't too bad. Go ahead and let the other shoe drop," Kaestner said.

"This is the bad news. The FBI found Foss's body. He died from a gunshot in the back of the head, execution style. Here, you can read the details."

"Oh, this is terrible. The guy seemed to have a knack for finding trouble and skating away. I guess his luck finally ran out." Kaestner handed the message back to the captain.

"That it did. The FBI is making the notifications. Do you know if he had any family in Newport?"

"No, Sir. I don't know. I'll check with the ship's office and see if we have anything on record."

"Too bad. He never caused any trouble onboard ship, but sure had his problems when ashore. I'll notify Mister Quinn and Chief Jones," Ellingham said. "Different topic, how's Mister Frankel doing?"

"He seems okay. Whatever you told him perked him up. Do you have any idea what's going to happen to him?"

"No. There will be an inquiry when we get home, but you never know how they will turn out."

"Wait and see, I guess. I'll check to see if we have anything on Foss." Kaestner turned into the pilothouse.

Ellingham moved to his command chair and sat. "Messenger."

A seaman approached. "Sir."

"Go find Mister Quinn and Chief Jones. I want to see them both in my office at 1000."

"Aye, aye, Sir." He pivoted and walked off.

The captain also stood and departed the bridge.

The phone rang as Ellingham entered his office. "It's the XO, Sir. Foss doesn't have any family locally. His home of record is Helotes, Texas and he listed a sister as his only next of kin."

"Okay, we'll let the FBI boys take care of everything. Have the office verify the NOK address so we can ship his personal effects, and tell Mister Riley so he can take care of the payroll matters. We'll also need a notification message to BUPERS with a copy to DESRON Forty-Two."

"Aye, aye, Sir."

The captain sat in his desk chair and stared at the blank bulkhead, reflecting on events. This is not a good development on top of everything else. He looked at his wife's picture. Maybe it's time to think about retirement, if I survive the inquiry over Sloan's death.

A knock on his door interrupted his thoughts. "Enter."

"You wanted to see us, Sir," Mister Quinn said.

"Yes, come in and have a seat."

Jones and Quinn faced their captain across his desk.

"We received some bad news on Bosun Foss. The FBI found his body yesterday. Apparently, he pissed off the wrong guys. He died from a gunshot to the back of the head with his hands tied behind his back. They found the body in an abandoned warehouse in old San Juan, an area off-limits to naval personnel, of course."

"That's a shame. The guy was one hell of a bosun, and the deck gang will miss him," Lieutenant Quinn said.

"Sir, we tried hard to find the guy and had some good leads, but couldn't get the local cops interested in searching for him. Maybe with more help and time, we could have saved him," Jones said.

"I remember the details. You two did the best you could. In the end, it's a matter of personal responsibility, and Foss had a screw loose in that area. Now he's paid the ultimate price. Brief the division at quarters tomorrow, Mister Quinn." He handed his copy of the message to the lieutenant.

"Chief, Commander Kaestner is trying to verify the address for Foss's sister, whom he identified as his next of kin. Once he has that sorted out, you can gather up his personal effects and send them to her."

"Aye, aye, Sir."

"Thank you both," Ellingham said.

The two rose and departed.

Mike and Jones met in the Chiefs' mess and sat for the noon meal.

"The captain received notification that the FBI found Foss's body in San Juan yesterday. Somebody had tied his hands behind his back and shot him in the back of the head," Jones said.

The conversation paused as the mess cook slid a food tray onto the table for each man.

"Thanks, Charlie," Mike said. After the mess cook walked away, he looked back at Jones. "I bet it took more than one guy to take him down."

"I'm sure it did. I never met a meaner, tougher fighter in my life. I don't think any one man alive could take him—had to have been several—with guns. You couldn't scare him with a knife. And no one ever accused him of fighting fair. He knew every dirty trick in the book."

"Odd how different he could be on the ship," Stafford said. "I've never heard anyone in the crew say anything against him. That guy, Gibbs, I sent you, worshipped Foss. Told me he saw the guy like the father he wished he'd had."

"I know," Jones agreed. "I never met a bosun better at helping boots when they came aboard. He could turn 'em into good, solid deck hands and make them like the job. I never had any discipline problems in the division with him up there running things. No one stepped outta line, more out of respect than fear, I think. He could whip any man on this ship, but never bullied anyone or pushed his weight around. He just knew more about the job and did it better that anyone else could.

"So far we're doing okay, but Dalton will never fill Foss's shoes, especially now that he's been busted to third class. Maybe a BM1 replacement will show up when we get back to Newport."

Chief Ford entered and sat down with his friends. Jones filled him in on the Foss situation.

"Paul, I'm sorry. I know how important Foss was to you and first division. He raised plenty of hell on the beach, but I always got along with him," Ford said

"Yeah, all his shipmates did. We were his family. It seemed like he couldn't get along with civilians. Every time he got in trouble, it involved a civilian, like that witch Bianca. I'm convinced she set him up, but they'll never prove it."

"Oh, well. Life goes on. You guys have any plans for Newport?" Ford asked.

"I have a big one. I'm taking off this uniform and never putting it back on," Mike said.

"I been thinking about doing that too," Jones said.

"Paul, I figured you for a thirty-year man," Mike said.

"Maybe, if I make senior chief. I'll have twenty-six years in come January, and the E-7 pay scale stops there . . . No more longevity pay-raises. Problem is, I don't know what I'd do if I got out."

"I lucked out when I retired last year. My brother came to the rescue and got me a job selling sporting goods to retailers around New England. I'm hoping they'll take me back after this little vacation," Mike said.

"They got to, it's the law. You were called back," Jones said.

"How much longer you got, Ken?" Mike asked.

"I'll finish twenty years in June. Mary Ann's been bugging me to retire. She wants to go back home and buy a house."

"All I can say is, when the fun stops, it's time to go," Mike said.

After Jones left the compartment, Mike said, "What do you make of the Foss thing, Ken?"

"I considered him a good shipmate, and he had a reputation in the division as a great bosun, but unfortunately he was a lousy citizen and petty officer. He wasn't a good leader because he set such a poor example for the men when he went ashore. I don't think he could have survived in retirement—that might have been the only thing in life he feared. I don't know, but I'll miss the big galoot."

CHAPTER 39

Home Sweet Home

Forty Miles South of Newport, Rhode Island

Monday, 19 November 1962

At 1945 EST, the Chairman of the Joint Chiefs' of Staff dispatched the following message: "Lift quarantine effective immediately. Return LANTFLT ships to homeports and normal operating areas at your discretion. Maintain one CVA with air group in ready status in Mayport Caribbean area. Instructions will be furnished later as to future movements and disposition of PACFLT amphibious forces. Anticipate requirement for sighting and photographing Soviet ships departing Cuban ports with IL-28 aircraft." [4]

As the order went out to dissolve the quarantine forces, more than 63 ships of the mighty force, which had clearly demonstrated its capability to respond quickly to their country's needs, had an opportunity to be home for Thanksgiving. [4]

*Admiral Anderson pointed out that the entire operation
had been a magnificent testimonial to the senior leaders
of our Government, and commanders at all levels. He
praised those who were so quickly able to move—large
numbers of troops—their ships—many ships—and their
aircraft of many types into position to carry out lengthy,
tedious, and often sensitive operations with a high
degree of leadership, professional competence, courage,
and diplomatic skill.*[4]

Boyington sprang to life at 0600, when the bosun piped *Reveille*. Division petty officers didn't have any problem getting their men out of their racks. In two hours, they would tie up in their homeport where wives and girlfriends would greet them in a grand homecoming.

After morning chow, the loud speakers crackled. "Attention, this is the captain speaking. Before we arrive in port, I want to take a few minutes to thank each one of you for your splendid performance during this mission.

"The country can be proud of what its president, his administration, our diplomats around the world, and especially the armed forces achieved. The tremendous show of force and the resolve to use it, if necessary, eliminated a serious threat to the peace and made America safer. We stood on the brink of a nuclear war with the Soviet Union, but it did not happen, and you played a significant role in bringing about that outcome.

"Every American has a great deal to be thankful for, and the national celebration of Thanksgiving is only days away. I ask you to remember the *Sibuyan Sea* pilot and our two shipmates who died during this deployment, along with our fellow serviceman in the air force who perished. Please keep all of them and their families in your prayers.

"We will try to relax the leave and liberty restrictions so that as many of you as possible can spend the holiday with your loved ones.

"Again, I thank you, and I salute you for a job well done. That is all."

The ship remained silent for a few moments, and then the normal chatter resumed.

Yesterday the crew had turned-to and cleaned the ship from bow to stern. The bright work, that is anything made of brass, glistened in the morning sun. Now the time approached for the crew to shine. All off-watch sailors changed into their sharply pressed dress blue uniforms with spit-shined shoes, and glistening white hats. Then they waited.

The task group sailed past Block Island, nearly home. Excitement grew.

Finally, the most anticipated command of the morning blared throughout the ship. "Now hear this. Now station the Special Sea and Anchor Detail. All hands, not on watch, prepare to man the rails."

The squadron formed into a single column, with the flagship, *Bartow* leading. Following her were *Browning, Boyington, Keffer,*

Negley, and *Spenser*. The carrier *Sibuyan Sea* trailed the destroyers. She would sail past as they turned east into the Naval Station Newport harbor for their special homecoming. Quonset Point Naval Air Station, the carrier's homeport, was several miles farther north on Narragansett Bay.

The crew donned their peacoats, squared their white hats, and headed for the weather decks.

Every few feet along the main decks, on both port and starboard sides, a proud sailor stood—proud of his ship, proud of his country, and glad to be home.

As they reached the harbor, the CRUDESLANT band struck up *Anchors Aweigh*. The large crowd cheered, and children waved tiny American flags. A few old disabled vets stood behind the crowd, their eyes moist.

Bartow slid into her berth behind the destroyer tender U.S.S. *Cascade* (AD 16), port side-to pier one. *Boyington* tied up behind *Bartow*. The other ships moored outboard from these two. Bosuns opened gangways and placed gangplanks between ships to provide access to the pier.

A cacophony of competing bosun pipes echoed around the harbor. Announcements boomed from loudspeakers, "Now secure the Special Sea and Anchor Detail. Set the in-port watch."

A frenzy of activity took place on every ship.

On the pier, the band played, and anxious wives talked as they tried to control excited children. Girlfriends checked their lipstick and patted their carefully coiffured hair.

Brows slid into place from the pier to the quarterdecks of *Bartow* and *Boyington*. The duty section sprang into action. Engineers connected water, electric and telephone lines as fast as humanly possible. Deck hands placed rat guards around each mooring line. No one would leave their ship until all tasks were completed.

Finally, liberty call sounded, and nearly two thirds of the crew headed for the quarterdeck. Naval tradition dictated officers disembark first, then chiefs and finally, the rest of the crew. Each man stopped and saluted the OOD, flashed his ID and either a liberty card or leave papers, saying, "Request permission to go ashore, Sir."

The OOD returned each salute as he eyed the documents. "Permission granted," the officer said. He would repeat those words hundreds of times before his watch ended.

After receiving permission, the departing sailor then turned aft, saluted the flag, and headed down the brow.

Before his feet touched the quarterdeck, Mike saw Sandy in the front row, holding Maria. Both were bundled up against the cold November day. Sandy's long golden hair reflected the sunlight like a beacon. Minutes later, he embraced her.

Paul Jones followed closely behind, looking about.

Ken Ford saw his wife and ran to her.

Stafford turned to Jones with a questioning gesture.

"I don't get it. Roxie said she would be here when we returned," Jones said.

"Maybe she got held up at the gate," Stafford suggested.

"Yeah, maybe, but I'd guess she could talk her way through most any situation she comes up against."

"She'll show up. Paul, meet my wife, Sandy and daughter, Maria. Sandy, this is my old friend, Paul Jones."

"Oh, I'm so happy to finally meet you, Paul. I think I've heard about every adventure you two have had over the years," Sandy said.

Paul turned a bit red. "I hope not all of them." He took her hand, and she kissed him on the cheek. He tickled Maria under the chin, and she smiled at him shyly.

"Let's go into town and find a restaurant before they all fill up," Mike suggested.

They started up the pier and met Ken and Mary Ann Ford. More introductions followed.

"Ken, we're heading downtown for lunch. You two want to join us?" Stafford asked.

"Sorry, Mike. I've got ten days leave, and we're heading straight for home. I have some big decisions to make and a lot of planning to do. You guys have fun—nice to meet you, Sandy." The Ford's turned and hurried off. Mary Ann waved as Ken pulled her other arm.

"Mike, can you hold on a minute? I want to step into the gedunk and call Roxie. Maybe she'll meet us in town."

"Okay, Paul. We'll wait right here."

"When can we go home?" Sandy asked.

"They have to cut orders to separate me. Technically, they have me for a year, but I don't think they'll hold me to that since the crisis seems to be over. I'm hoping to leave in a day or two. Do you want to stay down here or go back home?"

"Are you kidding? I need some serious loving and just look at all these sailors."

Paul overheard the remark as he approached. "If your man ain't getting' the job done, you just call on ol' Jonesy, sweetheart."

Sandy looked at Mike, "Well?"

"I'll get a motel room."

Sandy turned back to Paul. "Maybe next time."

Jones's mouth fell open.

"Any luck reaching Roxie?" Mike asked.

"No answer. Let's go"

They walked up the hill and found Mike's Ford. Dust and black ash from the ships that had moved in and out of port over the past month blanketed the car.

"Okay, but first we have to find a car wash, then we can eat," Mike said.

"I love it when a man has his priorities straight," Jones said.

Two days later *Boyington* ship's company formed up on the pier in dress blues for a formal inspection. When he completed the inspection, Captain Ellingham returned to the head of the formation.

"Chief Gunner's Mate Michael Stafford and Machinist's Mate Second Class William Bailey, front and center." Lieutenant Kaestner ordered.

The two men marched to the front of the formation and came to attention in front of the captain.

"Attention to orders," the exec called out. He then read the citation awarding Mike the Navy and Marine Corps Medal, third award, for pulling an injured airman from a burning plane at sea.

The captain whispered his congratulations as he pinned the medal on Staffords uniform. Mike saluted. The captain returned the salute.

"Attention to orders," the XO called out again. He then read the citation awarding Mike the Navy Commendation Ribbon, fifth award, for helping to save the Soviet ship *Svetlana* from sinking.

They repeated the award process.

"Attention to orders," the XO called out a third time. He then read the citation awarding Bailey the Navy Commendation Ribbon, first award, for helping to save the Soviet ship *Svetlana* from sinking.

When the award ceremony ended, and the captain dismissed the crew, an obviously angry Sandy approached Mike. "When did you plan to tell me about this?"

"Now, honey—"

"Don't you 'now, honey' me, Michael Stafford. You promised before you left home that you would be careful, and you wouldn't take chances. Now I find out you were swimming into a burning plane and on a sinking Russian ship. How exactly do you define being careful? Tell me that, Mr. Hero."

"Please, Sandy, keep your voice down. It might sound risky to you, but I had everything under control. I wasn't risking my life."

"I'm so mad and so proud of you. Kiss me and promise that there won't be any more heroics."

They embraced and held a long kiss.

"I promise," Mike finally said.

"Okay, but you better mean it, this time. Burning plane—sinking ship, humph."

EPILOGUE

Three days after arriving in port, Mike and Sandy drove home to Manchester-by-the-Sea, Massachusetts. Mike wore civilian clothes. His uniforms were carefully packed away in his sea bag, and a DD 214, Certificate of Release or Discharge from Active Duty, folded neatly and tucked safely in his wallet. He returned to work at the sporting goods company, but it would only be for a short time. The CIA needed help with the Cuban situation in the aftermath of the missile crisis and would soon come calling.

Before the *Boyington* sailed again, Chief Boatswain's Mate Paul Jones reenlisted to complete thirty years of service. Shortly thereafter, an enlisted selection board recommended him for promotion to Senior Chief Boatswain's Mate. He anxiously awaits the day he will advance to that lofty and highly competitive position within the noncommissioned officer corps.

Chief Boilerman Ken Ford retired after twenty-year's service and moved home to Mystic, Connecticut.

Following his two-year tour as captain of the *Boyington*, the navy selected Commander William H. P. Ellingham to attend the prestigious Naval War College.

Ten months after the Cuban missile crisis ended, Lieutenant Commander John R. Kaestner received a promotion to commander. His first assignment in that rank would be navigator of the navy's newest supercarrier, the USS Kitty Hawk (CV-63).

The investigation into the death of Photographer's Mate Third Class David M. Sloan is ongoing. Ensign Henry Frankel was relieved of duty and reassigned to shore duty on the staff of the commander, cruisers destroyers Atlantic, pending the outcome of the investigation.

SOURCES

The sources quoted or paraphrased in the chapter introductions are:

1. Chang, Lawrence and Kornbluh, Peter, Editors, *The Cuban Missile Crisis, 1962,* National Security Archive.

2. Burr, William and Blanton, Thomas, Editors, *The Submarines of October*, National Security Archive.

3. Utz, Curtis A., *Cordon of Steel, The U.S. Navy and the Cuban Missile Crisis,* Naval History and Heritage Command.

4. *The Naval Quarantine of Cuba 1962,* Naval History and Heritage Command.

5. John F. Kennedy Presidential Library and Museum, Reading List Oct 22, 1962

6. John F. Kennedy Presidential Library and Museum, Security Action Memorandum 199.

7. Ritter, Stephanie, *SAC during the 13 days of the Cuban missile crisis*, Air Force Global Strike Command.

8. Ball, Gregory, Capt. USAFR, *Cuban Missile Crisis*, Air Force Historical Studies Office.

9. John F. Kennedy Presidential Library and Museum, Reading List Oct 27, 1962

10. Naval Historical Foundation, U.S.S. *Joseph P Kennedy, Jr.*: Cuban Missile Crisis Veteran

11. Kennedy-Khrushchev exchanges, document 68, Foreign Relations of the U.S. 1961-1963. Vol VI. United States Department of State.

12. Kennedy-Khrushchev exchanges, document 69, Foreign Relations of the U.S. 1961-1963. Vol VI. United States Department of State.

13. Wikipedia, *Cuban Missile Crisis*, Crisis Continues.

ACKNOWLEDGEMENTS

This novel may have lingered in manuscript form for years without the urging, skillful editing and support provided by my devoted and talented wife, Kathleen. She spent countless hours reading and correcting my errors. Any that remain are mine alone.

Many others deserve a full measure of gratitude and credit: My dear friend and former shipmate, the real John R. Kaestner, struggled through the first "final" draft making suggestions that definitely improved the story.

The authors of the Daytona Writers Group also made dozens of invaluable contributions, and I sincerely thank each one: Leaders Veronica Hart and Chris Holmes and members, Amanda Alexander, David Archard, William Collins, Dr. Walter Doherty, Patrick Guttery, Dr. Robert Hart, Judith Lawrence, and Joyce Senatro.

Finally, I wish to commemorate once again four great naval officers, three of whom instilled in me a profound fondness of the sea, the

United States Navy, and especially their beloved destroyers: Captains Robert E. Adler, George J. Davis, and Edward G. Kelley. The fourth, Captain Peter A. Huchthausen, destroyerman, diplomat, and author, encouraged me to put my stories to paper. God bless them all.

GLOSSARY

The following U.S. Navy terms and definitions are representative of those in use during the early nineteen-sixties, the period of this story, and are not necessarily applicable to earlier or later times.

1JS. Sound powered telephone circuit connecting the bridge and the sonar operator.

1JV. Sound powered telephone circuit connecting bridge, CIC, lookouts, engine room and after steering.

1MC. A Shipboard public address system with loud speakers in most compartments and on the weather decks.

ADC (Air Defense Command). U.S. Air Force command responsible for the aerial defense of the continental United States (1946-1968). During the Cuban missile crisis, it assumed responsibility for missile defense as well as manned aircraft.

AOR (Area of Responsibility). The AOR is a defined geographical area where responsibility for all military operations is invested in a single commander.

Armed Forces Police (AFP). A joint service law enforcement organization with a permanent staff. Armed Forces police have jurisdiction over all U.S. military personnel. AFP units are located in areas having a large military presence.

ASW (Anti-Submarine Warfare). Term describing the weapons and/or activities involved in finding and destroying enemy submarines.

ASW Condition One. Modified general quarters, where only battle stations on the bridge, CIC, sonar, ASW weapons positions, and one five-inch gun are manned.

athwartships. Something (e.g. a passageway) running across a ship, from port to starboard.

attack director. ASW system that indicates the ship's position relative to a submarine in both true and relative bearing. It also displays the relationship between the ship and submarine's courses and shows the limits from which each ASW weapon may be fired.

battle station. The duty station of a sailor when the ship prepares for or is engaged in battle. Battle stations are manned when general-quarters (GQ) is sounded.

bilge. The bottom-most compartment of a ship, separating the hull (floor) from the lowest deck. It collects water, oil, and other contaminants, requiring constant drainage, cleaning and preservation.

boatswain's mate (BM). A rating with expertise in seamanship, deck maintenance, and small boat handling. Sailors in this rating are referred to as "Bosun" and may be informally addressed as "Boats."

bollard. A heavy post on a pier or ship's deck for securing mooring lines.

bow. The forward most section of a ship.

bravo-zulu. An U.S. Navy and NATO flag hoist signal meaning "well done."

bridge. Location from which a ship is controlled or conned, physically positioned on an upper deck for best visibility. The bridge is the duty station of the officer of the deck when a ship is under way.

brow. A heavy gangplank equipped with handrails for embarking or debarking a ship.

bulkhead. Any wall enclosing a compartment on a ship. Sailors tend to refer to any wall, ashore or afloat as a bulkhead.

bulwark. Vertical structure along the outboard side of a ship to protect sailors and decks from wind and seas.

BUPERS (Bureau of Personnel). The navy equivalent of a civilian corporation's human resources or personnel department.

captain. A senior naval rank (pay grade O-6) or the unofficial title of an officer of any rank in command of a vessel or installation.

captain's mast. A non-judicial procedure that permits commanders to discipline sailors, administratively, without a court martial. Sentences depend on the rank of the commander and the charges.

charthouse. A compartment near the bridge where quartermasters maintain navigation charts.

CIC (Combat Information Center). The tactical center of a warship where radarmen maintain a constant picture of the ship's location and every air or surface contact, friend or foe, within detectable proximity.

CINCLANTCOM (Commander in Chief Atlantic Command). The commander of all U.S. forces from the eastern shore of North America to Europe. Unified commanders report directly to the president.

CNO (Chief Naval Operations). Officer responsible for the recruiting, training, equipping, and assignment of all naval personnel and the procurement of all materiel required for the fleet. The CNO is a member of the Joint Chiefs of Staff, the military advisors to the president.

CNO Flag Plot. A room in the Pentagon displaying the location of all reported Soviet surface vessels and submarines in the Atlantic Ocean during the Cuban missile crisis. Naval personnel assigned contact numbers from this location.

CO (Commanding Officer). The officer in charge and responsible for all operational aspects or a ship or station.

COMDESCRULANT (Commander Destroyers and Cruisers Atlantic). The officer responsible for the manning, upkeep, and deployment scheduling for ships of these types.

COMLANTFLT (Commander Atlantic Fleet). Officer responsible for the operational employment of all vessels assigned to the Atlantic Fleet, also known as the U.S. Second Fleet. He is subordinate to Commander in Chief of the U.S. Atlantic Command (CINCLANTCOM).

commander. A senior navy rank (pay grade O-5) or the official title of a person in charge of a vessel, installation, or organization.

commodore. Title given the commander of a destroyer squadron (eight ships). The commodore's rank is captain (pay grade O-6).

conn. Navigational directions given to the helmsman, or having the responsibility for directing a ship.

coxswain. Enlisted sailor in charge of a small boat, pronounced "kok sun."

CPO. Abbreviation for chief petty officer.

crypto. Short for cryptography, the coding of information from a readable state to something void of understanding. The intended receiver must use a key or algorithm to decrypt the coded (encrypted) information. Encryption prevents unauthorized or unwanted persons from reading the message.

CTF (Commander Task Force). Officer responsible for the operational employment of a task force.

datum. Geographic coordinates of a ship or submarine's current or last known location.

dead reckoning tracer (DRT). A device linked to the ship's gyrocompass indicating the ship's current position, which allows CIC personnel to plot a record of the course being steered.

deck. Structural portion of a ship corresponding to the floor of a building.

depth charge. A non-guided, anti-submarine explosive device activated at a preset depth by water pressure.

DESLANT (Destroyers Atlantic). All destroyers assigned to the Atlantic Fleet.

DESRON (Destroyer Squadron). A unit of eight destroyers under the command of a commodore.

destroyer. A multi-purpose, lightly armored warship. Offensive weaponry may consist of three and five inch guns, torpedoes, rockets and depth charges. Defensively destroyers depend primarily on speed and maneuverability.

destroyer tender. A large ship equipped to service and repair destroyers.

engine order telegraph. System for transmitting speed and direction commands between bridge and engine room.

ETA. Estimated Time of Arrival.

ExComm. Executive Committee of the National Security Council. A presidential advisory committee established by President Kennedy during the Cuban missile crisis.

executive officer. The officer second in command of a ship or naval installation. The executive officer may be referred to informally as the "exec" or "XO."

fantail. Main deck in the stern or after part of ship.

fire control system. System of radars and computers for directing (aiming) and controlling gunfire.

fireman. Junior enlisted sailors (pay grades E-1 to E-3) in the engineering group.

fire room. Location of a ship's steam producing boilers, below the main deck.

forecastle. The main forward deck and the bow compartments below that deck. Pronounced, "foke'sul."

gedunk. A canteen or snack bar on a base or a large navy ship.

general-quarters. Condition wherein all hands man their battle stations.

gig. Small enclosed boat carried on a ship for the commander's use.

gipsy. Part of a hoist; a large drum on which cables coil.

Gitmo. Slang for U.S. Naval Station Guantanamo, Guantánamo Bay, Cuba.

gun mount. Lightly armored structure, open or enclosed, used to protect the gun crew.

gunner's mate (GM). A rating specializing in weapon systems. Sailors in this rating are informally referred to as "Guns."

gunnery officer. Ship's officer heading the gunnery department, responsible for all weapons systems. On smaller vessels, such as destroyers, deck maintenance is also a responsibility of the gunnery officer. He may have an assistant, called the "first lieutenant," (a title, not a rank) to supervise deck maintenance.

halyard. Line used to hoist flags.

handy billy. A small, portable, gasoline engine driven water pump.

hawser. Heavy line used for mooring or towing ships.

head. Toilet and shower room on a ship.

hedge hog. An antisubmarine weapon that simultaneously launches an array of multiple rockets.

helm. The "steering wheel" or tiller of a ship.

helmsmen. Sailor who steers the ship at the helm.

holiday routine. A schedule wherein off-watch personnel aren't required to work.

IRBM. Abbreviation for Intermediate Range Ballistic Missile.

jack. A small flag indicating a ship's nationality; the U.S. jack is the blue field and stars (union) of the national flag.

jack-o'-the-dust. The informal title given a sailor designated to assist the commissaryman by breaking out provisions.

jackstaff. A short mast at the bow of a ship. When in port, the jack flies from the jackstaff.

Jacob's ladder. A lightweight ladder made of rope or chain with metal or wood steps.

jay-gee. Slang for a lieutenant junior grade, pay grade O-2.

ladder. Any stairway on a ship, usually steep; sailors ashore tend to refer to any stairway as a ladder.

leave. Formally authorized time away from a sailor's ship or shore installation greater than forty-eight hours.

level. Partial decks above the main deck numbered in ascending order, preceded by a zero. Thus, the first level above the main deck is designated 0100 and called the "Oh 1 level."

liberty. Formally authorized time away from a sailor's ship or shore installation usually seventy-two hours or less, and within a limited distance.

loran. Acronym for "long range navigation," a system of shore based radio transmitters that permit ships to triangulate their position at sea.

M-1. Rifle, Caliber .30, M1: A semi-automatic rifle used by the U.S. military, also called the M-1 Garand.

M-1911. A single-action, semi-automatic, magazine-fed, and recoil-operated handgun chambered for the .45 ACP cartridge.

MAA (Master-at-Arms). An additional duty assigned to a petty officer. The MAA is responsible for enforcing law and order aboard a ship or shore station.

magnetic anomaly detection (MAD). Aircraft system that detects changes in the earth's magnetic field caused by the presence of a submarine.

main battery plot. Central location capable of firing all weapons (five-inch and three-inch guns, torpedoes, depth charges, and hedgehogs).

material conditions. Doors, hatches, and valves are marked for closing before going into battle. When damage is probable, all those designated with an X or Y are secured. When damage is imminent, all with an X, Y, or Z are secured.

mechanist mate (MM). A rating specializing in engine room operations and maintenance.

merchant marine. A professional civilian sailor; not a part of the defense department.

mess deck. The compartment on a ship where enlisted men, other than CPOs, eat.

mid-rats. Food (rations) served to the mid-watch before they assume the duty (0001-0400).

motor whaleboat. A small, powered boat, pointed at both ends.

MRBM. Abbreviation for Medium Range Ballistic Missile.

NOTAM (Notice to All Mariners). A warning of hazardous or special conditions at sea, broadcast primarily by governments of seafaring nations around the globe.

OIC (Officer in Charge). A non-command, often temporary, position with responsibility and authority to complete a specific task.

oil king. An informal title for the boilerman responsible for monitoring the levels and conditions of fuel in the various bunkers onboard Navy ships.

ONI (Office of Naval Intelligence). The naval organization responsible for the collection and dissemination of strategic intelligence. It also investigates criminal activity within the navy.

OOD (Officer of the deck). The captain's official representative who is in charge of the ship for the period of a watch. All personnel aboard, regardless of rank, are subordinate to the OOD except the captain and executive officer.

OPCON (Operational control). A defined level of authority given a commander over subordinate units.

open bridge. Portion of the bridge exposed to the weather.

operations officer. The head of the Operations Department on a ship, which may include radio and signal communications, the combat information center, radar and radio electronics repair and related functions.

OPLAN. Abbreviation for "operations plan." A plan for conducting operations in a hostile environment.

passageway. A hallway on a ship or in a navy building.

PCS (Permanent Change of Station). An official transfer from one duty station to another.

petty officer. Navy non-commissioned officer (pay grades E-4 to E-9).

pilothouse. An enclosed section of the bridge housing the helm for steering, the engine order telegraph for transmitting propulsion orders to the engineers below deck, and other and control and communications equipment.

pipe. A small, shrill whistle used by boatswain's mates to pass a call to the crew. The intonation pattern and duration of the call signals the activity the crew is to perform.

POD (Plan-of-the-Day). A schedule of events and notices of general interest to the crew of a ship or station, published by the executive officer.

pollywog. A sailor who has not crossed the equator. Once a he has crossed and a proper initiation completed, the pollywog becomes a shellback.

port. The left side of a ship, looking forward, or a harbor.

quarterdeck. A ceremonial area designated by the captain when in port or at anchor. The quarterdeck is duty station of the OOD under those conditions.

quartermaster (QM). A rating specializing in ship navigation and handling.

radar. (radio **d**etection **and r**anging), A system using reflected radio waves to locate distant objects (e.g. land, ships, planes), called targets, bogeys, or contacts. Most destroyers have four radars (Surface search, air search and two for fire control).

radarman (RD). A rating specializing in radar operation, image interpretation and air traffic control.

radarscope. A device that displays the information acquired by a radar system, also called a radar repeater or scope.

radio central. A ship's communications nerve center housing radio equipment and operators.

radioman (RM). A rating specializing in radio operation and message routing.

rank. Grade of a commissioned officer, pay grades O-1 through O-10, or warrant officer, pay grades W-1 and W-2).

rate and rating. Rate is the grade of an enlisted man (pay grades E-1 through E-9). Rating is the occupational specialty of a petty officer. Combining the rating and rate, describes a sailor's military specialty and grade. For example, GM3, GM2, GM1and GMC for gunner's mate, third class through chief.

S2F Tracker. A twin piston-engine aircraft purpose built to locate and attack submarines.

SAC. Strategic Air Command. A U.S. Air Force major command.

SACEUR. Supreme Allied Commander, Europe (NATO).

scuttlebutt. A drinking fountain aboard ship or slang for rumors.

seaman. Generally, a sailor, specifically the three junior enlisted grades, (Seaman Recruit, Seaman Apprentice, Seaman) pay grade E-1 to E-3, in the deck group.

seaman apprentice (SA). Pay grade E-2. Also unofficially called seaman deuce or two-striper.

shore patrol (SP). A detail of petty officers charged with maintaining order among naval personnel ashore.

SITREP (Situation Report). A report sent to a higher headquarters advising of an event in progress.

skipper. Slang for a commanding officer.

snipe. Slang for a sailor in the engineering ratings.

sonar. **S**ound **n**avigation **a**nd **r**anging, Sonar equipment transmits a sound impulse that when reflected back, as from a submarine, yields location (distance, depth and bearing).

sonarman (SO). A rating specializing in sonar operation and maintenance.

sound powered phone. A shipboard telephone system that does not use an external power source. The speaker's voice powers the transmission.

special sea and anchor detail. The senior personnel (officer and enlisted) who perform critical functions when entering or leaving port, or navigating narrow channels.

stanchion. A post or support on a ship.

starboard. The right side of a ship, looking forward.

steward (SD). A rating specializing in wardroom services: preparing and serving food, and in the general upkeep of officer's quarters.

striker. Designation given an enlisted man, in pay grades E-1 through E-3, trained for a specific rating. The striker includes intended the rating with his or her rate. For example, a seaman formally trained to become a quartermaster is a QMSN.

task force (TF). A large group of ships temporarily combined for a specific mission (e.g. the invasion of an enemy held island). When the mission is complete, the higher command reassigns the ships or task groups to other missions. A TF may consist of multiple task groups (TG).

task group (TG). A group of ships assembled to accomplish a particular task, (e.g. amphibious landings or anti-submarine warfare). Task groups may operate independently, or add their unique capabilities to a larger task force (TF).

tender. An auxiliary ship equipped to maintain and repair a particular type of warship (e.g. a destroyer tender).

torpedo. A guided explosive device used against threats underwater (e.g. a submarine or ship's hull below the waterline).

UCMJ (Uniform Code of Military Justice). The foundation of law pertaining to military personnel in all services of the United States.

U.S.S. (United States Ship). An abbreviation used only for warships.

wardroom. Officer's mess and lounge aboard ship, also used to mean the officers of a ship collectively.

watch. A duty period, usually either two or four hours in duration, when a sailor performs a specific function or task.

watch, quarter and station bill. A chart of every man's position in the ships organization and his station during special details or conditions, e.g. General-Quarters.

weather deck. Portion of a deck exposed to the elements.

whaleboat. Also known as a motor whaleboat, a small, powered boat, pointed at both ends.

XO. See Executive Officer.

yeoman (YN). A rating specializing in administration.

yo-yo. Slang for the U.S.S. Yosemite (AD 19), a destroyer tender and flagship of the commander, cruisers destroyers Atlantic (COMCRUDESLANT).

ABOUT THE AUTHOR

William E. Dempsey began his military career as an electronics technician in the United States Navy several years before the time of this story. During his enlistment, he served aboard the destroyer U.S.S. Blandy (DD 943) in the Atlantic and Mediterranean Fleets, and as an electronics instructor at the Great Lakes Naval Training Center.

In 1980, he received a commission in the Army medical service. Four years later, he made an interservice transfer to the Air Force where he concluded a twenty-eight year career. His time in uniform included five years in Washington, D.C. The first assignment was Chief of Combat Casualty Care Analysis at Headquarters, United States Air Force. A three-year Pentagon assignment followed, in the National Military Command Center, as an Emergency Action Officer, on the staff of the Chairman of the Joint Chiefs of Staff.

This is his second historical fiction novel based on the Mike Stafford character. If you enjoyed it, please let your fellow readers know by leaving a review at amazon.com. Bill, Mike Stafford and the Amazon readers will all appreciate it.

Visit Bill and Mike Stafford at williamedempsey.com

Made in the USA
Charleston, SC
11 October 2016